Unclouded
Day

Unclouded Day

Book One
The Stones of Song Series

by

William Woodall

Jeremiah Press · *Antoine, Arkansas*

Jeremiah Press
PO Box 3
Antoine, AR 71922

© Copyright 2012 by William Woodall. All rights reserved.
www.williamwoodall.org

Cover image copyright 2008 by Enya de la Jara. Used by permission. See her other work at http://treffoil.daportfolio.com

First published by Jeremiah Press on 04/09/2012.

Printed in the United States of America.

This book is printed on acid-free paper.

ISBN 978-0-9833298-2-4

For every child,
Who ever stood alone against the darkness,

And won.

He shall lead them unto living fountains of waters,
And God shall wipe away all tears from their eyes.

-Revelation 7:17

Quotable Quotes
By Brian Madaug Stone

"He was no different than any of a hundred other youngsters, except that he had a mind to dream, and faith to believe, and courage to set aside himself for the sake of those he loved."

"Many times, he'd looked at those distant mountains and wished he could run away to some shining land where there were no tears and no miseries, where fathers never disappeared, and mothers never gave their children black eyes, and all things were forever bright and beautiful. It was perhaps the dearest and deepest wish of his heart."

"Truth which is spoken without love can be cruel as a punch in the gut."

"In a way, it was worse to have tasted beauty and then have it snatched away, than never to have known it at all."

"There's nothing too good to be true. If the story isn't real, then it must be because it's not good enough to be true, not because it's too good, and in that case the real truth would be something even better."

"Nor did he dream, except the sweet and simple dreams of the pure at heart, of the kind that nourish the soul but are never remembered."

"The strong of heart shall drink of Me; the life-giving Life, and the Beauty that makes beautiful."

"To God Most High, may our taste of this fountain give you glory forever."

"He brought beauty to everything he touched. It was almost like he had the power to pull a grimy, obscuring film off the world which no one had ever noticed was there because they'd never seen things any other way. Without it, everything looked fresh and bright and new."

"The world has taught you to think it's not safe to be too glad, and that tears are more real than laughter. But that's not so. Joy is what the whole world was made for, even if people don't remember that very often nowadays."

"Nothing lasts forever in a dark and fallen world, and the best they could do was to plant memories of Heaven, to turn men's souls in that direction; not to make a heaven on earth."

Contents

The Fountain of Youth
By Oliver Wendell Holmes

The fount the Spaniard sought in vain
Through all the land of flowers
Leaps glittering from the sandy plain
Our classic grove embowers;

Here youth, unchanging, blooms and smiles,
Here dwells eternal spring,
And warm from Hope's elysian isles
The winds their perfume bring.

Here every leaf is in the bud,
Each singing throat in tune,
And bright o'er evening's silver flood
Shines the young crescent moon.

What wonder Age forgets his staff
And lays his glasses down,
And gray-haired grandsires look and laugh
As when their locks were brown!

With ears grown dull and eyes grown dim
They greet the joyous day
That calls them to the fountain's brim
To wash their years away.

And what are all the prizes won
To youth's enchanted view?
And what is all the man has done
To what the boy may do?

O blessed fount, whose waters flow
Alike for sire and son,
That melts our winter's frost and snow
And makes all ages one!

Prologue

Among the native tribes of America, it has long been told that deep underground, in a cavern green as emerald at the heart of the world, that the blessed of God might find a fountain clear and cold, and that anyone who drank of that water might live far beyond his years, young and beautiful till the end, and that his dearest wish might come true.

Now the fame and the echo of that story have gone far out into the wide world, and many heroes and great men have searched for the Fountain in vain. It is said that DeSoto himself tried to find it, and Ponce de Leon the Lion-Hearted, and perhaps many another whose name is no longer remembered. But none ever succeeded, for the way is hidden except to those who are chosen, and found worthy.

This is the tale of a boy who found himself chosen, though no one who knew him would ever have suspected he was anything but ordinary. He was no different than any of a hundred other youngsters, except that he had a mind to dream, and faith to believe, and courage to set aside himself for the sake of those he loved.

And although he would have laughed if anyone had suggested such a high calling for him, he learned in time not to wonder at the works of God, who may often choose to lift up the weak and humble things of this world to fulfill His purposes, when the strong stumble.

Chapter One

Brian found the amulet in an old cigar box in the attic. He wasn't looking for it, or anything in particular really. He just liked rooting around up there sometimes, especially on days when Mama was in a bad mood. He'd learned long ago that it was best to disappear for a while at times like that, if he didn't want a smack in the face. Out of sight, out of mind.

She'd finally passed out on the couch around two a.m. last night, and Brian had known even then that she'd probably wake up with a killer hangover the next morning. That was never something you wanted to stick around for; not if you were smart, so he'd planned to get up early and take Brandon fishing for a while. At least till she had a chance to mellow out a little bit.

But there'd been a cold gray rain falling when he opened his eyes that morning, forcing him to rethink his plans. It wouldn't do, to take Brandon out in the weather like that; the kid was always catching colds. Bran was still two weeks shy of four years old; a bit more than ten years younger than his big brother, and Brian loved him above all things in the world.

So instead he'd come up to the attic, to root around amongst Papaw's old Army trunks for a while. The whole place was full of junk his grandfather had dragged back home from all over the world, and no matter how often Brian dug through it, there was always something new to see.

Not all of it was pleasant, to be sure. Some of Daddy's old things were up there too, here and there, and it always made Brian a little sad when he stumbled across anything like that. He hadn't seen his father since Brandon was a baby, and sometimes that still stung. His name was Crush, and Brandon looked very much like him with his deep red hair the color of a ripe cherry. That was memory enough, without looking for more.

But he didn't come across things like that very often, and since fishing was a no-go, then treasure-hunting in the attic seemed like a good backup plan.

So he'd crept out of bed, leaving Brandon still asleep, and tiptoed quietly upstairs. He switched on the dusty old floor lamp before picking a trunk at random, close enough to the door that he could see if Bran woke up and came out into the hall. He'd probably sleep for hours yet after staying up so late last night, but then again you never knew.

In the meantime, Brian pulled up a chair, threw back the rusty iron latches, and lifted the lid of the trunk he'd picked. It smelled faintly musty inside, and as usual it was full of assorted junk; a baby cuckoo clock no bigger than an apple, a set of ivory throwing knives, postcards, a beeswax candle that still smelled like honeycomb, dozens of other trinkets and souvenirs like that. They were tossed in the trunk carelessly, with no particular order; just a random jumble of odds and ends.

Down at the very bottom he discovered an old cigar box buried under a piece of cardboard, almost like someone had tried to hide it down there for some reason. Probably no one had, of course, but the idea tickled his sense of adventure. He pulled it out and blew dust off the lid, then tore off an ancient strip of duct tape that held it closed. Inside he found some crumpled rice paper yellowed with age, and wrapped up inside it was a silver necklace with a small medallion-type amulet attached. It was badly tarnished in spite of the wrapping, but there was no doubt about what it was.

Brian was delighted; this was *real* treasure!

There were seven blue gems set in a circle around a carven picture of a flowing fountain on the front of the medallion, and there was a smooth crack that ran all the way round the edge of the back side, as if it was meant to open up like a locket. There didn't seem to be any catch or knob or button that he could push to pop it open and let him see what might be inside, but while he was looking for one he did find an inscription of some sort which he couldn't make out through the tarnish. His curiosity was strong now, though, and he wasn't to be put off by such difficulties. He spit on the edge of his shirt tail and rubbed hard till he could read the writing, but even then he was none the wiser. The words simply said *Thumb Here.*

The letters were sloppy and blocky, like someone had scratched them there with the point of a pocket knife.

"Thumb here?" he repeated aloud, thinking to himself what an odd thing that was for someone to put on a piece of jewelry. It was clear enough, though, so he shrugged his shoulders and stuck his thumb where it said, wishing the silver wasn't so gummed up and nasty. It might actually be worth something if he could get the tarnish off.

The instant he touched it, a sharp pain stabbed his hand, and he cried out wildly without thinking. It felt almost like he'd touched a burning hot coal, and he dropped the thing instinctively. He quickly inspected his thumb for injuries but saw nothing unusual, and since the pain had vanished as well, he was soon more puzzled than anything else. He wiggled his fingers to make sure they still worked, and everything seemed fine. Then he listened to see if anybody was coming to check on him after that wild cry, but the house was silent. He must not have been as loud as he thought.

He stared down at the amulet suspiciously, and then cautiously prodded it with his big toe. Nothing happened, but he couldn't help noticing that the gummy black tarnish was all gone. Silver gleamed brightly even in the weak light from the lamp, and he noticed for the first time that the flowing water in the fountain-picture was speckled here and there with tiny chips of what might have been diamonds, glittering and beautiful. It looked like someone had scrubbed the whole thing spotless in the blink of an eye.

In fact, it was almost like his wish had come true.

The thought came to him out of nowhere, and he felt a rush of excitement. Brian had always believed that there had to be something more out there than just the dull and humdrum world he was used to. So when something magical was suddenly dropped in his lap, he wasn't at all disbelieving, as some people might have been. When reality is harsh, one learns very quickly to look beyond it.

Eventually he got bold enough to pick up the amulet by the chain and examine it again, this time a lot more closely. A ring of tiny words was now etched sharply into the gleaming surface around the edge, but they were much too small for him to make out what they said and he soon gave up trying.

He thought back carefully, trying to remember exactly what he'd done. His head was full of vague ideas from a hundred fairy tales and movies about how things like this were supposed to work, but he couldn't remember doing anything special except touching his thumb to the medallion.

Well, fair enough. He'd give it a try. It was worth a hurt finger to find out the truth, if that's what it took.

He looked at his shirt tail, where the spit-and-tarnish mixture from earlier was gradually turning into a smudged brown stain as it dried, and decided that would make as good an experiment as any. Therefore he took the medallion in hand, and gingerly touched his thumb to the back. He was braced for the pain this time, and was puzzled when it didn't come. Nevertheless, he forged ahead.

"I wish my shirt was clean," he said distinctly, but this time he was disappointed. Nothing happened. Brian wasn't willing to give up just yet, though. He looked down at an old pair of socks on the floor.

"Come here," he ordered them in a firm tone. Again nothing happened, and Brian was frustrated. What was he not doing right?

He tried to think again what he'd been doing when the tarnish disappeared. He'd been looking at the medallion, thinking about how it would look if it was clean. He hadn't actually said a word, come to think of it. He'd just thought it. Okay then, so maybe he had to visualize what he wanted, instead of talking out loud. He decided to try it again.

This time he didn't say anything, just envisioned the socks rising up off the floor and landing beside him on top of the trunk lid. Now there was no doubt about it. The socks floated obligingly off the floor and came to rest beside his elbow, exactly where he'd wanted them to go. There was still no pain though, and Brian broke into a huge smile.

He was eager to try some more, but then he hesitated. Mama was somewhere downstairs, and he didn't dare let her catch him doing magic, of all things. The first thing she'd do would be to take the amulet away from him, and if that happened. . .

Brian felt a cold chill at the very idea. Mama was nasty enough already, without giving her magical powers to make things even worse. There was no way he could let *that* happen. What he really needed was a place where he could be sure she wouldn't walk in and catch him, but that was impossible as long as they were both under the same roof.

He glanced outside. The rain had stopped for now, and there was nothing to keep him from leaving the house for a while if he wanted to. Fishing was forgotten for the day, but the creek was still the best hide-out he knew of, far from Mama's prying eyes. He was sorely tempted to go snatch Brandon out of bed and slip away while they still had the chance.

Then a problem came to mind, and he hesitated. Brandon had a really hard time keeping secrets, and it wouldn't do much good to go hide in the woods to do his experiments if the kid came right back home and blabbed everything, now would it?

He thought about slipping away by himself and leaving Brandon at home with Mama for a little while, even though he didn't like the idea very much. He was pretty sure Bran would sleep for hours yet after staying up so late last night, but then again he might not. If he *did* wake up early, it was a pretty good bet that Mama would end up screaming at him for spilling cereal on the floor, or making too much noise, or some stupid thing like that. Not to mention she'd probably tear Brian to pieces for not watching him, as soon as he got back home.

Not a good outcome, either way.

Nevertheless, he was almost dying with curiosity to find out more about the amulet, and he was blessed if he could think of any other solution.

He decided to risk it, just this once.

He slipped the amulet in his pocket and crept stealthily down the painted wooden stairs, stepping lightly and near the edges to avoid creaks. A thin film of dusty grime had sifted out of the wallboards since the last time he swept, and tiny particles of dirt clung unpleasantly to the bottom of his bare feet every time he took a step. He made a face and wished for the millionth time that it wasn't so hard to keep the old place clean.

He didn't stop on the second floor, not wanting to wake up either Brandon or his mother. He wasn't sure if she'd ever roused herself enough to stagger her way to bed last night or not, but he didn't want to find out the hard way by disturbing her.

The kitchen was deserted when he got to the bottom of the stairs, and he surveyed the wreckage from last night glumly. Glasses half full of unfinished milk from supper stood huddled together on the dull green Formica countertop, and dirty plates were piled high in the sink. An empty Absolut vodka bottle lay at a drunken angle against the base of the refrigerator where Mama had thrown it, and a fleet of cigarette butts floated grotesquely in a pool of spilled beer on the floor. A slightly dried-out meatball lay in solitary splendor under Brandon's chair on a thin veneer of splattered spaghetti sauce.

There was more, but Brian had seen enough. The cleanup job would be bad enough without having to think about it ahead of time. He crept a little nearer to the archway that separated the kitchen from the living room, to see if Mama was still asleep on the sofa. She wasn't, but someone had turned on the TV, and presently he noticed muffled sounds of movement coming from the bathroom. It sounded like Mama was brushing her teeth, and before long he heard something clatter on the floor and the sound of cursing. It sounded like she was in an especially nasty mood, and he felt a strong urge to disappear again.

He suffered a fresh twinge of worry about leaving Brandon alone with her, and he glanced upstairs one last time with furrowed brow, half tempted to put off his expedition for another day.

But Brian was fourteen, and the thought of waiting for anything was hard to endure, let alone something as amazing as this. Therefore he tiptoed quietly across the faded yellow linoleum to the back door, reminding himself once again that Brandon was still asleep, and that the quicker he left, the quicker he could get back.

He shut the screen door slowly behind him, careful not to let the rusty hinges squeak too loud. It didn't seem to matter how often he oiled them, that high-pitched squeal always came back in a few days. He listened to make sure Mama hadn't noticed, and then he set off purposefully across the pasture.

He quickly covered the open ground and slipped through the rusty barbed wire fence on the far side, careful not to let his jeans or his shirt get snagged. Ripped up clothes were too hard to replace.

His bare feet crunched wetly on dead vines and pine straw as he followed the little path into the woods beyond the fence, and once or twice he had to wade through a flooded spot. That was all right, though; he knew the way. By and by the trail curved away northward, following the little valley up into the mountains, and before long he came to higher and drier ground again.

At one place, an outcrop of stone jutted out over the creek, with a beautiful view of almost the whole valley to the south and a deep swimming hole underneath where you could cannonball off the rock if you were brave enough, and beyond it there was the wooded mountainside where no one ever went. That's where Brian was headed.

He and Brandon had always called that place Black Rock, though Brian couldn't remember why. It didn't really look black, except when it was wet. It was Brandon's favorite spot when the weather was nice, because there were lots of lizards and bugs to catch while they basked in the sun, and there was a sandy beach beside the creek that was perfect for castle building. Brian liked to go there and read or throw rocks even when Brandon wasn't with him, because it was a good place to be alone with his thoughts, and in the fall he sometimes hunted on the mountainside.

Not always in the fall, actually, although he didn't like to talk about that very much. Hunting deer out of season was always risky, but there'd been several times when it was either that or go hungry. Not much of a choice, when you thought about it.

But for now, the most important thing of all about Black Rock was that Mama absolutely hated the place and never went there. Brian had no idea why she felt that way, but he was glad she did.

A low growl of thunder rolled through the dense pine woods, and he looked up at the sky anxiously. The clouds were still dark and heavy with rain, and he wondered for a second if maybe his expedition hadn't been such a good idea after all.

He hesitated again, not wanting to get soaked, but eventually curiosity pulled him onward. He could always stand under a tree for a while if he had to. It wasn't quite ten minutes later when he finally emerged from the woods and stood on top of the big stone outcrop. All around the Rock was a little meadow maybe a hundred feet across, full of wildflowers when the season was right, although at the moment it held nothing but thistles and sedge grass, most of it dead from the summer heat.

The castle he and Brandon had built last week on the sand bar had melted into a shapeless blob coated with pockmarks from the rain, and there were several fresh deer tracks coming down to the water to drink. Little bits of embedded mica twinkled on the surface of the Rock, which was still dark and wet in most places.

Brian pulled the amulet out of his pocket and toyed with it. The jeweled silver glittered like broken glass, even on such a dreary day. It was a beautiful piece of work, whoever made it. Strangely enough, there was no clasp or catch on it as you would have expected to find on a necklace. The chain was made all in one continuous piece. The only way to put it on was to slip it over your head.

Brian wasn't sure he liked that idea much. He wasn't on good terms with pain in any form, and he still remembered what had happened to his thumb earlier. It had only been just that once, sure, but what if the same thing happened to his neck or chest? He wasn't keen to find out the hard way. But a necklace is meant to be worn, and with a deep breath he whisked the chain over his head before he could change his mind.

It hung lightly around his neck, the silver disk lying flat against his heart. He grasped it in his hand and held it as far away from his body as he could before he tried anything else with it, though. Might as well be as careful as possible.

His legs were coated with mud and dirt up to the knees from the flooded path, and he could feel scattered smudges of thick red clay slowly pulling hair as they dried on bare skin. His face was slick with oily sweat, curling down in streamers from his forehead. He felt grubby, and this gave him an idea for his first experiment.

"I wish I was clean," he said, imagining himself just that way. Again he felt nothing at all, but when he looked down every particle of dirt had vanished from his body. His clothes were cool and fresh, and even his teeth felt newly brushed. Brian smiled with pleasure, more confident now. His eye fell on a nearby rock.

"Come here," he commanded it, holding out his right hand. The rock trembled and then gracefully floated into his outstretched palm. Brian laughed with delight, throwing the rock into the creek and casting his eyes about for more things to work his magic on. Nothing could have knocked a chip off his satisfaction at that moment.

He played with the amulet fondly, dreaming such dreams as would have seemed unbelievable just yesterday. But now! Now all things were possible.

The summer sun had scorched the tall grass around Black Rock into a wide field of standing hay, which not even the recent rains had been able to bring back to life. The dirt was pale and rocky, full of little white stones that looked like the bleaching skulls of field mice, and Brian eyed all these things thoughtfully.

Moving rocks and cleaning off mud was all very well, but surely there was something more dramatic and interesting he could do. The dead grass and gloomy skies didn't seem to offer very many possibilities at the moment, though.

It would have been a much different place in the springtime, full of wild flowers and swallowtail butterflies and sometimes a few deer grazing at the edge of the woods. That was Brian's favorite time of year, and for a fleeting second he wished it was March instead of September.

A wild thought entered his mind, and he began to smile at the very audacity of it. He walked slowly to the center of the little meadow, and his left hand reached up to clasp the amulet curiously. Could he do it?

"Give me spring," he whispered, conjuring up the vivid image in his mind. Before the last word fell from his lips, the meadow began to change before his eyes. The dry grass broke up into wispy fragments quickly swept away by the wind. Dormant seeds burst into new life in a spreading pool of green around his feet, sending up pale tendrils already heavy with the buds of flowers. Lavender stars peppered the ground with a sprinkle of blooms, and chains of golden daffodils appeared across the far side of the meadow.

For a second he was awed by his power, and stood staring at the changes he'd made. He thought about gathering up armfuls of the daffodils and carrying them back home to brighten up the drab old house just a little. Mama liked flowers. She might even. . . well, what *would* she do, actually?

When he stopped to seriously think about it, he realized he was dreaming with his head in the sand. Mama wasn't a fool. She knew it wasn't the right time of year for daffodils, and at the very least she'd ask him where they came from. And then what would he say?

It wasn't just the daffodils, of course. Anything strange that happened around the house might cause problems. Mama was suspicious, and he knew from experience that it didn't take much to set her off. The least careless remark, the most minor incident; anything could cause an explosion.

It came to mind again that Brandon would probably be the worst problem he had when it came to keeping the secret. He was seldom out of Brian's company, and he was way too curious about things. He just didn't understand the need to keep his mouth shut sometimes.

The cool wind had dried a sweaty trail of hair against the curve of his cheek, and Brian absentmindedly brushed it away. He turned his back on Spring, the thought of his mother having temporarily soured his taste for any more playing around. He unraveled a sprig of honeysuckle which had grown around his ankle and headed back for the downward path, feeling deflated. What good was magic if you couldn't use it?

He walked quietly into the leaf-scented shade of the hickory trees, paying no attention to anything above the tips of his toes. He was lost too deep in thought. Maybe if he was super careful and only did things Mama wouldn't notice, then he might get away with it. That was an unsatisfying compromise, but it was the best thing he could think of at the moment.

He sighed, and decided it was probably about time he headed home; he needed to be back before Brandon woke up, just in case.

While he thought thus, he felt a single fat raindrop land on his arm, and again he glanced up at the sky uneasily. This time dark thunderheads were piled up like play-doh in the west, and the wind was starting to pick up again. From where he stood, he could see rain falling in dark gray sheets maybe half a mile away, and it was moving his direction.

He made a run for it, gambling on the chance that he could make it to the house before the rain did. Brian was a fast runner, and if he'd been wearing his shoes he might possibly have made it in time.

But he was barefoot, and that slowed him down just a bit. He was crawling through the fence when the rain caught him, causing him to rip a long hole in the back of his t-shirt from trying to slip through the barbed wire too quickly. He cussed under his breath and ran across the pasture to the back door, angry at the fence, and the rain, and himself most of all. He didn't have so many shirts that he could afford to tear them up like that.

He quickly got a grip on himself as he reached the house, though. There were worse things in the world than holey shirts, and the slightest display of bad temper was as sure a way to provoke Mama to anger as he knew of.

He scuffed his feet and made sure to let the screen door slam (but not too loudly, of course) when he walked into the kitchen.

If he made a little noise he could let Mama know he was there without actually having to speak to her. She was out of the bathroom now; he noticed the back of her head where she sat on the couch watching one of her soaps. On the screen, an actress was passionately kissing a character Brian had never seen before, and Mama seemed rapt. She either didn't notice him or didn't bother to say anything. Brian didn't really care which, as long as she left him alone.

He didn't see Brandon with her, so he slipped upstairs as quietly as possible. A quick touch of his amulet wiped out the creak in the seventh step just as his foot touched it, and a second one swept the dust all clean. Those were things nobody would notice, or if they did then Brian could always say he'd fixed them by hand. Caution, caution was the thing to remember.

He didn't start to worry until he got to the bedroom and found no Brandon there either, and when a quick look in the upstairs bathroom and out the back window also failed to turn him up, Brian reluctantly decided he had no choice but to ask Mama, although he dreaded it.

He almost skipped the seventh step on his way down before remembering that he didn't have to anymore, and then he deliberately set his whole weight on it just to listen to the silence. He was starting to feel a little better about things. He might have to be careful, but his power was far from useless! He fixed two of the worst cracks in the wallpaper and removed a scratch on the banister without missing a beat, and then slipped through the kitchen as quiet as a whisper to stand hesitating at the entrance to the living room. Then he waited carefully for a commercial break before clearing his throat.

Mama didn't look back at him.

"What?" she asked irritably.

"Um, I just wondered if you knew where Brandon might be, Mama," he asked, in the humblest and most respectful voice he possessed. Mama hated disrespect above all other crimes.

"I don't know where he went. Go find him yourself if you want him," she said, in a tone that meant the subject was closed. Brian mumbled something that might have sounded like a thank-you, and then quickly retreated.

He searched rapidly through the house, checking all the places he could think of that were big enough for Brandon to be hiding in. He went back upstairs, looking in the hall closet and even venturing into Mama's room. No Brandon anywhere.

Then he thought of the attic. It seemed unlikely; Bran didn't usually go up there by himself, but there was always a first time for everything.

Brian quickly climbed up the narrow steps and poked his head through the door. It was too dark to see much, so he grabbed a rafter in one hand and felt his way forward, groping for the lamp stand. He couldn't remember switching it off earlier, but he guessed he must have.

When his eyes had adjusted to the darkness a bit, he immediately saw the lamp knocked over on the floor and the bulb smashed into a thousand pieces. He doubted Mama had been up there, so it must have been Brandon who'd done it.

"Great," he muttered.

He explored the boxes and piles of junk one at a time, being careful not to step on broken glass, and finally he found Brandon curled up in a ball in one corner, almost hidden behind a stack of old newspapers. Brian could barely see him at all except when he moved, and he seemed to be making no effort to come out. Then he realized the kid probably couldn't tell who he was in the dark.

"It's me, Beebo. Come out and tell me what's wrong," he said.

That got results. Brian staggered and barely kept from falling backwards into a mountain of rusty gas pipes heaped up behind him, almost bowled over by what felt like a human cannonball. Brandon wouldn't do anything but cry for a long time, and Brian soon gave up trying to ask him anything. It could wait.

Instead, he sat down and held him till he stopped crying before trying to talk to him again. Brandon still wasn't having any of that just yet, though, and the tears threatened to start all over again.

Eventually he calmed down to the point that Brian was able to pick him up and carry him out of the attic, and that was progress at least. It wasn't until they came out into the hall that he saw Brandon's left eye was almost swollen shut.

Brian went cold inside. Black eyes don't come from falling; only fists can do that.

Still, he said nothing, and took Brandon to their room. When he got there, he shut the door and sat down in his old rocking chair by the window. He knew, in a way, that this was just as much his fault as it was Mama's, because he was the one who'd wanted to go off and leave Brandon alone with her. He knew better. He couldn't pretend he didn't.

"Let me look at your eye, Beebo," he whispered. Brandon turned his head, looking up at him with one bright blue eye the exact same color as Brian's own. He couldn't see out of the other one, which gave him a strange, lopsided look.

Brian didn't care about being secret anymore. He closed his eyes, and imagined Brandon's eye the way it was supposed to be, and then kissed it. And when he looked again, there was no trace of the black eye left. Brandon looked at him soberly and laid his head on his brother's shoulder, and then it was Brian's turn to cry.

Chapter Two

"Where'd you go this morning, Brian?" Brandon asked him finally, when both of them were a little calmer.

"Oh, nowhere much," he replied, still not wanting to say too much about the amulet.

"Yes you did. I saw you cross the pasture and you was gone forever," Brandon contradicted. Brian shook his head and sighed. So much for secrecy.

"I had to go up to the Rock for a little while, bubba, that's all," he said. That was all Brandon really needed to know.

"Well, you stayed gone too long. Mama was mad cause you left and didn't tell her," Brandon told him. Brian tasted a fresh surge of guilt when he heard that.

"I'm sorry, bubba. I won't do that anymore, okay?" he promised. Brian figured a little humility never hurt anybody, and Brandon smiled.

Before either of them could say anything else, they were both startled by the sound of the front door slamming, followed by Mama's old green Monte Carlo spinning out of the pothole it had made in the driveway.

Brian glanced out the window just in time to see the car turn left at the end of the driveway, and then he knew without a doubt where she was headed. That was the way to the nearest liquor store, twenty miles away at the county line, and also the way to the nearest bar if Mama felt like venturing a little farther afield. That meant she wouldn't be back for at least an hour or two, maybe not even for the rest of the day if they were lucky. Brian felt a weight slip off his shoulders as he watched her leave, even though he knew what it probably meant for later.

The rain was falling heavily now, and it looked like it meant to keep on for a while this time. That was just fine with Brian, now that Mama was gone. He meant to catch up on some sleep for a few hours, if he could only convince Brandon to do the same. If Mama came home drunk again later on and started trouble, there was no telling how late it might be before she let them go to bed.

Of course, it was always possible she'd meet somebody interesting at the bar and stay out till midnight or maybe even all night long, but that was no sure thing. Brian knew better than to count on it.

So he found a more comfortable position in the chair, and started rocking while they watched the rain together. Before long, Brandon laid his head down on Brian's shoulder and his thumb crept slowly toward his mouth, a sure sign of sleepiness. Brian slipped an arm around and gently dislodged the thumb, but Brandon wasn't nearly asleep just yet and put it right back.

"Sing me a song, Brian," he asked suddenly. This was a normal request, and Brian didn't mind. Music was a thing that came naturally to a boy who spent so much time alone. He'd found an old guitar in the attic a few years ago and learned to play it by ear, but he had a good singing voice, too; a high treble that hadn't quite started to change yet. He would have died a thousand deaths before letting anybody else hear him sing, but for Brandon he didn't mind.

So Brian sang softly for a while, an old song he remembered from church and which both of them had always loved, especially the last verse:

> *Oh, they tell me that He smiles on His children there,*
> *And His smile takes their sorrows away,*
> *And they tell me that no tears ever come again,*
> *In that lovely land of unclouded day,*

By the time he finished the song Brandon was asleep. The thumb had fallen out of his mouth, leaving a thin thread of slobber stretching from his lip to his hand. Brian carefully pushed his mouth shut so he wouldn't get drooled on, and that was that.

The back of the rocker was high enough for Brian to rest his own head there, so he did. After a while, the wind shifted around to the south, blowing the rain in heavy sheets against the windowpanes and blocking most of his view. Brian closed his eyes, and before long he was fast asleep, too.

He slept for several hours, until finally the discomfort of sitting in the rocker woke him up. It was still raining a little, but other than that the house was silent. Brian listened carefully for the sound of the TV or anything else that might tip him off that Mama had made it back home, but there was nothing.

He yawned, and rubbed the sleep out of his eyes with balled fists. His neck ached from sleeping in such an odd position for too long, and the rest of him wasn't too comfortable, either. He wanted to stand up and stretch his legs. He carefully got up from the chair and laid Brandon on the bed without waking him, and then rubbed the back of his neck to ease the cramp.

As soon as that was done he padded downstairs to get a drink of water and possibly clean up the kitchen while he still had time. He knew Mama would be furious if she got home and found it still dirty, and she might show up at any moment. She'd been gone for hours already. He almost dared to hope that maybe she really *would* stay out all night this time. He knew it was almost too good to be true, but you never could tell.

He went to the screen door and peered outside at the rain. It had slacked off to a slow drizzle again while he slept, and there were heavy wisps of smoky white mist drifting across the face of the mountains in the distance. It made them look dreamlike and insubstantial, like a country in some fairy tale he'd never heard before but would have very much liked to hear. They were called the Crystal Range, and the name only made them seem even more mysterious and beautiful than they already were. Brian watched them for a few minutes, eyes unfocused, lost in thought. Many times, he'd looked at those distant mountains and wished he could run away to some shining land where there were no tears and no miseries, where fathers never disappeared, and mothers never gave their children black eyes, and all things were forever bright and beautiful. It was perhaps the dearest and deepest wish of his heart.

He knew it was nothing but a childish daydream, of course, and for a long time he'd told himself it was foolishness even to wish for such things. The world didn't work that way, and it was no use to break his heart with longing for things that could never be. So he'd told himself, many more times than he could ever remember, until he'd come to believe it for the most part.

Still, he was a little sad when he turned away from the mist-shrouded mountains, and no amount of reasoning about the way the world worked could quite shake it loose. He'd never spoken of these things to anyone; it was simply his own private sorrow, always there in the back of his mind but seldom thought of anymore.

He sighed, and turned his attention to cleaning up the mess in the kitchen instead. That was something practical he could think about, instead of empty pipe dreams.

He grabbed a wet dishrag from the sink and mopped up the meatball, which had somehow gotten crushed since earlier and was now smeared greasily across the floor in a long maroon trail. The empty vodka bottle by the refrigerator was quickly thrown in the trash, and he was in the middle of sweeping up the beer and cigarette butts when he suddenly realized there was no reason why he should have to work so hard.

He glanced at the stairs and listened, to make certain Brandon was still asleep. He hadn't seemed to think much about what Brian had done to his eye, but the less he saw, the better. Brian stealthily touched the amulet, then closed his eyes and imagined the kitchen to be spotlessly clean. He wasn't sure whether it was really necessary to keep his eyes shut or not, but it did help him form a clearer image of what he wanted, and surely that helped, didn't it?

When he looked again, no one would ever have guessed the kitchen had ever been messy. Not a speck or a stain was on anything, almost like someone had scrubbed the whole room with a toothbrush.

Brian smiled with satisfaction and then headed back up to his room. It always made him vaguely uneasy to be down there in

Mama's territory for very long, even when she wasn't home. Now that his work was done, he was ready to be upstairs again.

The room he shared with Brandon was the second one on the left hand side at the top of the stairs, and besides the attic, it was Brian's only real refuge. Mama did have obscure scruples at times, and one of them was that she let him do pretty much whatever he liked with his room.

On the wall above his bed was a tattered picture of his grandfather, and on the back of the door was a height chart for Brandon and a faded copy of the Ten Commandments. A single goldfish swam lazily in a glass bowl on top of Brandon's toy chest. In the corner was a dirty-clothes box that had once held Washington apples, and just above it a big red crayon scribble that he'd never been able to scrub off the wall. Other than that, everything was as spotless as Brian could make it. He liked order and stability in his world, and this was one of the few places he could make it happen.

On the desk was an old buck knife with his grandpa's initials *SDG* carved deep into the base of the blade; a parting gift from the old man not long before he'd passed away. On the wall behind it hung a cork board with a collection of photos pinned neatly side by side; mostly of Brian and Brandon, of course, with a handful of Grandpa Stephen or Aunt Carolyn, plus a few of Mama and Daddy back when they were still together.

Besides the bed and the desk, the only other piece of furniture was the big antique rocking chair. Brian had salvaged it from the dump a few months ago with one of the arms broken in half, but he'd fixed that by binding it tightly with half a spool of yarn, and then he'd wrapped the other arm so it would match. It was still a little wobbly, but not too bad.

Brandon was still sleeping, so Brian sat down in the rocker and soon fell to daydreaming about Spring in the mountain meadow, and all the great things he might do in the world.

He still had the hole in his shirt from climbing through the fence that morning, and it crossed his mind that it might be worthwhile to try fixing it. He wasn't worried about holding the amulet away from his body anymore; he simply let it rest against his chest. The metal had quickly picked up his body heat and lay almost unnoticed against his skin, just a round flattened lump under his t-shirt.

He traced the shape of it with his forefinger, and then with a silent wish he sealed up the hole in his shirt. He reached behind his back to make certain it was really gone, and his hand met nothing but smooth fabric. He nodded with satisfaction.

He glanced again at Brandon, but the boy still seemed dead to the world for the time being. Cleaning the kitchen had put Brian in the mood to try something else, but he was still afraid to be too obvious about it. So, what to do?

A tiny fleck of paint on one of the windowpanes caught his eye, and with a snap of his fingers it was gone. The windowsill was already as clean as he could scrub it, but upon further inspection he decided it still lacked something. He erased the paint off the surface and polished the wood underneath so that it almost glowed. Brian contemplated this change for a second, then dyed the faded curtains a rich midnight blue, at the same time mending every tiny run and spot-hole.

The colorful window was in such contrast to the rest of the room that Brian decided to go a little farther, just to see how it would look. He could always put it back the way it was.

He turned his attention to the wallpaper, which was cracked and peeling in spots. Some of the places were discreetly patched with scotch tape, but Brian thought that looked pathetic now. He soon fixed the problem, restoring the paper to like-new condition. He bleached the fly-specked ceiling to bright white, and polished the hardwood floor, too. He sealed up a rip in the mattress where stuffing was coming out, and fixed the tatters in Papaw's picture. Soon, the brass doorknob glittered like gold, every piece of clothing in the closet became brand new, and the fishbowl turned sparkling clear. Even the goldfish looked bigger and brighter than ever before. Within minutes, Brian had changed the room utterly, and he could hardly contain his pleasure.

He knew it couldn't stay like that, of course, and with a disappointed sigh he changed everything back the way it had been before. Almost. He didn't undo the floor polish or the new curtains, and he didn't dirty the fishbowl or dull the goldfish. He also left Papaw's picture alone. He thought those things were small enough that they wouldn't be noticed, and if somebody *did* notice then he could explain them pretty easily. In fact, if he was slow and careful enough, he thought he might even fix up the whole house little by little when Mama wasn't paying attention.

He had high hopes.

* * * * * * *

Mama came home at three a.m. that night.

Brian and Brandon were long since in bed asleep by then, but Brian snapped awake when he heard her kick the front door open. Sometimes the wood swelled up a little bit from the moisture when it rained and made it stick against the jamb. All it took was a little extra coaxing, but of course Mama was too impatient for that; especially if she'd been drinking.

Brian was instantly on edge, his heart pounding, and he half sat up in bed. Brandon hadn't stirred, and that much at least was good. The longer he stayed out of it, the better.

Brian knew better than to show his face unless he had to, so he kept quiet and listened instead of getting up.

He heard Mama talking downstairs, and then he caught the sound of someone else's voice too; a man this time. That wasn't good, and Brian strained his ears to see if he could figure out who it was or what they might be saying to each other, but it was too hard to hear.

He debated with himself about the wisdom of creeping to the top of the stairs and trying to figure out who the dude might be and just how drunk Mama really was. If she was already close to passing out then he didn't have much to worry about, but if she was just now getting started then he didn't dare go back to sleep for a while. He didn't like not knowing. But then again, if he got caught spying the consequences could be terrible.

After a while, he decided it was worth the risk. He stealthily got up and tiptoed across the room, where he paused to put his ear up against the crack of the door. They were still downstairs; that was good.

With utmost caution, he ever-so-slowly turned the doorknob, and then opened the door just enough to slip out into the hall on his hands and knees. It was dark except for the light welling up from the stairway, and that was all to the good, too.

Brian crept close enough to the top of the stairs so that he could hear what was being said, and then got down on his stomach with his chin cupped in his hands. Mama was laughing, and so was the man. Then he heard some other woman's voice, too. They all sounded just about medium drunk, but nowhere near ready to pass out yet. That was bad; it was the most dangerous time of all.

They seemed to be talking about politics, of all things. . . a topic which didn't interest Brian at all. He was pretty sure he'd never met either the man or the woman before, but at least they didn't seem like the kind of loud and dangerous drunk that you had to keep an eye on. Brian didn't care how many people his mother dragged home as long as he didn't have to deal with them and they didn't get mean.

Well, maybe on some level he *did* care, but that was another one of those impossible pipe dreams that did him no good at all to think about.

He listened long enough to make sure there was nothing going on except drunk-talk, and then shook his head in disgust and got back up on his hands and knees to crawl back to bed. Hopefully whoever-they-were would be gone before morning. In the meantime, Brian was glad it was no worse.

He wasn't as careful on his way back to the bedroom as he should have been, and his foot accidentally bumped against one of the little tables that held Mama's houseplants. It teetered over and fell to the floor with a loud thud, spilling dirt and baby spider plants everywhere.

It was too much to hope for that no one down below had heard the noise, and Brian's worst fear came true when he heard footsteps coming upstairs.

There was no chance to hide and precious little time to make up a story, but he tried. He scrambled to his feet just barely before Mama's head appeared in the stairwell, with a furious look on her face.

"What are you doing out of bed, Brian?" she demanded, before she even made it up the stairs.

"I'm sorry, Mama. I was just on my way to the bathroom. I'll clean it up," he promised, trying to sound as sorry and as scared as he could, not daring to meet her eyes. Then she noticed the spilled pot for the first time.

"You clumsy little. . . Get downstairs right *now* and find something to clean that up with!" she bellowed, and he hurried to obey.

He didn't quite make it past her. She caught him with a punch to the nose that made him see stars, and he stumbled against the stair banister, barely catching himself from falling. He gripped the wood tightly and took a deep breath to steady himself through the pain, and then headed downstairs.

His whole face was throbbing, and he could feel warm salty blood running down his chin and dripping onto his shirt, but he dared not stop to wipe it away.

He made it to the bottom and saw a burly man sitting at the kitchen table with a half-empty bottle of Absolut vodka in front of him, Mama's favorite brand. Next to him was a woman with stringy gray hair who looked like she'd seen better days. *Much* better days, as a matter of fact. Both of them were laughing.

"Sometimes you got to teach the little hard heads a lesson, dontcha, Peg?" the man called out, and Mama laughed too.

"All the time," she agreed, and cuffed Brian again to show him she meant it. She only caught the side of his head above his ear that time, but it hurt badly enough to make him stumble again. He grabbed the broom and the dust pan from beside the refrigerator with trembling hands, and said nothing at all while he rushed back upstairs to clean up the spilled flower pot.

He was very good about not letting himself cry in front of his tormentors, not till he got back upstairs and out of sight. But when he heard them still laughing and socializing in the kitchen just like nothing at all had ever happened, then he couldn't hold himself back any longer.

Still, he wept quietly, as he'd learned from long experience to do. And after he'd cleaned up the mess, he went to the bathroom and washed his face and his shirt to get rid of the blood. His nose and his temple still hurt something fierce, and his eyes were still puffy and stung from crying.

"You're really a mess, boy," he murmured to himself, staring at his reflection in the mirror. It wasn't all that funny, but he smiled a little. Then he winced, because the movement hurt his nose. Mama hadn't pulled her punch, that was for sure.

He washed his face again, mostly because the cool water felt good on his hurt spots, and then he swallowed three ibuprofen tablets and went back to bed. Brandon never woke up, and for that at least he was thankful.

He told himself again that it was just the way things were, and he cursed himself for being so clumsy as to knock over the plant, and even for being stupid enough to get up in the first place and try to spy on his mother. Didn't he know better, after all this time? If he'd had a lick of common sense he would have gone back to sleep without even thinking about trying such a foolhardy stunt as that. But he had, and so now he had to pay the price for it. Simple as that.

He found it hard to go back to sleep, partly from the pain and partly because his swollen nose made him snuffly and blocked his breath. Every now and then he heard Mama and her nameless buddies give an especially loud whoop of laughter that startled him wide awake again. They seemed to be having a merry old time down there, he thought to himself.

At that moment, Brian hated all of them with such a smoldering hatred that anyone who'd seen his face right then might have taken a step backward. But there was no one in the darkness to see, and no one to know it except Brian himself. And God, perhaps, if He was watching.

Brian was ashamed of himself for thinking such a thought, but sometimes he couldn't help wondering why God never seemed to lift a finger to save the people who suffered and didn't deserve it. Brian couldn't decide whether he personally fit into that category himself, but surely Brandon did? Sometimes he didn't know what to believe at all anymore.

"God, if you're really there, please do something to change this. If you don't then I guess you're not real anyway, but I hope you are," he whispered under his breath, and after saying this deeply bitter and disrespectful prayer, he finally slept.

The strangers were gone the next morning when Brian got up, and so was Mama for that matter. She had to work the day shift at the diner that day, Sunday or not. She probably had a hangover again from too much vodka; Brian certainly hoped so.

He felt a little better, himself. His nose was still tender to the touch, but it didn't look swollen anymore and the bruise on his temple was far enough back that it was hidden under his hair. That was good; he would rather have crawled through sewers than to let anybody notice his battle scars.

He told himself it could have been worse; he remembered one particularly horrible night not long after Daddy left, when she'd lost her temper and actually shot at him with the little pistol she kept in her purse. He couldn't remember anymore what it was that she'd been so mad about, that time. Brian had never been so terrified in his life, either before or since, and the memory was seared into his brain like a white-hot branding iron. In fact, there was still a bullet hole in the wall of his bedroom to remind him.

Brandon had been barely a year old at the time, and Brian dreaded to imagine what might have happened if that bullet had passed just three feet lower, through the place where he lay sleeping that night in his bed, totally oblivious to what was going on.

There were times, after an especially painful binge, when Mama wouldn't touch a drop of alcohol for weeks and hardly said a cross word to either of them. But as soon as Brian started to think there might be just a drop of kindness under all that hateful crust, she always fell right back into the same old rut. Brian didn't believe she would ever really change, but at least life was a little easier when she was trying.

A hard and bitter look crept onto Brian's face as he remembered these things, and he touched the amulet without thinking. He'd been caught off guard last night, but never, ever again would he let things get out of control like that. If Mama ever did anything to hurt him or Brandon again then he'd give her a taste of her own medicine, next time. He had the power now to deal with her in such a way as to make her wish she'd never laid a finger on either one of them. He could do that much, and he *would* do it, if he had to. He swore it on a stack of Bibles and on the heads of everyone he loved.

The oath left a bad taste in his mouth almost as soon as he formed the words, and he hoped it never had to come to that. Nevertheless, he meant what he said. He was no tear-stained and terrified little boy anymore; he had power that was almost invincible, and she had better watch out.

Chapter Three

He cooked sausage and scrambled eggs for breakfast that morning, and made cereal for Brandon, and after eating they walked the not-quite two miles to church, as they often did when the weather was nice or if nobody could give them a ride.

Brian sent Brandon to his preschool group and then sat next to Rachel McCray on the third pew, for lack of a better seat. They were the same age, but not particularly close. She lived on the road to Glenwood, maybe ten miles away, and they didn't see each other much except at church or at school. Brian had always thought she looked kind of like a rat; she was too thin, and her nose and chin were a little too sharp, and the Coke bottle glasses she always wore didn't help matters any. He vaguely remembered that there was supposed to be something wrong with her, but he'd never been curious enough to ask anybody exactly what it was.

He didn't particularly like her, but the only other seat he could find was next to Adam Crenshaw and Patti Sue Jackson, whom he liked even less. Adam was a football player and Patti Sue was a farmer's daughter; both of them were popular, good-looking, and fairly rich, and worst of all they both knew it. Brian always got the feeling they were looking down their noses at his raggedy clothes and cheap shoes, on the rare occasions when they talked to each other at all. He was in no mood to deal with all that today.

"Hey, Mad Dog," Rachel murmured when he sat down beside her.

"Hey, Raych," he answered, smiling tiredly at the nickname. His middle name was Madaug, after his great grandfather, and he'd made the mistake of letting that fact slip out a few years ago. It was supposed to be pronounced Madug, not Mad Dog, but people always seemed to think it was hilarious to mangle it like that. Yet another thing he felt like choking his mother for. Or maybe biting her, come to think of it. That might be a lot more appropriate.

"Are you okay? Looks like you've got a pretty good bump on your head," she said.

"Really? Is it that noticeable?" he asked.

"Well, no, not unless you're close up, I don't guess. What happened?" she asked.

"Oh, it was nothing much. I fell down the stairs last night, that's all. Busted my nose, bonked my head; it was just a stupid accident, really," he lied.

"Oh, okay," she said. Then she paused, as if choosing her words carefully.

"Everything's all right, isn't it, Brian?" she asked, awkwardly. It was almost like she knew what really happened, and for some reason that infuriated him.

"Sure. Why wouldn't it be?" he asked, with just the slightest tinge of a hard edge to his voice.

"No reason at all. I'm sorry," she apologized hastily. He hesitated, and then decided it was better to just let it go at that.

"No problem," he said, with a fake smile. In fact he was worried. If blind-as-a-bat Rachel McCray could see that something wasn't quite right, then probably other people could, too. Brian could imagine the gossip all too well, and he suddenly hated Mama even worse than before. The shame was worse than the punch.

He glanced at Patti Sue without thinking, half expecting to see a knowing smirk on her lips. But she was only reading the bulletin and didn't seem to have noticed Brian at all, actually.

He quickly looked away again and told himself to get a grip; just because Rachel noticed he had a bump on his head didn't necessarily mean the whole town was talking about him behind his back. It was crazy to let Mama make him so paranoid.

With some effort, he put on a mild and pleasant face that showed nothing of how he really felt inside, and after a while he managed to put the incident out of his mind.

After church they walked home again, and then Brian fed Brandon and sent him to watch *Tom & Jerry* cartoons in the living room. He had another project in mind to try out with the amulet that day, and it was one he definitely didn't want any witnesses for.

It had crossed his mind that it would be nice to have some money, and he'd been thinking about ways he could make that happen. He had several ideas he wanted to try, and hopefully at least one of them would earn him some serious cash. That was what he had in mind for his afternoon's project.

The first thing he tried was to pick up a sheet of notebook paper and imagine it turning into a stack of twenty dollar bills. But that turned out to be harder than he thought it would be, partly because he discovered that he wasn't totally sure what a twenty dollar bill ought to look like. Oh, he'd seen them before, of course, but he'd never paid close enough attention to remember all the minor details, and he was uneasy about getting something wrong. That could land him in a lot of trouble, if he made a mistake. He wasn't sure he had it in him to be a counterfeiter.

Well, okay then. If he couldn't print money, then what could he do to earn some? He thought vaguely about diamonds and gold and things of that sort, and he decided that would be his next experiment.

Brandon had a big bag of marbles in his toy box, and Brian quietly went upstairs to fetch them. They were only glass, but they sparkled prettily in the sunlight and reminded him of lost jewels. Maybe, with just a pinch of luck, he could turn them into *real* jewels. He picked one up between his thumb and forefinger, and tried to imagine what a diamond would look like. He found that rather difficult too, when it came right down to it, since he'd never seen a diamond the size of a marble before.

Still, he tried, and the marble did change into something that looked mighty similar to what Brian imagined a diamond ought to look like. He remembered that diamonds were supposed to be able to scratch glass, and so he tested his new-made bauble on the kitchen window above the sink. It scratched it, all right, but Brian still wasn't satisfied. There might be other things that could scratch glass, too. Besides that, a diamond that big was probably worth a lot of money, and for that very reason it would probably turn out to be hard to sell. There had to be a better option.

He picked up another marble and imagined it turning into gold instead. He knew what gold looked like, and this time the magic worked perfectly. He opened his eyes and saw that the marble was a bit smaller than before, but other than that it did indeed look exactly like gold. Brian nodded, much better pleased.

He didn't want to use up all of Brandon's marbles, though, so he put the rest of them aside and fetched a handful of pea gravel from the flower pot in the bathroom. Mama used it to put out cigarette butts whenever she was in there, and Brian washed the ashes off in the sink before he did anything else.

As soon as he got back to the table, he converted the gravel into a handful of gold nuggets that sparkled and glittered in the light. All the pieces were smaller than before, which he didn't quite understand, but he shrugged it off as unimportant.

After a bit of thought, he went up to the attic and removed a piece of loose floorboard near the back wall, his well-trusted hiding place. Inside was an old Crown Royal bag, and he pulled this out, listening to the coins jingle inside. Brian liked Crown Royal bags. The purple cloth and gold trim made him feel rich, like a king.

Feeling rich and being rich were two different things, of course. Brian's hoard contained not quite forty dollars, painstakingly collected over the past six months. Quarters left over from trips to the store, nickels and dimes salvaged from sidewalks and baseboards, all of it had gone into his hiding place. He'd learned to be tight as tree bark with his money, but now it seemed less important than before. He took out the change and hid it in an old shoebox where nobody was likely to look, and then he filled up the bag with his nuggets.

He didn't fill it up completely, but even so the bag was awfully heavy. He remembered reading somewhere that gold was supposed to be heavy, though, so he wasn't worried about it. He stuffed the bag in his pocket and decided to call it a day.

He thought he could probably sell the gold at the pawn shop that Mama sometimes used. They had a sign in the window specifically saying that they bought gold, and Brian knew the owner well enough to know that he was a greedy man who could probably be talked into making some kind of deal. With a little luck, he could slip away from school at lunchtime on Monday, get his business done, and be back before anybody realized he was gone. If things worked out right, he'd soon be a very rich young man. Let Adam and Patti Sue and everybody else chew on *that* for a while.

There was still the question of how to explain where he got so much gold, of course. He knew people tended to get mighty curious about things like that, but Brian had a ready answer for them. He'd just tell them he found it amongst his Papaw's stuff in the attic. Everybody in town knew what a pack-rat his grandfather had been, so it wasn't a totally unbelievable story. And even if people doubted it, they wouldn't be able to prove anything. It would never cross their minds to think he was manufacturing it out of pea gravel at his kitchen table, and that was all that really mattered. If they wanted to invent some other story about where it came from, then so be it.

So it was that Monday morning he went to school with a pocket full of gold nuggets and so much enthusiasm that he could barely endure his morning classes. He'd never felt so impatient for anything in his life as he did for the lunch hour to come that day, and when it finally arrived he wolfed down his food in record time and quickly slipped out to the parking lot.

This was technically against the rules if you didn't own a car, but enforcement was fairly spotty. Brian was counting on the fact that nobody would remember he was on foot.

Apparently no one did, because he wasn't challenged when he headed in that direction. Several kids were already out there, sitting on tailgates, talking on cell phones, and occasionally smoking when they thought nobody could see. None of them paid Brian any mind.

He crossed the entire lot and casually slipped into the trees on the far side when he was fairly sure no one was looking. Then he set out for downtown as fast as he could walk. The pawn shop wasn't far from the school, but then again he didn't have much time, either.

There didn't seem to be any customers at the shop when he got there, which was so much the better. He patted the Crown Royal bag in his pocket and fought down the nervousness that threatened to ruin the whole deal. He reminded himself several times that he was a customer, and he had just as much right to be there as anybody else did.

"Hey, Mr. Johnson," he said cheerfully when he walked in the door. Mr. Johnson glanced up from reading the newspaper, and he didn't smile back.

"What can I do for you, son?" he asked, in a bored voice.

"Well, I saw the sign in the window. It says you buy gold," Brian said, a little nervously.

"Yeah, we do. But I'll give you a piece of advice, kid. Whatever you've got, take it back to whoever it belongs to before you get caught with it," he said, in that same bored tone. Brian bit his tongue to hide the surge of anger he felt at the man's casual assumption; he couldn't afford to take offense, no matter how insulted he felt. He took a deep breath and told himself he was there to do business, not to make friends.

"I didn't steal anything, Mr. Johnson, honest," he said.

"Uh-huh. Well, let's see what you got, then," he sighed, putting his feet down on the floor and sitting up straight. Brian quickly pulled out the old Crown Royal bag and shook out a handful of nuggets onto the countertop. Mr. Johnson didn't look impressed.

"Painted pea gravel ain't worth much, kid," he commented.

"Just test it, please," Brian said. He knew Mr. Johnson had chemicals to test for whether gold was real or not; he'd seen him

use it on one of Mama's rings a few times. The man grumbled
and muttered under his breath, but nevertheless he pulled out a
vial of testing acid and dripped a little of it onto one of the
nuggets. There was no reaction, proving the piece was real. Mr.
Johnson looked up at Brian with wary eyes.

"Where'd you get this, son?" he asked, and Brian lost his
patience.

"Where I got it doesn't matter, Mr. Johnson. You can see it's
real, and I promise you I didn't steal it, and you can have it for
half the usual price if you'll just keep your mouth shut and not
ask me any questions," he said boldly. He'd never said anything
like that to a grown-up before in his whole life, but he figured if
Mr. Johnson could be rude then so could he.

For a second Brian was afraid he'd gone too far, but Mr.
Johnson didn't seem to care. He just knitted his brows while he
stared at the gold, and Brian could almost watch the wheels
turning in his mind as he considered the various aspects.

"I think we can do business along those lines, Mr. Stone," he
finally said, and stuck out his hand with a saccharine smile.
Brian shook it with a smile of his own, knowing perfectly well
that the man thought he was cheating an ignorant kid. That was
all right, though. Brian could make all the gold he wanted, and if
he had to give Mr. Johnson a cut rate deal then he was ready to
do it.

They weighed out the nuggets, and when it was all said and
done, Mr. Johnson laid nine hundred and forty-seven dollars into
Brian's hand. It was more money than he'd ever seen in his
entire life.

"You got any more nuggets like that?" Mr. Johnson asked
lightly, after he counted out the money. Brian could almost see
the greed in his eyes.

"I think I might could scrounge up some more; I'm not sure,"
he replied, just as lightly.

"If you do, then you'll bring them to me first, right?" he asked.

"Sure thing. We got a deal," Brian agreed, and that was that.

It turned out to be a sweetheart deal, indeed. Every day at
lunch after that, Brian slipped into the pawn shop to deliver
another bag of nuggets and carry home another wad of cash. He

kept it hidden under the same loose floorboard in the attic where
he'd always kept his stash, where Mama couldn't find it. God
only knew what she'd think or do if she came across a hoard of
money like that. Some of it he spent on things for the house and
stuff for him and Brandon, but by the end of the week he still had
close to ten thousand dollars stuffed away up there, if he counted
right. It was a good feeling, knowing that.

As he grew bolder, he started doing more things around the
house, too, gradually ceasing to care very much whether Mama
noticed or not. He still feared her at times, but not nearly the way
he had just a week ago.

Therefore by Thursday Brian had already fixed most of the
subtle things around the house. . . the scratches and cracks, the
ground-in grime, the creaky wood and the flaky paint. The place
still didn't look all that different at first glance, but the details
were already very clear to anybody who looked close enough.
Mama couldn't help but notice, but so far she hadn't said
anything. Not yet. She surely knew Brian was behind it all, but
apparently she hadn't thought it was anything beyond an
inexplicable attack of cleaning. After all, he hadn't yet changed
anything which couldn't be explained with a lot of elbow grease,
and he never changed anything at all unless she was gone first.

But that wasn't all. He used his newfound wealth to do all
kinds of things he'd never had a chance to do before. He bought
anything he wanted, without even looking at the price. He went
places and hung out with people who would barely have spoken
to him a week ago. Even Adam Crenshaw started acting like
they'd been best buds since kindergarten.

Brian wasn't stupid; he knew the only reason Adam and the
others suddenly liked him so much was because he was generous
with his money, but for the time being he honestly didn't care.
He was enjoying himself too much.

And then there was his main project, the one he lavished more
care and love upon than any other, and that one he shared with no
one but Brandon.

If anyone had visited Black Rock about that time, they might
have noticed something different about the place. Brian
remembered what he'd done to the little meadow that first day,

and in his enthusiasm he decided to beautify the whole area. He worked unceasingly on the land all round the Rock, until it gradually became a radically different place than it had ever been before. The first thing he did was to kill all the bugs and snakes and creepy-crawlies. He destroyed every thorn and every thistle, every weed and every wasp. Nothing dangerous or ugly was allowed to invade his little kingdom. It was reserved exclusively for all things bright and beautiful, and he set an invisible barrier to keep any new pests from getting in.

About forty acres was the limit of his power to maintain all this, but within that circle the land was becoming like a page from a fairy tale in which every day is high spring and there is no stain to be found on a single leaf or stone. By Thursday evening it was almost perfect, with only a few little touch-ups remaining.

If Brian had thought about it, he might have connected all this with that old, heartbroken longing he'd felt when he gazed at the misty mountains of the Crystal Range after the rain, when he imagined some place where no bad thing could ever come, or when he sang *Unclouded Day* to Brandon and dreamed of the same thing. But Brian was young, and it never crossed his mind to connect the dots in that way. All he knew was that the place touched his heart and made him happy, and that was good enough.

He spent as much time up there as he could, when he wasn't busy with Adam or other things. Sometimes he didn't even come home till after dark. That wasn't so *very* unusual, of course, but at first he'd worried that Mama would get suspicious and maybe even come up there looking for him. But she still seemed oblivious for the time being, and if she noticed anything different about the house or about Brian's behavior, she didn't see fit to mention it.

So it was that on Thursday evening he was planting white oaks, setting acorns with one hand and then making them grow into tall trees in less than a minute. He kept one eye on his work and the other on Brandon, who was playing in the dirt not far away. Brian had never left him alone again since the day he got the black eye, and that meant he had no choice but to take him along up to Black Rock, even if it meant partially letting him in on the secret.

He still worried sometimes that the kid might slip up and say something about what he saw to somebody who didn't need to hear it, but so far he seemed to accept it all without question, like it was the most natural and ordinary thing in the world. He hadn't even asked how any of it was possible. Brian told himself that even if he *did* mention it to somebody, they'd probably just think he was imagining things. Nobody paid much attention to what a little kid said, especially not a wild story like that.

At least he hoped not.

Still, Brian always wore the amulet under his shirt and never said a word about it, just in case. The less Brandon knew, the less he could talk about.

Brian stood up from planting acorns and wiped a trickle of sweat off his forehead. It was hot work, growing trees. But he loved white oaks, and he didn't grudge the effort. It was well worth it.

He looked down the trail at Brandon playing in the dirt, and with a half-smile lifted him up off the ground and dusted him off. Brandon had loved that at first, but he was starting to get tired of it.

"Put me down!" he cried, struggling uselessly against the breeze. The sun was beginning to slant low across the ravine, and it was almost time to call it a day.

"I think I might just carry you home that way, Beebo," Brian replied, teasing him. He wasn't serious, but from Brandon's howl you would have thought he was pulling hair. Brian floated him closer and set him down on his feet.

"I didn't mean it, silly boy," he said.

"Yes you did," Brandon said, crossing his arms and scowling furiously.

"All right, I'm sorry then, okay?" he asked. Brandon thought about that for a few seconds, and gradually stopped scowling.

"Okay," he agreed.

Brian took his hand, and they walked home together with no more ado.

There were limits to his power, of course, and through trial and error he'd gradually figured out what these were. He couldn't affect anything more than about a thousand feet away, and he couldn't create something out of nothing. He couldn't make things with complicated parts that he didn't understand. He couldn't bring things back to life if they were dead, and he couldn't affect anybody's thoughts or feelings. But he could move things, and he could change one thing into another (if he had the same amount of mass to work with), and he could usually heal wounds on living things and make them grow.

He wasn't inclined to complain about the things that were beyond his reach, though. What he *could* do was plenty awesome enough.

He was sure there was still a lot he didn't know, but that didn't worry him very much anymore either. He looked forward to finding out everything there was to know, little by little. He had all the time in the world, and it was a pleasure he had every intention of enjoying to the fullest. Still, there were times when he wished the amulet had come with an instruction manual.

Mama was working the evening shift that night, so she wasn't home when they got there. Brian cooked a pot of macaroni and cheese and cut up some hot dogs in it to give it a little extra pizzazz, and after supper he gave Brandon his bath and put him to bed. He enjoyed all these normal things very much, perhaps because he associated them with the nights when Mama wasn't home and therefore he had peace and freedom for a little while.

That night, in the simple happiness of his heart, Brian gave up on secrecy. Mama could think whatever she wanted to think; he was determined to fear her no longer.

Therefore he walked through the house with a critical eye, changing anything he felt like changing. He denied himself nothing his heart could wish for, from marble floors in the bathroom to crystal goblets in the kitchen. The place became beautiful as the castle of a king long ago, and Brian was delighted at what he'd done.

There were certain things he could only do with money, so he snatched up some cash from his hiding spot and called Adam to give him a ride to town.

Adam was cruising the streets with Patti Sue when Brian called, but both of them were more than happy to do him a favor. Patti Sue even offered to stay behind and watch Brandon until they could get back from the store. It was truly amazing how things had changed, Brian couldn't help thinking. But that was all right; he appreciated it anyway.

Once they got to the store, he bought a big-screen TV and a high-definition stereo, a brand new computer and a dirt bike, among other things. Adam was suitably impressed, and Brian favored him with a hundred dollar bill just for the pleasure of giving it away.

All these things he set up in the house, and when he was done, he was awed all over again by the power he held in his hands.

He enjoyed it all for a little while, and then quietly went upstairs to bed. Mama could think whatever she liked when she saw it; he could deal with her, if he had to.

He quickly changed into a more comfortable t-shirt and some shorts without switching on the lights, then laid down on the bed beside the already sleeping Brandon, listening to the old house creak and settle for the night.

Brandon made a vague sleepy sound and moved closer to him, not really awake. He settled comfortably against Brian's side and then grew quiet again. Brian reached down and smoothed his soft red hair, just starting to get long again now after being shaved off for the summer back in June. It looked like he was dreaming about something from the way his eyes moved, and Brian felt a gentle wash of love for him.

"Good night, Beebo," Brian whispered, and snuggled close beside him. He wasn't especially sleepy yet, but he knew that would come soon enough, if he lay still for a little while. In the meantime, he said his prayers and dreamed about the future, and his thoughts were good ones.

Brian was happier than he could ever remember being in his whole life, and he foresaw no end to the good times and the good work he could do with the amulet in his hand. He'd barely scratched the surface. He had power and wealth beyond his wildest dreams, and what could he not do now? The amulet had been the greatest thing that ever happened to him.

He smiled again, and then slowly drifted off to sleep.

Chapter Four

He fully expected Mama to say something to him about the house at breakfast the next morning, because there was no chance whatsoever that she hadn't noticed what he'd done. But she was strangely silent about everything, even dazed-looking, and if he hadn't known better he could have sworn he saw a glint of fear in her eyes when she looked at him.

That was impossible, of course, but still, the very idea of it made him feel awkward and uncertain how he ought to speak to her, or if he should even speak to her at all. He was used to living in fear of her, but to have the shoe switched so suddenly to the other foot left him at a loss for how to behave.

So neither of them said much of anything, and Brian was relieved when the bus finally came to pick him up.

School was uneventful that day, but Adam had invited him to come to a tailgate party before the football game that night, just to hang out and have a good time for a while. Brian had never been invited to such a thing in his entire life, and he was determined to go.

He hadn't asked Mama for permission, nor did he much care anymore whether she liked it or not. She was working the evening shift at the diner again, and Brian had hired a babysitter for Brandon. . . another thing unheard of in all the days of his life up till then. He knew Mama wouldn't have liked that at all, if she'd known about it, but he didn't care much about that either. There was nothing she could do about it either way.

He put it out of his mind and met Adam in the school parking lot as soon as class was out.

"Hey, Mad Dog, you ready to go?" he asked cheerfully as soon as Brian made it to the truck.

"Yeah, but where's Patti Sue?" he asked, looking around. Normally she was stuck to Adam like super glue.

"Oh, she's already home. Her mom came and checked her out early today so she could go to the doctor. But hurry up if you're going, cause she's already texted me twice wanting to know where I'm at," Adam said.

Brian shrugged and got in the passenger seat, not really interested in Adam and Patti Sue's love life. If she wanted to act like a clinging vine and he wanted to put up with it, then that was their business.

The party was supposed to be at Patti Sue's place, down by the river. Her daddy raised several hundred acres of rice and soybeans down there in the flat bottomlands, and he didn't mind if they used one of the empty fields.

Adam turned off the highway onto a rough dirt road that led way back into the soybean fields, and before long Brian spotted the orange glow of a bonfire.

"There it is, Mad Dog," Adam said, smiling eagerly.

When they got there, Adam stepped on the gas and spun his tires in the dirt before he slid to a stop, and Brian heard several people holler and clap appreciatively.

Most of the kids were a year or two older than Brian, which made him feel both slightly uneasy and deliciously grown-up at the same time.

Several people had brought radios and coolers full of Cokes, and Patti Sue was handing out wieners and marshmallows to roast over the bonfire. Brian helped himself, and he was in the middle of roasting his second marshmallow when Adam came up behind him and clapped a hand on his shoulder.

"Come on, Mad Dog, let's go get some mud on the truck," he said.

"Sure," Brian agreed, and climbed into Adam's 4x4 with two other guys he didn't know. Adam revved the engine till it sounded like it might blow up, and then let off the brake. The field was still pretty soggy from the rain a few days ago, and Adam's big tires tore the ground to pieces and sprayed mud everywhere.

"Won't Mr. Jackson get mad if we mess up the field like this?" Brian asked during a lull when Adam could actually hear him.

"Nah, he won't care. Nothing grows down here anyway," he explained.

Brian shrugged. If Adam didn't care, then he sure didn't.

Before long it was time to go to the game, so they doused the fire with river water and cleaned up the empty Coke cans and such. Brian rode with Adam and Patti Sue, but once they got to the game those two disappeared together and left him to fend for himself.

He didn't mind. He just found a place to sit in the front row of the stands and cheered when there was a good play, eating hot dogs and popcorn to his heart's content. He was sorely tempted a few times to make the ball fly just a little bit farther and help the team score a touchdown, but he didn't meddle. It was enough to know that he could have done it if he'd wanted to.

The game was over at nine, and since Adam and Patti Sue were still nowhere to be found, Brian hitched a ride with someone else. He decided on a whim to have them drop him off at the post office instead of at home so he could walk for part of the way. He was in the mood for some solitude after so much socializing all evening, and besides, it was only about two or three miles from there to his house. He was used to walking that far.

The night breezes were cool against his skin, carrying with them the faint scent of late-blooming jasmine from somebody's yard. He felt at peace with himself and the world, and inclined to do a good deed if anything happened to present itself.

He came to Annie Summerford's house before long, and on impulse he left a crisp hundred dollar bill in her mailbox. Miss Annie had once been the school librarian, but Brian knew she was old and poor now. If anybody could use some extra money, he was sure she could. Leaving that much cash left him nearly empty-handed, but that was okay, too. He had plenty more at home.

Helping Miss Annie made him feel good, and as he went on he kept an eye out for anything else he might do.

He passed the old stone gym and the little white church by the creek without seeing anything else worth doing. He removed a few smudges of gray lichen from the rocks on the gym, but that wasn't very satisfying. He wanted something more dramatic than that.

A few stray leaves were beginning to turn yellow on the sweet gum trees, more from the heat than the season. Brian was tempted to move things up a bit and see what fall would look like in September, but he decided that might attract more curiosity than he felt like dealing with. So he left the trees alone and told himself he could always try it with the white oaks around Black Rock if he liked. He could turn them green again anytime he really wanted to, if he didn't like it.

He crossed the bridge, and saw his Aunt Carolyn's place sitting dark and silent on the far side of the creek. A few really determined weeds were growing up through the old cattle guard, and Brian quickly killed them for her.

A full moon was shining through the trees behind him, flooding the highway with pools of silver. Brian waded through them, following his footsteps home. On another day he might have been frustrated by the lack of opportunities to do anything meaningful for people. One would have thought there were more needy folks in the world than just one old woman. But he was feeling good that night, and it would have taken a lot to darken his mood. Maybe another day, he thought to himself.

At long last he opened the back door and went inside the house, pleasantly tired from the long walk but not really sleepy just yet. The babysitter was on the couch watching a movie, and he paid her and sent her home. Brandon was already long since in bed, and Mama wouldn't be home till after midnight.

Brian washed the dishes, and then sat down on the big overstuffed couch in the living room to watch a movie for an hour or two until he felt like going to bed. He picked one at random, which turned out to be *Predator,* with Arnold

Schwarzenegger. Brian liked that just fine; anything with that many guns and explosions was always reliable entertainment.

He hadn't been watching long when he was startled by the sound of a key turning in the back door lock, and he turned around just in time to see Mama coming into the kitchen.

This was an anomaly; she shouldn't have been home for at least two more hours yet. But before he could get up or think to say anything, she shut the door behind her and looked at him steadily.

"Brian, we need to talk," she said, in a tone which he couldn't quite figure out. She didn't seem angry, and certainly not drunk. Worried, maybe? Whatever it was, he couldn't put his finger on it.

Mama put down her things and came to sit in the recliner across the coffee table from him. She seemed nervous, and she kept twisting the ring on her finger and picking at the hem of her uniform, like she didn't know what to say.

This was so out of character that Brian had no idea what to expect. But he'd learned from long experience not to rush her, so he sat in meek silence while she gathered her thoughts, whatever they might be.

"When did you find it?" she finally asked.

"Find what, Mama?" he asked.

"Brian, don't play dumb. You know exactly what I'm talking about. The necklace," she said.

He was momentarily shocked that she knew about the amulet, but he quickly recovered himself. It didn't matter anymore whether she knew or not; there was nothing she could do about it anyway.

"Last week," he answered, truthfully enough.

"What *day,* Brian?" she insisted urgently, and he couldn't help wondering why it was so dadgummed important.

"Saturday. Why?" he ventured to ask. Asking Mama questions was always a risky move, but his power had made him bold. Mama ignored the question.

"Saturday, saturday. . ." she said softly, half to herself, as if thinking hard. He still had no idea what was on her mind, and found himself irritated by her foot-dragging. If she had something to say, why didn't she just go ahead and say it?

"What all have you done with it?" she asked suddenly, looking at him intently.

"What do you mean?" he asked.

"I mean I know about all the stuff you did to the house and I know you got some money from somewhere. I don't care about all that. I want to know what else you've done, if you've messed with anything alive or anything that belongs to somebody else," she asked.

"Why do you need to know?" he asked. This verged on downright disrespect, and he knew it, but Brian was determined to stand his ground this time. He could see that his answer angered her, but for once she forced herself to speak calmly.

"Because you don't know what you're playing with, that's why. You could cause terrible things to happen and not even realize it, Brian," she explained.

"What kinds of things? And why does it matter how long it's been?" he asked.

"Because it only works for seven days, that's why, and if you found it last Saturday then tomorrow at midnight is the end of it all. There's no way to fix anything stupid you already did, but there's still the next twenty-four hours to think about. I don't want you to make any more mistakes between now and then," she said. That sounded more like the old Mama; insulting and high-handed as usual. Still, Brian could tell she was making a real effort to bite her tongue and talk to him reasonably. And somehow that scared him more than any harsh words she might have used, because it meant she was deadly serious about whatever she said.

He was gripped by a sudden terrible fear that she might be telling the truth, and he had to swallow hard to keep his calm. The thought of losing his power was horrible to even imagine, especially when the idea was sprung on him so suddenly that way, and when the deadline was so near. *Tomorrow!* He could never finish everything he'd wanted to do by then, not even close.

It might be a lie, of course; but even the possibility was enough to make his throat dry and his chest tight.

"How do you know?" he asked. It came out almost as a whisper, and Mama noticed his fear. She smiled a bitter smile.

"Did you bother to read the thing before you went off on your little spree? No? I didn't think so. Stupid boy," she muttered under her breath, and Brian felt hot blood rising to his cheeks. She seemed to have a supernatural talent for making him feel like a complete fool.

"No, I couldn't read it. The writing was too small," he said, surly now.

"Uh-huh. Never heard of a magnifying glass? Even an idiot would have known that much," she said, scornfully.

Brian had had about as much of her attitude as he could take. He looked up at her with smoldering eyes that held more than a little hatred, and when he spoke there was ice in his voice.

"What difference does it make to *you* if I do something stupid or not? You never cared about me or anything I ever did anyway," he blurted. A week ago he would never have dared to say such a thing to her, and perhaps if she hadn't been speaking to him that way he wouldn't have said it now. But as it was, the cold and bitter words spilled out before he could think to hold them back.

That silenced her, but Brian took no pleasure in it. The accusation left a bad taste in his mouth, and he was almost immediately sorry he'd said it. The words might be true, but that was no excuse. Truth which is spoken without love can be cruel as a punch in the gut. Didn't he know it all too well himself? He could see clearly that his words had stung, but hurting her only made him feel worse.

"I do love y'all, whether you believe that or not," she finally told him. Those were never cheap words from his mother, and he knew he must have cut her deep to make her say them now. There were even tears in her eyes, shocking as that was. Brian didn't have the faintest idea what to say to her. So he said nothing at all, taking refuge in silence as he'd done so many times before.

But the hurt didn't last very long, and his silence seemed to infuriate her.

"Go on, then, rockhead. Don't listen! You'll find out soon enough what happens, and then we'll see how much damage you've done!" she screamed, and then proceeded to curse him with every foul name she could think of and then some.

Brian didn't wait to hear more. He got up from the couch and left the room without another word, and Mama let him go.

He couldn't have gone to sleep just then if his life depended on it, not till he calmed down a bit, so he left the house through the back door and slammed it behind him, not caring if it angered his mother. In fact he hoped it did.

The full moon gave plenty of light to see by, and after a moment's thought Brian set out across the pasture toward Black Rock, not caring how late it was. He needed some time alone, and that was one place he knew he could get it. He couldn't decide how he felt, except that it wasn't good. He wanted to hit something and he wanted to cry while he did it, and what kind of a messed up mood was that?

Nothing disturbed him until he emerged onto the flat surface of the Rock, where he took a seat at the foot of one of his perfect white oak trees. He was a little calmer by then, and the peace and beauty of his sanctuary soon lulled him yet further. The soft breeze in the oak leaves and the quiet gurgle of the creek flowing over stones were sweet balm for his jangled nerves, just as he knew they would be.

He pensively tossed a few pebbles over the edge of the Rock into the swimming hole, lost in thought. Mama had given him a lot to think about, even if he wasn't sure how much of it to believe.

Now and then his fingers chanced across a larger rock nestled among the tree roots, and these he threw hard and fast across the little gorge until they smacked with a satisfying *thwock* into the old sweet gum tree on the far bank. Its trunk was gnarled and deformed by a thousand previous impacts, silent proof that it had been used as a rock tree since long before Brian's time. He hadn't used the amulet to fix it; it was too much of a landmark.

He wasn't sure who the last stone-thrower at Black Rock might have been, but he could still see the faded craters whoever-it-was had left behind. The only clue he'd ever found was the name *Jack,* carved with a pocketknife into the trunk. Who Jack might have been was anybody's guess.

Brian couldn't remember anyone ever teaching him how to throw. It just seemed like he always knew how. He seldom missed the mark anymore when he chose to try, so the exercise hardly occupied his mind.

He soon decided that, whatever else she might have said, Mama had a good point about reading the words on the amulet. He really should have done that to start with, if he hadn't gotten so caught up in the excitement of the whole thing. It galled him to admit that she might actually be right about something, but there it was.

All he could do was wait till morning and see if he could find a magnifying glass somewhere. There wasn't one in the house, as far as he could remember. He guessed he'd probably have to get a ride to Wal-Mart and buy one.

That was one thing decided, at least. As for the rest of it, about losing his power after seven days and all that. . . well, he'd know one way or the other soon enough. There was nothing he could do about it either way. If Saturday came and went with nothing happening then he'd have proof that she was a liar and he'd never have to believe her again.

On the other hand, even if he did lose his power, there wasn't *much* he could think of that still needed doing. He had plenty of money now from the gold, and it wouldn't take long to beef up his nugget stash a bit. Other than that, he'd already done everything he cared the most about doing, if it came right down to it.

There was still the problem of dealing with Mama with no amulet to back him up, but Brian was a lot less scared of her than he'd been before. If the amulet had done nothing else for him, it had at least given him a healthy dose of courage.

He wondered if the seven blue gems on the front of the amulet had anything to do with the seven days Mama was talking about, and then decided it didn't matter.

As he mulled all this over, Brian began to feel the first twinges of sleepiness gnawing at the edges of his mind, and he decided to take a dip in the swimming hole to clear his head.

He stripped down to his underwear and took a running dive off the Rock into the deep pool below it, making a huge splash when he hit the water. The creek was clear as crystal, and he could see the bottom even by moonlight. In fact that was almost what it seemed like. . . swimming in a tank full of liquid moonlight. He liked the image, and when his head popped back up above the surface he shook it to scatter droplets of water out of his hair like a dog. He swam back and forth for a while, and then floated on his back with his fingers laced behind his head to keep his ears above water.

The night was warm and tranquil, and he felt no inclination to go home just yet. So in the meantime, he wished the stars a little brighter and the song of the crickets a little sweeter, and drank in as much of the peace of the place as he could.

After a while, his spirit calmed and refreshed, he climbed out of the pool and used the amulet to dry himself off before he put his clothes back on. He'd certainly miss little things like that if he lost his power, he thought to himself. But he was calm enough now that the thought only made him smile.

When he finished dressing, he made his way back home through the woods and across the pasture.

The house was dark when he got there, and he supposed Mama must have gone to bed already. Just as well; he didn't feel like talking to her anymore at the moment, not even to say goodnight. He tiptoed upstairs as quietly as he'd ever done in the bad old days, to lie down beside Brandon and hope for a better day in the morning.

He was very careful to wear a tight t-shirt that night, and to tuck the amulet firmly inside it so that no one could sneak in and take it from him while he slept.

That done, he prayed for everything to work out as it should, and then closed his eyes.

* * * * * * *

In the morning the goldfish was dead.

The bowl had turned gray with pollution, so dense and thick that nothing could be seen through the murk.

Brian could smell it even before he opened his eyes, and he quickly got up and threw it away before Brandon had a chance to see it. He silently promised himself to get a new one in a few days, whenever he had the chance. He wouldn't try to pretend it was the same one, but when something died it was usually better to replace it quickly.

He didn't give the dead fish much more thought after that, although he was soon to get a nasty surprise that gave him plenty of reason to think about it. But in the meantime, it was a gloriously bright and beautiful day, with the first scent of fall hanging crisply in the air, and Brian was happy with the world. Mama and all her dark and ominous words seemed like no more than a bad dream, to be swept away and forgotten in the morning light.

He changed clothes, whistling softly to himself, and then went to wake up his brother.

"Come on, Beebo, get up! Time to go!" he said cheerfully. Brandon groaned, and Brian tried tickling him. That usually worked, but not today. Brandon just rolled out of reach and pulled the covers back over his head.

"What's wrong with you, sleepyhead?" Brian laughed.

"Don't feel good," Brandon finally said.

"Well what's wrong? Does your stomach hurt, are you bleeding; what is it?" Brian asked.

"No, just don't feel good," Brandon answered. Brian touched his forehead, but it didn't feel especially warm. Nothing was wrong, as far as he could tell.

This was a complication. He needed to go get that magnifying glass, and beyond that he had a vague idea that they might go the lake for a few hours with Adam and Patti Sue. Brandon enjoyed things like that, as long as he had something to occupy his attention. But not if he wasn't feeling well.

Brian wrinkled his eyebrows and thought for a while. It was unlikely that he'd be able to find a babysitter for a sick kid on such short notice, but the trip to Wal-Mart was absolutely necessary if he wanted to read those tiny little words on the back of the amulet. He could put off going to the lake, but not that.

The only person he could think of to ask was Carolyn. Fortunately she turned out to be agreeable, and by the time she got there about thirty minutes later, Brian had to admit that Brandon did look sickly. He was pale and had dark circles under his eyes.

Carolyn took him home with her, and Brian promised to come fetch him later that afternoon.

He felt a little bit guilty about going off elsewhere when Brandon wasn't feeling good, but he told himself Carolyn would take good care of him and it wouldn't be for very long anyway.

That done, he put the matter out of his mind and called Adam.

They had to run all the way to Hot Springs to get to the nearest Wal-Mart, and when all was said and done it took almost two hours before Brian got back. He didn't dare try to read the words on the amulet in front of Adam, so he had to wait till he was home again before he gave it a shot.

As soon as he got there, he sat down at the kitchen table and took the amulet off, then laid it down flat on the tabletop so he could study it. The writing was so tiny that it was hard to read even using the magnifying glass, but after a few minutes he figured it out, and this is what he read:

Seven days you have the power.
Touch no living thing.
If the chain is broken, all is lost.

Brian felt a sudden chill in the pit of his stomach, replaced almost immediately by fear. Seven days. Touch no living thing.

That was the part which laid an icy finger on his heart and filled him with dread. Because he'd touched many living things, in all kinds of ways, and he dared not guess what the consequences might be. His mind jumped instantly to Brandon, and the goldfish, and Mama's warning about terrible things. He swallowed hard.

He abruptly stood up from the table and slipped the amulet back around his neck, telling himself sternly that he had to get a grip. He didn't know anything for sure yet, and panic wouldn't help anybody. The thing to do was to find out, if he could.

He couldn't quite bring himself to check on Brandon first; that cut far too close to the bone for him to face it immediately. But he could check on the trees and things at Black Rock, and maybe that would tell him what he wanted to know.

He hurried across the pasture and through the woods so quickly that he was soon out of breath, so anxious was he to find out whether his worst fears were true.

Almost as soon as he crossed the invisible barrier between his protected land and the everyday world, he noticed that something wasn't right. Many of the leaves on the trees were yellowed and withered, and some even looked dead. In places he noticed a jelly-like brown fungus growing on the branches, and that certainly hadn't been there before.

Brian felt another thrill of dread, but he refused to give in to despair just yet. Whatever it was, he might still be able to fix it. He used the amulet to kill the fungus and make the plants grow healthy new leaves, but there was nothing he could do about the dead ones. He turned those to dust instead. There were only a few of them, so the gaps were not very noticeable. He worked as he walked along, patiently fixing whatever was wrong.

It was strangely silent in the woods that day, a fact which he didn't notice for quite some time. But presently, as he worked his way up the path, he found a dead cardinal on the ground, and Brian's heart came up right into his throat when he saw it. It was brilliant red, even more so than normal. Brian had given it a little extra color at some point, just to make it look nicer. It was hard to say what had killed it. It didn't seem hurt, other than the fact that it was dead. Brian turned it to dust as he'd done with the withered trees, and it was then that he first noticed there were no birdsongs.

Indeed, Brian saw almost nothing living except the trees. He came across several dead or dying birds, and once a dead fox. He'd changed all the animals in his little patch of woods in some way or other; brightened their colors, made them bigger, given them blue eyes or softer fur or something like that. All of them had been fine yesterday, but now everything seemed to be dying.

Even during the little time he'd spent in the area, the leaves had yellowed and dropped off several more trees. Even the grass was dying.

He fought hard against the spreading destruction that had dropped like a stone into his peaceful kingdom, until he was exhausted from the battle. He couldn't keep up. Barely did he grow a new tree before it began to die too, and within an hour it was a dead trunk like so many others. He tried healing a few of the birds that were still alive and found that it lasted only a few minutes before the bird was dead. Brian was at his wit's end, unable to figure out what was happening or how he could stop it. His beloved sanctuary was beginning to look like a wasteland. By sundown there was hardly anything left but dead sticks and bare dust, like a bomb had exploded and destroyed every living thing.

Just as the sun slipped below the horizon, Brian abruptly gave up all hope of doing any more good up there. He ran down the trail towards home, paying no more attention to the dead and dying region he'd spent so much effort to cultivate.

When he got home, he went directly to the phone. All he cared about by then was getting hold of Aunt Carolyn and finding out whether his worst fear of all might really be true. He got her voice mail three times, and that only made things worse.

He left the house, running down the road to his aunt's place as fast as he could go. There was no car in the driveway, but he hoped against hope that maybe somebody was home, that maybe Carolyn had just gone to the store for something. He came to the front door, still breathing hard from his run, and found a note pinned to the mailbox. He snatched it up, and slowly read what was written there.

Brian, if you read this, we're gone to the hospital. Brandon is very sick. I already called your mother and she's coming up here. Stay home and we'll try to call you later.

That was all it said, but that was enough. Because he knew what was wrong, without a shadow of a doubt. Every living thing he'd touched with the amulet had sickened and died, and he'd used it on Brandon to heal his black eye.

Which he wouldn't have had in the first place, if Brian hadn't been so careless. So whose fault would it really be, if he. . .

Brian couldn't bring himself to even finish thinking that thought, and he sat down on Carolyn's porch and wept for the third time in a week.

Presently he went home and sat in the gleaming kitchen beside the phone, anxious not to miss any calls. He soon found that doing nothing was unbearable, so he fixed a frozen pizza and ate as much of it as he had the heart for. Then he wandered slowly through the quiet rooms in silence, touching things here and there. It was beautiful, yes, but he would gladly have traded all of it just to have Brandon home safe. What were money and things, compared to that?

Eventually Carolyn did call, and the news wasn't good. Brandon was still alive, just barely, but he wasn't doing well. Carolyn tried to say that nobody knew how it might turn out yet, but Brian could read between the lines well enough; what she really meant was that nobody expected him to make it for much longer.

He stayed calmer at that news than he thought he would. It might have been because he already expected it, or it might have been because he was too numb for words. Maybe both.

He got off the phone with his aunt not long after that. He felt dead inside, and couldn't think of anything else to say. He knew he must have seemed cold, but right then he didn't have the heart to care.

Brian pulled the amulet out from under his shirt and looked at it with hatred, wishing he'd never found it in the first place. If Brandon died then he'd never forgive himself. He studied the medallion forlornly, praying that he might find something to show him a way to save his brother, anything at all that he might have overlooked. But the only things he saw were the glittering fountain and the seven bright gems, and the flowing script around the edge.

Seven days. *Touch no living thing.* If the chain is broken, all is lost.

He wished bitterly that he'd known those three things a week ago.

Except, of course, he knew he *could* have known them a week ago, if he'd only made the effort to try. It hadn't been so very hard to figure it out. All it had taken was a crummy dime-store magnifying glass. But he'd been careless about that too, and now Brandon would be the one who paid for it.

He wondered very much about that third line, and what it might mean that all would be lost. Everything he'd done with the amulet? He'd gladly give all that up, if it would help.

Brian seized at the tiny scrap of hope like a drowning man snatches at a life preserver, and prayed to God he wasn't wrong. He took the necklace of the amulet in both hands, closed his eyes, and then, with a hard yank, he snapped the chain.

Chapter Five

As always, there was no fanfare, nothing to show that the magic had worked. Brian heard and felt nothing except the breaking of the silver chain. But when he opened his eyes, he found a world utterly changed. The kitchen was full of the exact same mess he remembered from last weekend, right down to the spilled beer and cigarettes on the floor. There was no trace of any of the changes he'd made all week. It was almost like he'd stepped back in time.

Brian blinked stupidly, and had a surge of *déjà vu* so strong that he honestly wasn't sure what was real and what wasn't anymore. He had to pinch himself to make sure he wasn't dreaming. He still didn't believe it and pinched himself again.

After a minute, he noticed that everything wasn't *quite* the same as before. The wide-screen TV and the computer he'd bought were still there, and so was anything else he'd purchased with money. It seemed to be only the things he'd directly used the amulet for that had disappeared.

He had a fleeting, idle thought of all that gold he'd made, suddenly turning back into pea gravel in somebody's bank vault somewhere, and wondered how he could ever sort *that* out. He sighed and thrust the idea out of his mind; he could deal with that later. Right now the only thing he cared about knowing was whether Brandon was safe or not.

The sudden reappearance of the nasty kitchen, beer puddle and all, gave him a wild hope that Brandon might even be back home already, just like nothing had ever happened. He'd been forced to believe stranger things lately.

He listened, just in case, but the bottom floor was empty and silent as the grave all around him, so Brian quickly ran up the filthy stairs to check the rest of the house.

He opened his bedroom door slowly, hardly daring to hope. Just like the kitchen, everything was exactly as it had always been before he found the amulet. He hadn't bought anything to put in there; it had all been done directly.

There was a vaguely human-shaped lump under the covers, and Brian crept to the edge of the rumpled bed, trembling. Then he pulled the corner of the blanket down, and found nothing there but a crumpled pillow.

He felt another surge of sickening fear and near-despair, but he refused to give in just yet. He methodically searched the rest of the house until he was certain there was no one else there, and when he was sure, he went back to the kitchen and called his aunt.

She answered on the first ring.

"What is it, Brian?" she asked.

"Is Brandon any better?" he asked immediately, hoping against hope.

"He's pretty much the same as he was thirty minutes ago," she said dryly. For a second Brian was startled that so much time had already gone by, but when he glanced at the clock he couldn't doubt it.

"Okay, sorry to bug you so much," he said.

"It's fine; I know you're worried," she said.

"So they think he'll be all right, then?" he insisted hopefully, and she hesitated before answering.

"The doctors are doing everything they can, Brian. That's all I can say for now. We'll just have to take it one day at a time and see what happens," she said. That was a far cry from what he wanted to hear, of course, but he bit his lip and tried to stay calm.

"Okay. Just let me know if anything changes," he finally said.

"I will. I promise," she said, and that was that.

After the call, he went back to the kitchen table to wonder what it could all mean. It seemed like breaking the chain had erased everything he'd done with the amulet, but if so then why was Brandon still sick? That part didn't seem to have changed at all, and Brian told himself he should have known it could never be that easy.

He buried his face in his hands and wallowed in misery for a few minutes, racking his brain desperately for something else he might do, anything at all he could try. He couldn't bring himself to believe there was nothing to be done, in spite of all the setbacks and failures in the world.

He looked at the amulet again, and for the first time he noticed that the little crack around the back side had popped open just a bit, enough for him to grab the edge with his thumbnail and open it.

This was something new, although Brian was too miserable to let himself hope that it could possibly mean very much.

Still, he couldn't help but try it. He hooked his thumb nail at the edge of the crack and spread the two halves apart, not sure what to expect.

As it turned out, one side contained something rather like a compass, with a needle that pointed in the same direction whichever way he turned the amulet. The only odd thing about it was that the needle seemed to be pointing northeast instead of north, and no amount of shaking or twisting could convince it to change its mind.

Brian could make little sense of that, but when he turned to the other side he was none the wiser. The back side contained some kind of verse centered across the middle, in the same flowing script he'd seen on the back. It was just as tiny, too.

There was just the barest sliver of hope in that, if the words could tell him anything useful. Brian had nothing else to cling to, so he hauled out the magnifying glass again, and this is what he read:

For the one who loves life more than things,
To whom love is more precious than power,
For the one who has strength of desire,
Who can bear length of days with pure heart,

Come drink, if you will, of the Fountain free-flowing,
At the heart of the world, where wishes come true.

Brian quickly scribbled the words onto a sheet of paper, just in case he couldn't get the amulet back open again later, wondering all the while what on earth all *that* could mean. He hardly dared guess or imagine.

He shut the amulet and tried to open it again, just to test the matter, and he found that it wasn't at all hard to open anymore. That *must* have changed when he broke the chain, because it had always been impossible to open before.

Then he noticed another oddity. The chain wasn't broken after all. It was all in one piece, smooth and whole, just like it had always been. That confused him more than anything, because he knew perfectly well that he'd broken it. He'd felt it snap, he'd even *heard* it.

That was another mystery Brian couldn't even begin to fathom, but in the meantime he was much more interested in that last line of the poem, the part about wishes coming true.

He wasn't sure he trusted the amulet anymore after everything he'd seen. He thought of Brandon, still lying there dangerously ill at the hospital, and he remembered the blasted devastation at Black Rock. Maybe he hadn't been quite as careful as he should have been, true, but still. . . using the amulet was like playing with dynamite. It could do wonderful things, but it could also blow up in your face and kill people, too. He didn't know if he wanted to take that chance again.

But he also remembered wiping away Brandon's black eye, and the light and the beauty that had seemed to glisten from every leaf and every blade of grass before the end came, and when he glanced around him at the poor and tattered room he sat in, his heart broke at the memory. In a way, it was worse to have tasted beauty and then have it snatched away, than never to have known it at all. Surely all that couldn't have been just a trick and a lie, could it? He wasn't sorry for giving it all up to save Brandon, for life was indeed sweeter than anything in the world, and love was more precious than all his powers. There was no trace of a doubt in his mind about those things, and never would be again. He hadn't realized how much treasure he really had, until he almost lost it.

But still. . .

He remembered, all too well, the way things used to be. He might have learned a thing or two and found a bit of courage he'd never known before, but the rest of the world had seemingly gone right back to the way it always was. Mama would still be a drunk, and Daddy would still be gone, and Brandon still might die, and he was pretty sure he'd end up having to give all the money back once people discovered that his gold had turned back into gravel. He might even go to jail for it.

At the very best, nothing would have changed from before. Brandon would come home to the same sad and broken place as always, and life would gradually settle down into the old familiar pattern. There was a time when Brian would have told himself there was nothing better to hope for, but he found that it was hard for him to accept that kind of thinking anymore.

He couldn't help wondering (just a little) what might happen if he really followed the amulet to the heart of the world and drank from the Fountain. Surely that's what the compass-thing was for, wasn't it, to show him the way? Wishes coming true was a pretty strong promise, when you stopped to think about it.

Was he being offered something more than just wealth and power, perhaps? Did he dare to believe that he might, just might, get all those impossible things he *really* wished for? Might he soften Mama's heart, and bring Daddy back, and make Brandon really well, and turn home into as beautiful a place as ever he'd tried to make Black Rock to be? It was almost too good to be true.

If Brian had been a different sort of person, perhaps he wouldn't have had the courage to believe such a thing for a second time. But as it was, hope and fear both nagged at his heart until he was almost torn to pieces inside.

Then again, what did all the rest of it mean, about bearing length of days with a pure heart, and where exactly was the Heart of the World?

Brian swallowed hard, and tried to judge which way the compass was telling him to go. It seemed to point north and a little east, toward the Crystal Range and whatever might lie beyond them, the land of his fantasies and daydreams since childhood. It seemed fitting, in a way, that that was the direction the amulet would tell him to go. But the question of how he was supposed to get there and what he might find when he did; for that he had no answers at all.

He walked slowly to the back door and looked out through the screen at the distant mountains, and beyond them the Heart of the World. Did he dare to believe? For that matter, did he dare *not* to dare?

He felt very alone at that moment, and unsure what he ought to think or believe, let alone do. His choices so far hadn't turned out all that well. He would have liked to talk to someone, anyone, but there was nobody he could think of. Mama and Carolyn were out of the question, and somehow he didn't think Adam or his other new buddies would be much better. He needed a friend, and for the first time in a long time he realized that he didn't have any.

That only made him feel worse than ever, though. So he took refuge in a chat room on the Internet, that last bastion of lonely souls.

The room was supposed to contain people who wanted to talk about mythology; Brian's best guess for where he might find some information and not get laughed at for asking such questions. So he posted the verses from the inside of the amulet, asking if anyone had seen them before and what they might mean.

It seemed like a long shot at best, but an hour later he was rewarded with an answer from a girl in Mississippi.

"It reminds me of a story I heard once, about a flowing fountain at the heart of the world, where people could drink from it and stay young and beautiful forever, and have all the wishes of their hearts come true," she said.

"You mean like the Fountain of Youth?" he typed back, thinking immediately of the diamond-crusted fountain emblazoned on the front of the amulet.

"Sort of like that, I guess. But not just anybody could find it; only the ones who knew the way. The ones who got invited, you might say," she replied.

"Invited?" he asked.

"Yeah. There was something about having to pass a test of some kind, as to what you'd choose when you really had to; power and wealth, or love. That's why that verse you posted reminded me of the story," she said.

"Do you think it's true?" he asked, not stopping to think how flaky that might sound, even on a mythology forum. She didn't answer right away, and after a while Brian thought he must really have put his foot in his mouth. But eventually he got his answer.

"I guess I believe there's nothing too good to be true. If the story isn't real, then it must be because it's not good *enough* to be true, not because it's *too* good, and in that case the real truth would be something even better," she finally said.

Brian pondered that, and couldn't decide what he thought about it yet. He'd never heard anyone put things quite like that before.

"Do you know the name of that story, or where I could find it?" he asked.

"I don't remember, but I'm pretty sure you could find it at the library or online, if you searched a little," she told him.

"Okay, thanks a lot," he told her, and again she didn't answer for a few minutes.

"I hope you find it," she finally said, and for a second he was startled at her words, until he realized she might only be talking about the story, not the Fountain.

Brian knew a little bit about how to search for things online, but not so much that he was able to do it quickly or well. It took him at least two hours to find anything, and the story he finally did locate turned out to be very difficult to read. The language was awfully old-fashioned, full of words and expressions that confused him. Nevertheless, he could puzzle it out if he tried. It was pretty much just like the girl had told him, but still, the story was well worth reading, for it mentioned one small but extremely important detail that the girl had left out.

Maybe she just hadn't remembered it, or maybe she hadn't thought it mattered enough to mention, but all the people in the story were led to the Fountain by a guide of some sort, which they were warned never to lose or to part with, lest they never find the way and be lost forever.

That was enough to make a believer out of Brian, for he knew beyond a doubt that the amulet he held in his hands must surely be his very own guide. And that verse inside it, whatever else it might mean, was an invitation to come and drink. It had to be. So he knew the way, and apparently he was invited, if he had the courage to follow through with it.

He thought again about Brandon, and that decided him.

"All right, I'll come," he said out loud, and once the decision was made he felt a great weight slide from off his shoulders, and he felt calmer and quieter than he'd felt all day.

He put the amulet safely in his pocket and switched off the computer before trudging upstairs to the attic. His money stash was still there, just as he'd left it, and he took a thousand dollars with him, for whatever he might happen to need. He wasn't sure what that might turn out to be, but he knew he didn't want to be broke. On the other hand, he didn't want to take all the money, either. That was just an invitation to get robbed, or worse.

He left a note for Mama, telling her he'd be back soon. It'd probably infuriate her that he hadn't asked first, but it might possibly keep her from calling the cops or coming to look for him herself. For a while, at least.

That done, he kick-started the dirt bike and rode it to the store by the crossroads, where he bought some leather gloves and a pair of sunglasses to keep the wind out of his eyes, and also a warmer jacket. The bike wasn't really made for long-distance riding, and it wasn't even street-legal for that matter, but since it was all he had it would have to do. He'd just have to be careful and not go too fast, and ride the ditches and back roads as much as he could, unless he could find something better at some point.

He thought about going home and getting a fresh start early in the morning, but then quickly decided that probably wasn't a good idea. Mama might come home, and that would make things difficult. It was better to go ahead while he still could.

He soon discovered that he couldn't follow the way the amulet told him to go; not exactly. The road didn't run quite that way, and the best he could do was to pick the road that seemed like it went in more or less the right direction. His best bet seemed to be the main highway that led into Glenwood.

He didn't plan on riding that far until morning; his main goal at the moment was to find somewhere other than home to sleep for the night, so he could avoid Mama if she happened to show up.

After a little while he passed a lonely barn in the middle of nowhere with no houses nearby, and he decided that it looked like an excellent choice. It was getting late, and he was more tired than he would ever have believed possible.

He killed the bike and walked it up the lane to the barn, so as not to make so much noise. The place looked deserted and ramshackle, and a bit spooky if the truth was told, but it must have still been used from time to time, because the loft was full of fresh hay. Brian parked his bike in one of the horse stalls and covered it with a ratty old blanket that he found hanging on a nail. Then he climbed up the ladder into the hay loft and found a place as close to the wall as he could, for the sake of getting a little breeze. The late summer night was still warm.

He kicked off his shoes and curled up in the hay as comfortably as he could to wait for daylight, and in spite of the strange bedding he fell asleep surprisingly quickly.

Nothing disturbed him during the night, and nothing looked down on him except a barn owl returning from the fields near morning. Nor did he dream, except the sweet and simple dreams of the pure at heart, of the kind that nourish the soul but are never remembered.

He woke later the next morning than he usually would have, perhaps because the day before had been so full and difficult. It must have been almost eleven o'clock when he opened his eyes, and he might have slept even longer if a finger of sunlight hadn't crossed his eyes just then.

He got up and stretched, yawning while he did so. Then he put his socks and shoes on, and made his way down the ladder to where his bike was hidden under the horse blanket.

He consulted the amulet to make sure he was still headed in the right general direction, and checked his map to make sure the road would keep going that way. All seemed to be well, so far.

It was a sunny, breezy day; good biking weather. Still, by the time he came into Glenwood he was beginning to feel cramped and uncomfortable. He wanted very much to get off and stretch his legs for a while.

It was way past noon by then, and Brian felt that it was high time for some food. There was a little convenience store not far from one of the city parks, and on a whim he decided to get some picnic supplies and have his lunch right then and there. He got cheese and bread and Miracle Whip, some smoked turkey breast, a bag of potato chips, and a two liter bottle of sweet tea. Then he went to one of the tables as far from the street as he could, within sight of the Caddo River splashing and glittering in the sunlight, and there he fixed himself a sandwich and some chips and laid them out on a paper towel. He ate slowly, taking time to savor the food and also to enjoy the warmth of the day.

He wondered if anybody would be looking for him at home yet, and somehow doubted it. He probably still had a while before anybody even noticed he was gone, much less cared.

Still, he took the time to call the hospital and talk to Carolyn for a few minutes to check on Brandon. There was still no change, and Brian wasn't sure whether to be pleased or worried by that news. It sounded good at first, but then again, the longer somebody stayed in bed, not moving or breathing on his own, the worse his chances were. Even Brian knew that much. People got pneumonia after a while, and Brandon had always been worse than most people about that kind of thing. He got chest colds all the time.

Brian told himself not to paint things blacker than they already were, but it made him twice as determined to find the Fountain as soon as possible, before things had a chance to turn bad. One wish would cure everything, and he could never rest easy till it was done.

Beyond telling Brian to go over to her house if he got hungry or needed anything, Carolyn didn't show much interest in where he was or what he might be doing. So much the better, he thought to himself.

Afterwards he had another sandwich and then got up to stretch his legs a bit, stopping long enough to toss three pennies into the river. The only other person in the park was a girl sitting with her grandmother and tossing bread crumbs to the sparrows. Or at least the grandmother was; the girl seemed more than a little bored. She saw Brian toss the pennies into the water, and smiled at him.

"You won't get much of a wish for three cents," she said. They were close enough that she could talk to him without shouting, and he smiled back at her.

"I didn't know this was such a high-priced river," he said. It was a mild joke at best, but she laughed.

"Well, no, I guess it's not. So what did you wish for?" she asked. He knew she was just making idle conversation for the sake of having somebody to talk to, but he didn't mind.

"I wished I could find the heart of the world," he said, truthfully. There was no particular reason to keep it a secret; she'd never take him seriously anyway, or even understand what he was talking about. But whatever the girl might have thought about his wish, she never got a chance to answer him.

"Here now, what's all this talk about the heart of the world?" the grandmother broke in, staring at Brian with the oddest sort of look in her eyes. It was almost a hungry look, he thought, like she wanted to eat him alive. He noticed for the first time that she was uncommonly pretty for an old lady, and for a moment Brian stared back at her, curious. She had on a pair of knitted gray mittens and a matching shawl that looked much too hot for the weather, but then Brian remembered that old people were always cold.

"It's nothing. I just heard a story once, about a fountain at the heart of the world where wishes come true, and I thought it'd be cool to find it someday, that's all. It was a silly wish," he said, apologetically. The girl smiled again when she heard all this, but Brian noticed that the old woman wasn't smiling at all.

"Who told you about the Fountain?" she asked, still staring at him.

"You've heard of it?" he asked eagerly, almost unable to believe it. This time she smiled slightly.

"Oh, indeed I have, child. Indeed I have, long ago. I even drank from it with my own lips," she declared. The girl glanced at her grandmother with exasperation, and then gave Brian a pained look.

"You have to forgive Granny; her mind isn't quite what it used to be, I'm afraid," she apologized in a low voice. Brian was crestfallen, and could barely hide his disappointment.

"Oh, I see. It's all right," he said. But the old woman cackled and gave him that hungry look again.

"You have to forgive Janette; she thinks I'm bonkers. But I meant what I said, young man. Come see me, *alone,* at Pinecrest, room 208, tomorrow, and I'll tell you the whole story," she told him.

"Sure, I'd love to," he said automatically, and Janette gave him another embarrassed look.

"Thanks for humoring her. Come on, Granny, I think it's about time we headed home," she said, turning to her grandmother.

"Bonkers. Nobody listens," the old woman muttered, but she roused herself when her granddaughter stood up and took her hand. Janette never looked back, but the lady gave him one more keen look as she was getting into the car.

Brian wasn't sure if the old biddy was really crazy or if she might actually know something worth hearing, but he finally decided it couldn't hurt to wait till tomorrow and go see her. At worst he would have wasted some time, and at best he might find out some things well worth knowing.

But first he had to find out where he was supposed to go. She'd said Pinecrest, room 208, wherever that was. Brian guessed it was a nursing home, but he couldn't remember hearing of it before. He'd been to Glenwood pretty regularly, but only to go to the grocery store and sometimes a few other places. Other than that, he didn't know his way around all that well. He'd never needed to.

A quick look at the phone directory gave him the address of Pinecrest Retirement Village, and since the town was fairly small, it didn't take him long to find the place. It was a long brick building with three wings and a flat roof, with a bunch of elderly folks sitting on a patio out front. It looked old and run-down and depressing, and choosing a cutesy name like "retirement village" didn't change the reality of what it was.

But the old lady had said to come see her tomorrow, not today, so there was no point in lingering.

The first thing he had to do in the meantime was to find a place to stay for the night, and he didn't much feel like sleeping in a barn again. Then he'd see what the morning would bring.

Chapter Six

The first thing he found was Tabitha's House, an old ramshackle Victorian-looking house downtown which advertised itself as a bed and breakfast inn. Brian wasn't fussy, and since there didn't seem to be anything else nearby he decided it would do well enough. He parked his bike in the little parking lot and trudged up the worn concrete walk to knock on the door.

It was opened, eventually, by a bald man wearing jeans and cowboy boots. That by itself might not have been so unusual, except that they were dark green fake alligator skin. Real leather was never that shiny, and never that green, either. Brian was looking down at the man's feet and couldn't help but notice such a spectacle, but he didn't comment on the man's taste in fashion.

"Can I help you?" the man asked. He sounded friendly enough, in spite of the fake alligator boots, and Brian looked at him and smiled.

"Yeah, I'd like to rent a room for the night, please," he said, trying to look as serious as he could.

A skeptical expression crossed the man's face, and Brian wished he could have looked a few years older; it would have simplified things so much. But however skeptical the man might be, he apparently decided to err on the side of caution.

"Of course, sir. We do have a couple of rooms available," he agreed.

"How much for one night?" Brian asked.

"Two hundred dollars, sir," the man said. Brian almost choked with sticker-shock, but he'd learned long ago from Mama never to show anything on his face that he didn't want people to see. Therefore he remained cool as a cucumber, and didn't betray how he really felt. He was tempted to walk away and look for something cheaper, but the thought of the smirk on the man's face if he did was enough to change his mind. He'd been laughed at way too often for being poor.

"Sure thing," he nodded. The man's eyes opened a little bit in surprise; he'd probably thought the price tag would get rid of a kid without having to go to the trouble and risk of refusing to rent him a room. Most times it probably would have worked, too, Brian thought, trying not to smile. But as it was, he'd offered a price and Brian had agreed, and that put him in an awkward position to weasel out of it. He tried, though.

"I hate to do this, sir, but since you don't have a reservation, we'll have to ask for cash before you can check in. Will that be all right?" he asked.

"No problem," Brian agreed, pulling out his billfold and taking out a couple of hundred dollar bills. He took his time about it, making sure the man could see that he had plenty more where that came from.

The innkeeper took the money, somewhat ungraciously Brian thought, but he offered no more objections and stood aside so Brian could come in.

Then he led his guest to a bedroom near the back of the house, on the second floor.

"This is the Tyler Room," he intoned pompously after opening the door, and Brian wanted to laugh again. The place really wasn't fancy enough to deserve having all the rooms with their own names. But once again, he kept his thoughts to himself.

"I hope you'll find everything in order, sir. If you need fresh towels or if you'd like anything from the kitchen, just push the intercom button by the door and we'll be glad to bring it to you," he said. Then he excused himself, leaving Brian alone.

The room was decent, with polished hardwood floors and a handmade quilt on a big four-poster bed. There was a portrait of

President John Tyler on the wall, for whatever reason. Maybe the room was named after him, though Brian couldn't have guessed why to save his life.

The window looked out on a street view that wasn't particularly interesting, and there was a private bathroom. It was nice enough, but Brian had halfway expected golden faucet handles and crystal chandeliers for the price he'd paid.

Still, he didn't much care. He could spare the money, and it was a lot better than the hay loft. He'd only have to stay one night, just till he could go visit the nursing home sometime in the morning. In the meantime he enjoyed a hot shower and put on some clean clothes, and after that he felt much better.

Almost as soon as he finished getting dressed, there came a knock on the door, and a girl's voice.

"Room service!" she called cheerfully. Brian was a little bit puzzled; he hadn't ordered anything, and the girl sounded vaguely familiar for some reason.

"Come in!" he called.

She opened the door, and he suddenly found himself confronted with Rachel McCray, standing right there in the doorway with a big smile on her face.

Brian cursed under his breath. Here he was trying his best to keep secret, and right out of the gate he had to run smack into somebody he knew. Could his luck get any worse?

"Is anything wrong?" she asked, seeing the shock on his face.

"Oh, no. . . I just wasn't expecting to see you, that's all," he explained, lamely. She laughed.

"Oh, that. Yeah, I just work here a little bit now and then on the weekends and after school. It's a good job. Helps me make a little money, you know. Anyway I was in the kitchen and I saw you coming up here with Mr. Croydon, so I just wanted to come say hi," she added.

This could be a problem, Brian thought to himself. If Rachel went home and told somebody where he was, then it might get back to his mother and wreck everything. He thought quickly.

"Well, hey, come in for a minute if you want to. I needed to ask you something anyway," he told her.

"Oh, yeah? What?" she asked, coming into the room and sitting down on the bed.

"Um. . . this might sound weird, but I need you not to tell anybody you saw me here, okay, Raych? It's really, really important," he told her. That piqued her curiosity, and she looked at him with her head cocked to the side, like a bird watching bread crumbs.

"How come?" she asked simply.

"It'd be a long story, I'm afraid. Let's just say I've got some things I need to do, alone, and if anybody finds out where I am then they'd drag me home before I could finish," he said.

"You mean you ran away from home?" she asked, wide eyed.

"No, no, nothing like that. I'll be back home in just a few days. Just got some things to do, first," he told her hastily. She hesitated, and he could tell that she wasn't sure whether to believe him or not. That would never do; he had to find a way to get her on his side, no matter what.

"Raych, listen. If I tell you what's going on, will you promise me you won't say anything to anybody?" he pleaded.

"Brian, I don't know if I can-" she started, but he interrupted.

"Just listen first, before you say anything one way or the other. Will you do that much? Please?" he asked.

"All right. I'll listen," she agreed reluctantly.

"Brandon is sick, maybe dying," he told her flatly, getting right to the point.

"Oh, Brian, I'm so sorry. I heard he was at the hospital but I didn't know it was that bad," she said. He had her sympathy, but now came the tricky part.

"Okay. The reason I'm here is because I heard about something that maybe could save him, but I knew nobody would let me go find it if I told them," he explained.

"What are you talking about? Why wouldn't they? What kind of a something?" she asked. Brian took a deep breath; the next part was even trickier.

"They say there's a fountain at the heart of the world, and if you drink from it then all your wishes come true. I think if I find it, then I can save him," he told her. She looked at him skeptically, like she was trying to figure out if he was joking or not.

"You're serious?" she finally asked.

"I've never been more serious in my life. My brother might die if I don't figure something out; I wouldn't joke about something like that," he reminded her.

"Brian. . . " she started, but he cut her off again.

"Listen, I know it sounds crazy, but look here," he told her, pulling out the amulet and opening it up to show her the pointer.

"What's that?" she asked.

"It points the way to the Fountain. All I have to do is follow it," he explained, and read her the verses from the opposite side. Then he quickly told her about finding the amulet and some of the things he'd done with it. He left out the part about Brandon's eye, and Black Rock, and a few other choice things; she didn't need to know all that, not by a long shot. He just had to tell her enough so she wouldn't think he was nuts.

"You really believe all this?" she finally asked. She still didn't look convinced; she looked more like a person who has no idea what to think.

"Yeah, I do. There's an old lady here in town who's been to the Fountain herself, a long time ago. I'm supposed to go see her tomorrow morning," he told her.

"I don't know, Brian. It just sounds crazy, you know. Like a fairy tale," she said, shaking her head.

"I know it does, but what if it's not? What if I *don't* go, and Brandon dies, and then I have to live the whole rest of my life wondering if he didn't have to," he pleaded. It was his last card, and if she didn't believe him after that then he wasn't sure what else to say to her. But her face softened when she heard those words, and she was silent for a long time, thinking.

"I guess I can understand that much, anyway. I'll tell you what I'll do, okay? I'll keep it a secret, but only if you'll take me with you," she finally told him.

"Huh?" he said, too startled to think of anything else to say.

"You heard what I said. If there's really such a place as that, and it's not just a story, then take me with you to find it," she said, and he could find no trace of anything except sincerity in her eyes. But her attitude mystified him.

"Why?" he asked.

"Well. . . let's just say Brandon's not the only one who needs fixing up," she said cryptically.

"What's that supposed to mean?" he asked.

"It means I'm sick, Brian," she told him simply, with a little shrug. He'd heard rumors about this before, of course, but nevertheless he pretended to be surprised. She might not like it if she thought people were gossiping about her.

"Sick like how?" he asked neutrally.

"It's called Batten's Disease," she said.

"I never heard of it before," he said.

"No, most people haven't. It's a rare genetic thing. But anyway, what happens is that you gradually go blind, and forget how to walk and talk, and then usually you die by the time you're twenty years old," she said. Her tone was offhand and matter-of-fact, like she was talking about the weather or a homework assignment, but somehow that only made it seem even more brutal and horrifying. Brian didn't know what to say.

"You don't *look* sick," he said, lamely.

"No, not right now. Not yet. Just my eyes, mostly, and I have to take medicine for seizures. But it gets a little worse all the time, and one of these days it'll get bad enough that I won't make it," she explained.

"There's no medicine or anything you could take?" he asked, still in shock.

"Well. . . sort of. There are some experimental treatments to slow it down for a while, but there's no way to cure it. I've got maybe five or six years left, if I'm lucky," she said.

"You're not scared?" he asked.

"Yeah, a little. But I know I'll go to heaven when I die, so I guess it could be worse. Besides, I decided a long time ago I wasn't going to let it ruin whatever time I do have left," she said.

"That's pretty brave," he told her.

"No, it's really not brave at all. I have to be that way, so I won't go crazy thinking about it all the time," she told him.

"Still sounds pretty brave to me," he said, and she shrugged.

"You do whatever you have to do. But I'm not quite as laid back and calm about the whole thing as you seem to think. I'm still snatching at every straw I can get my hands on. Even crazy fairy tales about magic Fountains," she told him, with a small laugh.

"I'm not sure I could be that strong," he told her, humbled.

"Sure you could, if you had to. I try to remember all the things I love to do, and how much there is to live for. That helps a lot, when I feel like giving up," she told him.

There was a long pause.

"So, can I come with you, then?" she finally asked, catching him off guard again.

"But how would you do that? I mean, wouldn't people be looking for you?" he asked.

"Aren't they looking for you, too?" she asked, reasonably enough.

"Well, yeah, I guess you have a point," he admitted, thinking hard.

"Can you. . . I mean, are you up to some hard traveling? I don't know how far it is, and I don't know what might happen between here and there. I've already had to sleep in a barn last night. It's not much fun," he pointed out.

"I can do pretty much anything you can do, as long as I have my glasses and my medicine," she said. He was still doubtful.

"Are you *sure?*" he asked again.

"Yeah, I'm sure. I can handle whatever I have to, and I won't gripe and moan about it, either. Like you said before, if I don't at least try then I'll always have to wonder what might have happened if I did," she reminded him.

"Well, yeah. . . I see what you mean," he said.

"So you'll take me with you?" she repeated again.

Brian still had serious doubts about the idea, but he had to admit that it would be nice to have somebody to talk to and chew things over with. And, as she herself said, she had an excellent reason not to give up until they found the Fountain.

"Sure, why not?" he finally agreed.

"Good!" she smiled, and then glanced at her watch.

"Got a hot date?" Brian asked, and she laughed.

"No, but I need to get back to work. I've already been up here longer than I should have been, and Mr. Croydon is probably already mad. But I tell you what. Come down to the verandah at supper time and we can talk some more. I'll take my break and then he can't say anything," she told him.

"Okay, that sounds good," he agreed.

"All right, then. Supper's at six. We're having steak tips with mushroom gravy, and I think baked potatoes and green beans," she said.

"Wow, fancy," he said dryly, and she laughed again.

"See you then," she told him, and then she went back to the kitchen.

It was only about three o'clock, and Brian still had a few hours to kill before he had to be back for supper. He went to a secondhand store to buy some fresh clothes while he had time, and while he was there he also got a handful of used books to read and a backpack to hold his things. After that he didn't particularly feel like sitting in the motel room doing nothing, so he decided to take a walk.

Glenwood was built on a little bluff beside the river, surrounded by patches of flat valley bottomland and boxed in on three sides by steep mountains and rolling hills. The sleepy downtown was good for walking, with a lot of old buildings and historical sites to occupy Brian's attention.

Eventually he came to a red brick Methodist church, with the grass neatly clipped and seven steps leading up to the double wooden doors. It was a pretty building, and Brian thoroughly approved of churches that made an effort to be beautiful instead of imitating a warehouse or a doctor's office.

He sat down for a little while on the top step to rest and to watch the occasional traffic go by, trying not to let himself think too much. There was no one else nearby, so he quietly shut his eyes for a few minutes to pray for Brandon, and while he was there he added a prayer for Rachel too.

That done, he felt a little more at peace than he had before, and he left the church in a better mood. It was getting close to suppertime by then, so he turned his footsteps back toward the hotel.

The verandah turned out to be a nicer place than he expected. It was full of wicker furniture where guests could sit and relax, and there was a view of a goldfish pond and some woods behind the house. Much better than the view from the Tyler Room, that was for sure.

He took a seat as far from the other guests as he could, and then slouched back in his chair to wait for Rachel. It wasn't long before she came outside and spied him sitting there.

"Hey, stranger. Are you ready to eat?" she asked.

"Yeah, I think so," Brian told her.

"Just one second, then. I'll be right back," she answered. She disappeared into the house for a few minutes, and then returned with two glasses of tea and two covered plates on a platter. She put the food on the table and then sat down in a chair beside him and handed him his glass.

"Whew! Time for a break," she said.

"Mmm. . ." Brian said, nodding.

"So how was your day?" she asked, putting her feet up on an ottoman that sat nearby and making herself comfortable.

"Oh, it was all right. Just wandered around town a little," he said.

"Yeah, dull place," she agreed.

"No, it was kinda interesting, actually. I'd never been downtown before," he said.

"I guess so. But anyway, I thought of something I need to ask you," she said.

"Fire away," he said.

"How are we getting around? We can't just walk all the way to the Fountain, can we?" she asked.

"No, I'm pretty sure it's too far for that. I've been riding my dirt bike up till now, but that might not work so well with two people," he said, doubtfully.

"Yeah, that's what I was afraid of. But I've got an idea, though," she said.

"What is it?" he asked.

"Well, can you drive?" she asked carefully.

"Um. . . maybe a little bit, if I had to. Why do you ask?" he asked.

"Because my sister has a car we might could use, that's why," she said.

"Aw, come on. Your sister would let you borrow her car to go who-knows-where, for who-knows how long, with a boy she barely ever met, when you're not even old enough to supposed to be driving by yourself?" he asked, skeptically.

"I wasn't exactly thinking of asking her first," she said defensively.

"You mean you want to steal your sister's car?" he said, dumbfounded.

"No, not at all. But she's out of town for three months and she told me I could use it now and then while she was gone, as long as I was careful with it," she explained.

"I'm pretty sure she wasn't thinking about something like this," Brian said.

"I'm sure she wasn't. But she didn't say I couldn't, either. All she told me was to be careful with it," she said.

"Don't you think that's splitting hairs?" he asked.

"Maybe it is. But you're forgetting one thing," she told him.

"Which is?" he asked.

"If we really find the Fountain, and it can really do what you say it can, then I don't think my sister will be sorry at all that I maybe took the car a little farther than she meant for me to," she explained.

"Well. . . yeah, I guess I can see how that might kinda change the way she saw things," he admitted after a while.

"Can *you* drive?" he asked suddenly, thinking about her eyes and her seizures. It didn't sound like a very safe combination.

"Yeah, I can drive okay most of the time. I've got my learner's license. Never drove around by myself very much except to go to school or to work sometimes cause you can get a special permit for that, but driving is pretty much the same wherever you go, isn't it?" she said.

"I guess so," he agreed, doubtfully.

"I could bring the car over in the morning, if that's what we wanted to do," she offered.

"Sure, let's do it," he agreed.

They didn't talk much longer, because Rachel's supper break ended and she had to get back to work in the kitchen for another hour or so, and then after that she was expected back home.

Brian sat for a while longer on the verandah until he finished his tea, and then he went back upstairs to his room to watch TV for a little while before bed. There was nothing on, so he dropped that idea before long.

He thought about going to bed, and even went so far as to turn his light off and lie down on the mattress. But he found himself restless and full of thoughts, and however hard he tried it was impossible for him to go to sleep.

As he lay there in the dark quiet, he noticed a quick flash of blue light against the white muslin curtains of his window, quickly cut off. He might not have noticed it at all if he hadn't been looking the right way, but as it was, his suspicions were aroused. He quietly got up to see what was happening, peering out through the curtains without moving them, and sure enough, down on the street he saw a county patrol car parked in front of the hotel. Mr. Croydon was down there in his fake alligator-skin boots, talking to a cop on the sidewalk. After a few minutes Brian saw the man look up and gesture vaguely toward the Tyler Room.

That was enough to make Brian's heart start pounding, and he quickly put his clothes back on and threw everything he had left into his backpack, ready for instant departure should it prove necessary. As soon as that was done, he went back to the window to look outside again. He might be worrying for nothing, but he'd rather be safe than sorry.

The deputy and the innkeeper were both gone from the sidewalk, and seconds later he heard footfalls on the staircase. The sound of boots against the hardwood floor was unmistakable.

Brian wasted no more time. His door was locked, but he knew that wouldn't delay them more than a minute or two if they meant to find him. The innkeeper surely had an extra key, and if Brian tried to leave the room before his adversaries arrived then he was like as not to bump right into their faces. The door was no way out; at least not for now.

Instead, Brian opened the window as quietly as he could and crawled out onto the roof, then shut it behind him so they might waste a little more time wondering where he was. If he left the window open then that was almost a dead giveaway.

The roof was a lot higher and a lot steeper than he would have liked, and he crawled gingerly across it to keep from falling or making noise. He had to find a way down as fast as he could.

He couldn't immediately think of any way except maybe to shimmy down a drain spout, but he doubted seriously whether the frail aluminum gutter work would hold his weight or not. What if it broke and sent him crashing two stories to the ground? If he didn't break his neck or a leg, then at the very least he'd make a horrible racket and get himself caught. There had to be a better way than that.

Next he thought about crawling into one of the other windows to hide somewhere else in the hotel until his pursuers gave up, but he soon rejected that idea, too. The other rooms in the hotel were the first place they'd look when they didn't find him in his own bed, and there weren't that many of them to start with. Not to mention the fact that he didn't know which ones were empty and which ones had guests in them. The last thing he needed was to break into an occupied room and get shot by somebody who thought he was a burglar.

On the other hand, he couldn't just stay on the roof, either. He showed up like a fly on an ice cream cone under the glare from the street lights; they'd spot him the second they came back outside.

He crept slowly and carefully toward the back of the house, hoping the shadows would give him a little more cover while he tried to think of some other solution.

What he finally found wasn't ideal, but it worked. The verandah at the back of the house was only a single story, which meant he could jump half the distance onto the verandah roof and then the rest of the way to the ground from there, like a giant staircase. Two short jumps was a lot better than a single long one.

The only thing that worried him about that plan was the noise. If he made a huge thump when he hit the verandah roof, they'd hear it inside the house and know where he was almost instantly.

He hesitated, not liking the idea, but finally decided it was the best option he could come up with.

He tried to muffle the sound by lying down on his belly and sliding backwards off the edge of the roof before he let go, but it was harder to hold on than he thought it would be. He slid the last few feet or so, scratching his arms on the gritty shingles and falling heavily onto the roof of the verandah ten feet below. So much for being quiet.

He wasn't hurt except for a few scratches from the shingles. He didn't know if anybody had heard him hit the roof or not, but he dared not hang around to find out. With only the barest nod to keeping quiet, he scrambled to the edge of the roof and jumped the rest of the way down to the grass, being careful not to twist an ankle.

He immediately took off running, trying to lose himself amongst the side streets as fast as he could. The hotel disappeared behind him pretty quickly, but it didn't take him long to realize that he could never hope to stay hidden that way for very long. There was almost nobody on the streets, which made him a glaring target. His only friend at the moment was the darkness.

When he'd made it far enough from the hotel, he took cover behind a hedgerow at the same church where he'd stopped to pray earlier. It was far from an ideal hiding place, but much better than roaming the sidewalks.

After a while his heart slowed down and he was able to think a little more calmly.

His mother must have come home and found the note he'd left her, and then called the cops to go round him up and haul him back home. That was the only explanation he could think of for what had happened. It didn't surprise him; it was exactly the kind of thing he'd been afraid she might do.

The only thing that puzzled him was how they'd managed to find him so soon, especially in such an obscure little hole-in-the-wall place. The only thing he could come up with was that Mr. Croydon must have said something.

Looking back, Brian realized that going to the hotel had been a mistake, and a stupid one, too. Fourteen year olds didn't do stuff like that, and they didn't usually walk around with fistfuls of hundred dollar bills, either. No wonder the man thought something fishy was going on.

Brian sat down and pulled his knees up to his chest so he could lay his head down, then let out a long breath. A few more stupid moves like that and he'd end up in juvenile detention for a week or two. Mama wouldn't hesitate to have him locked up if she thought it was the only way to knock some sense into his thick head. She'd probably use those same exact words, matter of fact. He knew her too well.

The idea scared him, but not as much as she probably hoped it would. Brian had lived cheek and jowl with fear for an awfully long time. He thought he could probably keep his head down and not get caught, as long as he didn't do anything else dumb to attract attention to himself.

But in the meantime they already knew he was somewhere in Glenwood, and that was bad enough. He didn't dare go back to the hotel to get his bike, and even the thought of sneaking back there long enough to wait for Rachel in the morning was enough to make his blood run cold. What if somebody had overheard their conversation last night and they had a squad car waiting for him the minute he showed up? But on the other hand, there was no way he'd get very far on foot, either.

He wished he knew where Rachel lived, or even her phone number, but he'd never thought to ask. Now he had no way to get in touch with her when he really needed to. But then again, maybe it was better he didn't. Calling her at home could make her parents suspicious, too, and that was the last thing they needed.

He drummed his fingers against his knees, thinking hard. The only thing he could do was try to catch up with Rachel in the morning, no matter how dangerous it seemed. He might be able to go back to the hotel and wait for her, *if* he could find a place to lay hid while he waited. If anybody had been eavesdropping on their plans last night then he might find himself walking right into a trap, but what choice did he have?

But surely tonight's escapade would have changed things, wouldn't it? They surely wouldn't expect him to show up at the motel in the morning just like nothing happened, would they? It would either be incredibly brave or incredibly stupid; he couldn't decide which. Maybe it was both, for that matter.

He chewed on the idea for a while but couldn't come up with anything better. He'd just have to try it and hope for the best.

In the meantime, he decided the hedgerow was probably a safe spot to stay put for a few hours, at least till they gave up looking for him. He could figure out his next move when he was sure the coast was clear.

His run from the law had left him drained, so he stretched out beside the hedge as comfortably as he could, and did his best to sleep awhile.

He didn't have much luck with that, because the roots kept digging into his back most uncomfortably, and the mosquitoes nearly ate him alive. He was able to doze a little in fits and snatches, but that was about all.

Chapter Seven

He was back on his feet not long after the first blush of dawn lit the sky, bleary eyed and tired, and wondering what time it was.

He figured they'd probably given up looking for him by then, and he felt safe enough to use the sidewalks without running the instant he saw a car on the road. He made his way as inconspicuously as he could to within two or three blocks of the hotel, and there he stopped, afraid to go any closer.

It was almost full daylight by then, and he felt a strong urge to hurry up and hide. It would have been easier if he'd known which way Rachel would be coming in, because then he wouldn't have needed to go near the hotel at all. He could have just waited beside the street until he saw her.

But he didn't know, so there was no choice but to inch his way closer to the hotel and hopefully find a hiding place which would let him see the street without being seen himself.

That was harder than he expected. He didn't dare lurk too long behind fence rows or outbuildings; there was too much danger of being spotted and reported. Nor did he dare break into an empty building or ask anyone to let him into their house. That was another excellent way to get caught.

He thought about crawling underneath the floor of the verandah at the hotel and peeking out through the trellis, but he couldn't remember if there was an opening he could use, and there wasn't time to hunt for one.

The best thing he could find was a huge, untrimmed magnolia tree growing in the front yard of the house next door to the hotel, with thick branches that grew all the way down to the ground and heavy leaves that might possibly keep anybody from seeing him, if he slipped in behind them. He quickly decided it would have to do.

He nonchalantly dropped to his knees in front of the magnolia tree, and made a show of looking around on the ground as if he'd dropped something. But he knew perfectly well that it was better to be quick than clever, so he wasted no time crawling up under the spreading branches, praying nobody had seen him do it. His luck had been so bad lately that he didn't trust it.

It was almost as dark as night under the magnolia leaves, dark enough that no grass could grow and he found himself crawling on bare dirt. He quickly found a vantage point from which he could peek out through the leaves at the street in front of the hotel, and there he waited.

It seemed like a long time, as it always does when there's nothing to do but wait. The sunlight gradually grew stronger until it was full day outside, but Brian's lair was still dark as a cave. That suited him just fine. The blacker the better.

He kept a sharp eye out for police cars, but saw none. Of course, that didn't mean they might not be there, he thought nervously. It only meant he didn't see them. There was nothing to prevent one of them from hiding somewhere and keeping a stake-out on the place, just like he was doing. He kept telling himself it was stupid to think they cared about finding him that much; he wasn't exactly on the *Ten Most Wanted* list. Still, it was nerve-wracking.

At eight-thirty, he saw a black Honda Civic pull up to the curb in front of the hotel and park there. He couldn't see who was inside, because someone had put window tint all over the glass. They hadn't done a very good job, either. It was full of bubbles, and it was already starting to peel off at the edges and turn purple. There was a slew of old and new bumper stickers on the back, from *I Love Chocolate* to *Biker Chick,* and almost everything imaginable in between.

Whoever was driving the car didn't get out right away, and Brian decided to take a gamble. If it wasn't Rachel and if the cops were hiding somewhere around then he might find himself in serious trouble, but if he dallied too long and it *was* her then that might be even worse.

He quickly crawled out from under the magnolia tree and trotted over to the car as fast as he could without running. He peered through the purple tint on the window and saw that it was indeed Rachel, and then he wasted no more time. He yanked open the door and slipped into the passenger seat as fast as he could.

"Where were you? I thought you'd never show up," she hissed, as she pulled away from the curb.

"There was some trouble last night. The cops showed up and I had to run. I almost didn't get away," he told her.

"What happened?" she asked, alarmed.

"I don't know. I couldn't sleep, so I was still awake when I noticed blue lights against the curtain. I got up to look and I saw the hotel manager talking to a cop down on the sidewalk and pointing to my room. Then they headed inside, so I thought I better get out while I still could," he explained.

"How'd you get away?" she asked.

"I had to crawl out the window onto the roof, and then I jumped down onto the verandah and then to the ground. I'm sure they knew I was up there, but I lost them in the dark," he told her.

"That was crazy, Brian. No wonder they call you Mad Dog. Don't you know you could break your neck trying to jump from that high?" she scolded him.

"Well, yeah, but I couldn't think of anything else to do at the time," he shrugged, and she sighed.

"I'm sorry. I'm sure you did the best you could. It just scared me when you said the cops showed up, that's all. So what did you do for the rest of the night?" she asked.

"Hid behind a hedge and then under that magnolia tree back there, and tried to sleep a little. Didn't work very well," he added thoughtfully.

"Well, I guess you can sleep in the car for a while after you tell me which way to go," she suggested.

"I can't sleep yet. We have to go see that old lady first and find out whatever she knows," he told her.

"Where does she live?" Rachel asked.

"At Pinecrest Retirement Village, room 208," he told her.

"Oh, okay. I know where that is," she said.

"Let's go, then," he told her.

Rachel threaded her way through town, and eventually came out onto the same leafy residential street Brian remembered from the day before. Uneasy as he was about getting caught, he was determined to talk to that old lady first before they left town.

"Coming?" he asked Rachel when they pulled into the parking lot.

"No, I think I'll wait out here with the car. I know too many people in there and it wouldn't be a good idea for them to see me skipping school like this. They might say something to somebody. You won't be in there too long, will you?" she asked.

"Hopefully not," he said.

He walked through the front doors like he belonged there, and soon found himself in an open area with an old fireplace and some threadbare couches, from which three wings diverged to the left, the right, and straight ahead. There was an office to the left, but he was reluctant to go in there and ask for directions. They might want to know who he was there to visit, and then what would he say? He had no idea what the old lady's name might be, just the room number she'd given him.

It turned out not to be all that difficult, though. He soon noticed that all the room numbers that started with 2 were on the middle wing, so he quietly made his way down the hall until he reached number 208, where he found the door shut. An old handwritten nameplate read *Sadie Jones,* and Brian tried to think if he'd ever heard of such a person before. It didn't seem to ring any bells.

He hesitated before knocking, remembering that some people did like to sleep late, but then he figured there was no more time left to dawdle. So he knocked, not very loud.

"Come in," said someone from inside. The voice was a little muffled, but he thought he recognized the sound of the old lady from the park. He turned the knob and went in, and there indeed she was, sitting in a leather chair beside the window, with a pink afghan spread across her lap and a steaming cup of black coffee in front of her. She was wearing the same pair of knitted mittens and matching shawl from yesterday, and she seemed to have been looking through the curtains at something outside. He caught a glimpse of roses through the dirty window before she dropped the curtains and turned to face him with a smile.

"Come in, young man, come in! I knew you'd come. Shut the door behind you so we can have a little privacy, and then come over here and sit down so we can talk," she said, waving toward another leather chair in front of the window. She didn't seem the least bit nutty, at least not this morning, and Brian relaxed. He shut the door behind him, as he'd been told, and then sat down in the other chair.

The old lady studied him for a while after he sat down, as if she might read all the secrets of the universe in the shape of his face. The intense look made him a little uncomfortable, but he endured it for as long as he could. At last he cleared his throat and spoke.

"Um, I was hoping you could tell me-" he began, but she interrupted him before he could finish the thought.

"All in good time, child, all in good time. We haven't even been properly introduced yet. My name is Sadie Jones, and you are?" she asked.

"Brian. Brian Madaug Stone, that is," he told her.

"Pleased to meet you, Brian Stone. What an unusual name you have," she commented.

"Yes, ma'am, so I've heard," he said dryly. As long as she didn't call him Mad Dog, they'd get along just fine.

"I imagine so. But tell me now, how did you hear about the Fountain, and why are you looking for it?" she asked, getting right to the point.

So Brian briefly told her about finding the amulet in his attic and some of the things he'd done with it, and how he'd broken the chain to save Brandon, and how it popped open and showed him the verses. He told her about the girl in Mississippi who first told him the story, and how he'd looked it up and decided to find the place.

She listened to all this without comment, and when he'd finished she asked him only one thing.

"You still haven't said why you want to find it, child," she told him.

"But I told you why," he said, confused.

"You told me how it happened, child, not why you want it. There's a difference," she pointed out mildly.

"Well. . . I guess the main thing is that I want to make sure my brother is okay. I thought it could probably do that much, if it makes wishes come true," he said.

"I see. Is that really your only reason?" she asked, keenly. He was tempted to say yes, partly for shyness and partly because it seemed churlish to care for anything else at a time like that, but something held him back.

"No, that's not all," he finally confessed, looking down at the floor.

"Ah, I thought not. So what might the rest be, then?" she asked.

"I want my mom to stop drinking and be nice again, like she used to be when my dad was with us. I wish he'd come back home, too. Things haven't been too good at home, the past few years," he said. It was hard for him to admit all this, especially to a complete stranger, but he forced himself to do it.

"Hmm. . . anything else?" she asked again, and Brian was surprised at the question. Wasn't that enough? He glanced at Miss Sadie, who was looking at him with a very solemn expression on her face. She really wanted to know.

"I'm not sure," he told her, uncertain what she wanted to hear.

"Are you not?" she asked, raising one eyebrow. This forced him to think, and Brian found that hard, with Miss Sadie watching him.

"I don't know what you want me to say," he finally said.

"I want you to tell me what you most dearly wish for, Brian Stone. Think, now. What did you do, while you had all that power? What did you try to make happen? What mattered to you more than anything else?" she asked. Brian had to think again, and it made his head hurt. What had he done, except make the house nice and make some money? There wasn't much else he could think of, except his silly project up at Black Rock. He might have loved that the most, but it sounded foolish and stupid, even to him. Surely she didn't want to hear about *that,* did she?

But he was at a loss to think of anything else, and so he fumblingly tried to tell her about it.

"When I grew the white oak trees, and made the stars shine brighter, and the cardinals redder, and all those things; that's what I loved the most, I guess. I wanted to make the whole world beautiful like I did up at Black Rock. I wanted to make it so there were no bad things ever anymore," he said, almost in a whisper, not daring to glance at her face to see what she might be thinking. If he had, he might have seen a faraway smile on her lips, and something very like a tear at the corner of her eye. She dried it away before he could notice, and when she spoke her voice was serene.

"That's what I wanted to hear, Brian Stone. That's a good wish, and a strong one too. But I still have to ask you one more question. Do you love this world enough to live far beyond your years, and to spend your whole life for that wish, pouring light into the darkness? Be certain before you answer me, because it'll be harder than you think. There's always a price to be paid," she said.

"Do you mean if I drink from the Fountain, I'll really live forever?" he asked, wide eyed.

"No, child, not forever. That's forbidden. But I know you could live for a hundred years or more. Maybe even *much* more, God willing, and that's far beyond most. And for most of that time you'd keep your youth, and your health, and you'd be just as beautiful and perfect as Adam was when he took his first breath before the Fall. How could it be otherwise? For you will have drunk from the Fountain that was put here at the beginning of days by God Himself, the life-giving Life, and the Beauty that makes beautiful," she said, in a sing-song kind of voice, as if she might be repeating something she'd learned long ago.

Brian was left speechless at this, and knew of nothing whatsoever that he might say. It wasn't what he'd expected at all.

"I thought it just gave you wishes," he said weakly.

"Oh, but it does, child. It does! It gives you the deepest desire of your heart, and nothing less. But only if your deepest desire was already for the one thing it can give you," she said cryptically.

"I don't understand," he told her, confused.

"You will, someday," she said. It was an unsatisfying answer, but there was one thing he had to be sure of, though.

"So does that mean I'll be able to make Brandon well again?" he asked.

"Among other things, yes. But that's the least of it. Let me show you something, child, and then maybe you'll understand," she said, raising an arm toward the grimy widow. Brian looked up, and saw nothing unusual except the flower garden outside.

"What am I looking for?" he asked.

"This," she said softly, and pushed open the glass.

A faint breeze blew in, carrying with it a scent of roses so sweet that they might once have bloomed in the meadows of Heaven. They were so bright and so red that they almost seemed to glow from within, and every dew drop glittered like gold in the morning sunshine. Brian thought he'd never seen anything on earth more beautiful. It reminded him of Black Rock, and he stared, wide-eyed, while Sadie Jones watched him.

"Yes, that's what it's like. You can take away every sickness, every scar, and every stain from anything in the world, and make it to be what it always ought to have been if the world was never broken. That's what you really always wanted, child, just like I did. And if you don't give up, then very soon you'll have it," she told him.

"You did this?" he whispered, still staring at the roses.

"God did this. But I was the one who touched them, if that's what you mean. The gift has faded over time, along with everything else I got from the Fountain. But it's still enough for these few little bushes, if I tend them every day," she told him.

"But what about the amulet?" he asked, still staring at the roses.

"What about it?" she asked.

"Why couldn't I do this before? I mean, I know sometimes I did, but why was I not supposed to? Why did it have to turn out so bad, if that was what I was supposed to end up doing anyway?" he asked.

"I couldn't say for sure, child. Things didn't happen quite the same way for me as they did for you. I never had an amulet like that, so it's hard for me to tell you what the purpose may be. But if I had to guess, I'd say it's likely because of what you said about the seven day limit. No doubt it's hard for living things to stand the shock of going back to normal again, once you touch them like this. I wouldn't be surprised if it made them sick, or perhaps even killed them. I'm sure that's why you weren't supposed to touch them. But the Fountain is forever; that much I know," she said.

"Then why not just show me how to get there to begin with, instead of letting me make such a mess of things with the amulet?" he asked.

"I don't think that's the right question to ask, child. The story of the Fountain has always been out there, for anybody who wanted to listen. It may well be that God has a million different ways to lead His chosen ones to the place He wants them to go, and I dare say most of those paths don't include an amulet at all. I wouldn't know about that. But it doesn't much matter how He deals with everybody else, child. What matters is whether *you* would have had faith enough to be sitting here right now, if it hadn't been for that amulet," she said.

"No, I guess I wouldn't have," he finally admitted, after thinking it over.

"Well, then, there you go. God always gives us what we need, not what we think we want. That amulet was exactly what you needed to make you believe," she said.

"You really think so?" he asked, frowning.

"Yes, and I think it was exactly the right test for you, too,"

"Why do you say that?" he asked.

"Because the test always has something to do with the darkest and the strongest temptation of your heart; the thing you're most likely to choose in place of love. We all have our different weak spots, you know, and that's why the testing can never be quite the same for any two of the chosen ones," she said.

"So what do you think my weakness is?" he asked, feeling suddenly very naked and vulnerable under her keen eyes.

"I think you know that already, child. Power and wealth. Most likely because you've had so little of both in your life," she said.

Brian didn't know quite what to say to this, even though he felt the truth of it painfully. It was hard, knowing that his most selfish desires were so completely transparent. But Miss Sadie pretended not to notice his discomfiture, and saved him the need to come up with a suitable answer.

"So it's really very simple, you see. You were given a taste of all the power and wealth you could imagine, just for a few days, partly to see what you might do with it, and partly to find out what your ultimate choice would be. There's no way of knowing where a man's heart will lead him, you know; not till he's actually put to the test somehow. You might have used your power to hurt people you hated, or to build up mountains of all the silly baubles and trinkets the world can offer. And worst of all, you might have decided those things were more important than love, or the whispers of your heart to go out and make the world beautiful. Then you wouldn't have been the right kind of person to drink from the Fountain, and so the way would never have been shown to you. And perhaps God on His throne would have wept at the sight, but I suppose that's nothing to the purpose," she murmured.

Brian wondered briefly what kind of test Miss Sadie might have faced, and what kind of path God had shown *her* to the Fountain all those years ago. She didn't seem to want to talk about it much, and he dared not pry.

"But I *did* try to get money," he pointed out instead, remembering the gold.

"Yes, you did, but that was never what you cared about the most. And when it came down to a choice between keeping all those things and saving your brother's life, you didn't hesitate," she reminded him.

"But he's still just as sick as he was before, Miss Sadie. Breaking the chain didn't help him at all," Brian said.

"Oh, but it did! You have a real chance to save him now, if you go on and drink from the Fountain. Indeed, that's likely the only hope he ever had, and you never would have found it if you hadn't done what you did, flinging aside all your treasures for the sake of love. Your choices matter, child, more than you could ever possibly imagine," she said.

Brian thought about this for a second.

"But could I really have kept all that stuff anyway, if I hadn't broken the chain? Or would everything have just disappeared no matter what I did, after the seven days was up?" he asked.

"That I don't know, child. I passed the test, and so did you. I couldn't say what happens to a person who chooses wrongly. It may be that those people get to keep whatever it was that they loved more than love, empty and pitiful as that is. Or it may be that it all turns to dust and ashes and leaves them with nothing but a broken heart. I have moods when both those things seem likely, but I'd only be guessing if I tried to tell you which one is the truth. And it doesn't matter, anyway. Would you really have let your brother die for the sake of some riches, even if you'd known for certain that you'd get to keep them all?" she asked.

"Not in a million years. Not for all the money in the world," he said quickly.

"That's what I thought," she agreed.

"But how did the amulet end up in my attic in the first place? Why me?" he asked.

"Now you're asking questions that nobody can answer, child. All I can say is that I think you were *meant* to find that amulet, just like I think you and I were meant to bump into each other at the park yesterday. Things like that are never left up to chance," she told him.

There was a pause while Brian considered all this, and Miss Sadie seemed content to watch her roses and let him think in peace.

"So what do I do now?" he finally asked, and she laughed.

"What silly questions you ask, child! Follow your compass all the way up into those mountains yonder, wherever it leads, till you come to the heart of the world. They say no one ever finds it in the same place twice, but all the same, you'll know it when you get there. You'll find a cavern green as emerald, with a gushing fountain of cold, clear water and a golden cup beside it. Then drink, if you have the courage," she said.

"And then what?" he asked.

"Then do what you love, child; that's all. I myself became a nurse for a good many years, since that's what I cared about the most. All I had to do was lay my hands on the sick to make them well, and for a long time there was never anything so bad that I couldn't cure it. The blessing has faded now, it's true, but even now it's still not gone completely," she explained.

"But mostly?" he guessed.

"Yes. . . it's like my roses. Now and then I can still do a little bit, but not much. There's a lot of pain in this place, and I soften it when I'm able to. It's part of the reason I agreed to come live here last year. Everybody thinks the reason the people at Pinecrest are so healthy is because they take such good care of us, but I know better," she said, with a small chuckle.

"Yeah, that's what I thought," he sighed.

"I can guess why you asked me that question, child. I know you're still thinking about this brother of yours that you love so much. But he was far gone by the time you got here, and I wouldn't have the strength to heal something like that anymore. But *you* will. If you make it to the Fountain, then you'll have the power to undo any hurt in the world, including his. Remember that, whenever you're still afraid for him," she told him.

"I'll do my best," he agreed, heavily.

"Shh. . . have faith, child. Everything will work out the way that it should," she told him.

"I hope so," he said.

"Don't hope; believe," she said, looking at him earnestly, and then she opened the top drawer of her bureau and took out a pair of scissors.

"What's that for?" he asked.

"Take this, to help you remember what you're working for," she told him, and then snipped off one of the brilliant red roses. Brian took it from her without thinking, and put it in the inside pocket of his coat.

"Thanks," he said automatically, not sure what he would do with such a gift. But Sadie Jones only smiled.

"You may find it more use than you think. Now go, child, while time is," she said.

He left the nursing home not long afterward, with many thanks and a humbled heart, not to mention a sense of fresh urgency to find the Fountain.

"Did you find out anything?" Rachel asked as soon as he got back in the car.

"Yeah, lots. But let's get out of town first and then I'll tell you all about it," he promised.

"Okay, which way do I go?" she asked. He consulted the amulet, which still pointed northeast.

"That way," he said, pointing toward the highest part of the mountains.

They stopped to gas up the car at the edge of town, and while they were there Brian took the opportunity to call Carolyn to check on Brandon again, and while he was at it to see if he was right about Mama finding the note. This time she didn't even let him get a word in.

"Where are you, Brian? Everybody's been worried sick, trying to find you since last night," she said.

Yeah, just like he'd thought.

"I was with a friend, that's all," he said.

"And you couldn't have called and told somebody that? Like things are not bad enough already right now with your brother maybe dying, and you have to go pull some crazy stunt like this. What's *wrong* with you?" she scolded.

"I. . ." he began, but she cut him off before he could say another word.

"Where *are* you, Brian? Wherever it is, you better get home as fast as you can get there," she finished. This was the moment he'd been dreading.

"I can't do that yet, Aunt Carolyn," he said firmly.

"What do you mean, you can't do that? Why not?" she demanded.

"I can't explain it right now, but I've got something I have to do for a few days. I'll be home as soon as I can, though," he said. Carolyn must have been shocked beyond words, because it took her almost a full second to think of anything to say.

"Have you lost your mind, boy? What could possibly be so important that you've got to drop everything and go do it at a time like this?" she asked.

"I can't tell you, but it matters a lot," he said.

"Nothing could matter that much, Brian. Go home, *now.* Your mother already has the police out looking for you, do you know that? And if they find you first then she's mad enough she might just let you sit in jail for a while till she decides to come get you," she said, and there was a hard edge to her voice that he didn't like at all.

"I know. Tell Mama I'm sorry, and tell Brandon I love him. I'll be home as soon as I can," he told her, and then hung up the phone before she could answer him.

It wasn't five seconds before the phone started ringing, and Brian knew it was Carolyn without needing to answer. But he had no time to argue with her anymore, and if she was angry, then she'd just have to be angry.

On the other hand, it probably wouldn't be too hard for her to call information and find out exactly where he was, using the number from the pay phone. It was time to go, before they got busted.

"What is it?" Rachel asked when she saw his face.

"Oh, nothing. Just my aunt, freaking out. I called her to check on Brandon and she said my mom's got the cops looking for me now, like I didn't already know that after what happened at the hotel last night. I didn't even get to find out how he's doing. Same old drama," he said bitterly.

"I'm sorry, Brian," she told him.

"Oh, well. Let's just not get caught, okay? Drive back the other way for a couple of blocks if you can, just in case the cops come by here and ask the people at the gas station which way we went," he said.

"Sure thing," she agreed.

This they did, and after the gas station was out of sight behind them, Rachel turned onto a side street and made her way back onto the highway with no more problems. Soon they crossed the county line into another jurisdiction, and he heard her give a little sigh of relief. Brian's heart was still too bitter from the phone call to do anything but stare moodily at the empty road ahead of them and wonder how bad things would have to get before they ever started to get better.

"So we're out of town now. What did the old lady say?" Rachel finally asked. Brian almost told her he didn't feel like talking for a while, but then he thought better of it; she was just trying to help.

"She said a lot of things," he said, and then proceeded to tell her everything Sadie Jones had told him. Rachel listened quietly to the whole thing, only rarely asking a question.

"And then she gave me this," he finished, pulling the rose from his inside pocket. A few of the petals were crumpled, and he thought it might already have faded just a bit, but it was still a thousand times more beautiful than the fanciest rose on earth. Rachel's eyes opened wide when she saw it.

"Is that real?" she whispered.

"Yeah. She said this is the kind of thing we'll be able to do, after we drink from the Fountain," he said.

"So it's really true after all," she said, still staring at the rose.

"Surely you didn't think I was making it all up, did you?" he asked, surprised at her reaction.

"No, it's not that. If I hadn't believed you then I wouldn't be here right now," she said, shaking her head.

"Then what is it?" he asked, mystified.

She didn't answer right away, and he watched her chewing on her lip while she thought about it.

"It's hard to explain. I guess till now there was still a little part of me deep down that kept wondering what if you're wrong, or what if we can't find the place. . . stuff like that. See, the first thing everybody told me when I found out I had Batten's Disease was not to believe in miracles, ever. All it does is break your heart when they don't come true, and things are hard enough

already without that. They always told me to make the best of
the time I've got, and if I don't hope for too much then I'll never
get disappointed. I guess it's just hard to get over all that and
start believing there's really a chance things could change," she
told him, glancing back at the road.

It sounded like something he might have said himself not all
that long ago, he couldn't help thinking. Not about dying, of
course, but about Mama and the way she acted. He knew exactly
what it felt like when hope seemed too good to be true. He
couldn't really blame Rachel for having some doubts about the
Fountain. He probably wouldn't have believed it himself,
without the amulet.

"It's okay. I know exactly how you feel," he told her, thinking
about his own impossible wishes.

"Really?" she asked.

"Yeah, I think so," he said, and then hesitated. He wasn't sure
how much he wanted to tell her, honestly, but then he bit his lip
and took a deep breath.

"Uh. . . you remember last week at church, when I told you I
fell down the stairs?" he finally asked.

"Yeah, I remember," she agreed.

"That's not really what happened. Mama came home drinking
Saturday night, and we got in a fight," he confessed, watching her
closely to see her reaction. But she only nodded.

"I thought it was something like that," she said. She didn't
seem shocked or upset at all, and she didn't look at him like he
was a lost puppy, either. He hated it when people did that.

He decided maybe it was worth the risk to tell her a little bit
more.

"She does stuff like that a lot. To me and Brandon both. She
blacked his eye the same day she punched my nose. It's been
that way for a long time," he said, keeping his voice flat and
steady.

"I'm sorry, Brian. I always wondered a little bit but I never
thought. . ." she said, and then trailed off awkwardly.

"I never told anybody before," he said thickly, and swallowed
hard.

"It's all right; I won't tell anybody, I promise," she told him.

"Anyway, I used to think it was just something I had to live with, you know. Something that wouldn't ever change no matter what I did. But then I found out all this stuff about the Fountain, and I started to wonder if maybe things could really get better. I didn't want to believe it at first, because it seemed like it was too good to be true," he told her.

"Yeah. . . that's exactly what I meant," she agreed.

There was a pause while neither one of them said anything, and Brian took the chance to pull himself back together.

"So what made *you* decide to believe it enough to go looking for it?" she finally asked.

"Well. . . I'm not sure I would have, if it wasn't for Brandon. But it was the only thing I knew of that maybe could save him, you know. He's pretty bad off, and then like I said earlier, things are not too good at home even if he makes it back. I don't want him to have to grow up that way, Raych. It hurts too much. I just want him to be happy and safe, you know. I always have, and the Fountain is the only thing I ever heard of that maybe could make that happen. Even if it's only a maybe, I have to try. I couldn't take a chance on letting him down. Not a second time," he said.

"A second time?" she asked.

"Yeah, the whole reason he's in the hospital right now is because of me," he said, and then quickly told her the story of the amulet again, with nothing left out this time. She shook her head when he finished.

"Brian, none of that was your fault. You didn't know what would happen," she said.

"Yeah, it was, though. I knew better than to leave him with Mama when she was in a bad mood, and it was stupid of me to use the amulet on his eye when I didn't know if it was safe or not. I'm not saying it's completely my fault, but some of it is," he said.

"Well. . . yeah, all right. I can see what you mean. But don't keep beating yourself up over it, okay? I don't think Brandon would want you to do that, anyway. Just try to make it right, if you can. That's all anybody can ask," she said.

"I guess so, but what if we don't make it back before it's too late?" he asked, remembering Carolyn's words about Brandon maybe dying. He hadn't paid too much attention at the time, but that was a pretty high-voltage expression for her to use, now wasn't it? He hoped it didn't mean anything except a bad choice of words, but who knew?

But just then they came to the foot of a treacherous hill and Rachel had to turn most of her attention back to driving, so he never got to hear her answer. Maybe there wasn't one.

The road was steep and crooked for several miles after that till they reached the summit, and then in front of them the mountains marched on, ridge after ridge, as far as the eye could see. It seemed to Brian like he could see for a thousand miles, till the air grew hazy and blue with the distance. Ahead was the wide world, and behind them lay everything he'd ever known.

For a second he was almost homesick, and he couldn't help wondering how much farther they'd have to go. If they kept going this direction, they might eventually end up. . . where? Missouri? Canada? Some island way out in the middle of the ocean, even? The Fountain couldn't be *that* far, could it? Because if it was, then that was impossible.

Or if not strictly impossible, then at least it would take so long that there was no point in even thinking about it. But Brian had no way of knowing; the pointer only told him which way to go, not how far it was or how difficult it might be to get there.

"Are you sure you'll be okay if I go to sleep for a while?" he asked presently.

"Yeah, no problem. I'll be careful," she promised.

"Wake me up if anything happens, okay?" he asked.

"Sure," she agreed, and he curled up in the passenger seat to sleep.

Hours later, the sunlight shining in his face woke him, and he sat up and rubbed his eyes.

"Where are we?" he asked sleepily, shading his eyes.

"Somewhere on the highway, that's all I know. Did you have a good nap?" she asked.

"Yeah, I feel better. Hungry though," he added.

"I guess we could get something whenever we pass another place. Are we still headed in the right direction?" she asked.

"Yeah, looks like it," he told her, after checking, "How long do you think it'll be before somebody starts looking for this car?"

"I'm not sure," she said, glancing at the rearview mirror in spite of the fact that there was absolutely nobody else on the road.

"Did you say anything to anybody before you left?" he asked.

"Yeah, I told them I was late for school this morning and that's why I needed to drive Sissy's car, and that I'd probably just go directly to work after class. They didn't say much about it," she explained.

"So how long have we got before they'll be expecting you home?" he asked.

"Maybe nine o'clock. Supposed to be eight thirty, but now and then I have to work a little bit late if the kitchen was busy that night. They won't think anything of it till at least nine, I'm sure," she told him.

"That's still not very long," he fretted.

"I'm sorry, Brian. It was the best I could do," she said.

"No, it's all right. I wasn't blaming you. I was just wondering what they'll do when you turn up missing tonight," he explained.

"Probably have the National Guard out looking for me, if I know them," she said, giggling a little. Then she saw the look on Brian's face and sobered.

"I guess that wasn't really funny, was it?" she said.

"Do you really think they would? Seriously?" he asked.

"Well, maybe not that, but I'm sure they'll call the police and report me missing, and I'm sure they'll tell them to be looking for this car. They may even go out and look for me themselves. They'll find out pretty soon that I wasn't at work or at school today, and that'll scare them. Mr. Croydon will probably tell them I was with you last night at supper, so you'll get connected to the whole thing pretty soon, too. I'm not sure what all they might do, but they won't just sit still, I know that much. They might even think you kidnapped me," she told him.

"That's a fun thought. We can't keep driving this car, then, if that's the case. At least not for long," he told her.

"Yeah, I thought of that, but how else will we get anywhere?" she asked.

"We'll have to think about it for a while. Maybe we can find something else," he said, wishing he'd brought more money along.

Not long afterward they came into a little town whose name Brian didn't notice, and stopped long enough to have a cheeseburger and some fries at a local diner. It made them both nervous to be in such a public place, but Brian reminded himself that nobody had any reason to be suspicious just yet. Rachel and the car wouldn't be missed till that evening, and as for him. . . well, he was a hundred miles from home and there was nobody to recognize him.

He hoped.

Still, they didn't linger any longer than they had to. They ordered a few extra burgers for the road so they wouldn't have to risk stopping anywhere else that evening, and then they got back under way.

They drove for hours like this, crossing the Arkansas River at Dardanelle and then climbing the steep southern face of the Ozarks.

After a while, Brian noticed that the pointer had slowly veered around to the northwest, and he realized immediately that it wouldn't have done that unless they were getting pretty close.

Chapter Eight

"I think we're getting close," he announced, trying his best not to sound too excited about it.

"How do you know?" she asked.

"The pointer is moving. If the place was still a long way off then a few miles wouldn't matter much about the direction we needed to take. But the closer we get, the more it affects it. So it's got to be pretty close," he explained.

The effect became more and more noticeable as the day wore on, until Brian was certain they had to be very near indeed. Eventually, just outside the town of Snowball, they found themselves forced to turn onto a gravel road, because the highway was actually taking them farther away at that point.

"You're sure we won't get lost?" Rachel asked worriedly.

"We can't get lost. We've got the amulet," he reminded her.

"Yeah, I know that. But I meant what if we get way back here on one of these dirt roads and can't find one that goes the right way? We don't know our way around up here, or at least I don't," she clarified.

"Neither do I, but we'll just have to do the best we can," he shrugged, pretending the idea didn't bother him. They drove on like this for another hour or two, working their way ever deeper into the mountains. In places the road was so steep and narrow that Brian was afraid the car would never make it, or even worse, never make it back out. There were rocky creek beds that had to be crossed, and deep washouts, and now and then humps of limestone that nearly blocked the way completely. But they crept ahead, slowly and carefully, always trying to keep following the pointer as best they could.

At last they reached a place where they could go no farther. A huge pine tree had fallen directly across the road, blocking the way completely.

"There's no way we can drive past that," Brian said, as soon as he saw it.

"Then I guess we'll just have to walk from now on. How close do you think we are?" she sighed.

"I don't know. Hopefully not too far," he said.

"Well, let's get with it, then," she said.

"Wait a minute, first. Is there anything we need to take with us from the car?" he asked.

"I don't think so. Just the keys, maybe," she said.

"Is there a flashlight anywhere? It'll be getting dark soon," he pointed out.

"Yeah, there's a little one in the glove box," she said, reaching inside to grab it.

"I don't guess your sister keeps a gun in here, does she?" he asked without much hope. He didn't really expect to need one, but it might be better to be safe than sorry.

Rachel laughed.

"Nope, no gun, but there's supposed to be a tire tool in the trunk, if you think we might need to bash somebody in the head," she told him, amused.

"No, it's not that. I was thinking more about wild animals," he said, getting out of the car to fetch the tire tool. She watched him with a smile on her face.

"You're crazy, Mad Dog, you know that?" she finally said, obviously amused.

"Maybe so, but if we meet a bear I'd just like to have something to fight with, that's all," he said defensively.

"Well. . . okay, point taken," she agreed.

They gathered up the remains of their lunch and their water bottles, and then Brian looked at the amulet one more time.

"That's the way," he said, pointing to a bluish peak far in the distance. It couldn't have been more than five miles away, but it looked like a walk to eternity.

"Do you think we can make it?" she asked doubtfully, gazing at the peak.

"We have to," he said simply.

They struggled on through the woods for a long time, following the pointer as best they could. At times they had to detour around deep gorges or sinkholes in the rough limestone, and this often led to long delays before they could get back on track again.

Perhaps an hour after they left the car, the sun slipped down below the mountains in the west, and it quickly began to get dark.

"I don't think we'll find it tonight," Brian said, stopping to take a drink of water.

"Yeah, I guess we need to think about making camp somewhere," she agreed.

"Oh, joy," he muttered, thinking how uncomfortable that was likely to be. He wouldn't have minded if they'd had a tent, or even sleeping bags, but lying on the bare ground was no fun at all.

"It'll be all right," Rachel said, and he was ashamed of himself for griping. If she could tough it out, then so could he.

They went on for a little longer, keeping an eye out for likely spots.

"I think this'll do," Brian finally said. It was nothing but a dense grove of pine trees, where the needles had fallen down for uncounted years and made a deep drift. It softened the bare ground, at least, and the trees would shield them from any unfriendly eyes that might come along.

There didn't seem likely to be any eyes at all, unfriendly or otherwise, but it never hurt to be careful.

The leaf litter was more comfortable than Brian had thought it would be, so they sat cross-legged on the ground to eat leftover burgers and drink water.

"This is nice, Brian," Rachel said at last.

"It is?" he asked, surprised.

"Yeah, it really is. Here we are, maybe getting close to the Fountain, doing something that really matters. It makes me feel ten times more alive inside than I would if I was just sitting at home right now watching TV or doing homework. Don't you think so?" she asked. He considered it.

"You know, you're absolutely right. I *do* feel that way," he agreed, and she laughed.

"You sound so surprised," she told him.

"I guess I never thought of it like that before," he admitted.

There wasn't much else to do, so they turned in early on their pine-needle beds, hoping they'd reach the Fountain before noon the next morning.

Unfortunately, they didn't. Most of the next day was spent very much like the previous afternoon, pushing their way through dense woods and avoiding obstacles, until they began to despair of ever making any progress.

"I hope it's not much farther," Rachel finally said, early in the afternoon. It was the first time she'd even mildly complained, but Brian couldn't blame her. He was tired, and dirty, and hungry, and this endless walk through the woods was wearing them both down.

"Surely it won't be," he said, as much for his own benefit as for hers.

They sat down on a fallen log beside a little creek to eat the last scraps of food and drink some water, and neither of them had enough.

"I'm worried, Brian. If we don't find the place soon, we'll have to turn back just for food," she said glumly.

"Yeah, we definitely can't go on like this," he agreed.

"Any ideas?" she asked.

"No, not really. I've still got some money, but that won't help us out here," he said.

"Do you think we could catch some fish? We've passed a few creeks now and then," she asked hopefully.

"What would we catch them with?" he pointed out.

"Well. . . I don't know. Can't you tickle them out of the water with your hands? I saw them do that on TV once," she asked.

"Do you know how to tickle fish?" he asked, raising one eyebrow.

"No," she admitted.

"Well, neither do I. So scratch that idea, then. I don't think I can go deer hunting with a tire tool, either," he said. The words came out a little sharper than he meant for them to, but Rachel ignored him.

"I bet we could gather some mussels and crawdads, if we had to," she finally said.

"That'd be pretty nasty, Raych," he pointed out.

"Not if we cooked them. We could make some soup, you know; put some clover in there, maybe some other stuff," she insisted, and Brian had to laugh.

"Clam and clover soup. Now I've heard everything," he said.

"We could *try* it, at least," she shrugged.

"Even if we wanted to, we still don't have anything to cook it in," he reminded her.

"We could use one of the water bottles, if we cut the top off," she suggested.

"It's plastic. It'd just melt if we put it over a fire," he said.

"True, but we could heat up rocks and drop them into the bottle. That'll heat up the soup," she pointed out.

"I guess we could try it," he agreed, doubtfully.

"Okay. You go get the mussels and whatever else you can catch, and I'll start a fire and gather some greens," she said.

"Sure, why not?" he shrugged.

He went down the slope to the creek and found a place where there was a gravel bar, and then started digging for mussels. It turned out to be a time-consuming process, and by the time he'd filled both his pockets full his stomach was starting to grumble about the long wait. There were no crawdads to be found, and he finally decided that the mussels would have to do.

He carried them back up the hill to where Rachel had built a fire, and saw that she'd gathered two or three handfuls of clover greens.

They carefully cut off the top of one of the bottles and heated water in it with hot rocks, as Rachel had suggested. The process seemed to work, and in the end they had a steaming bowl of food.

"Well, it *smells* pretty good," Brian admitted.

"Yeah, it does. I just hope it tastes good, too," she agreed.

"I'll taste it first, just in case it's nasty," he volunteered, eyeing the bottle. It might smell good, but it certainly didn't *look* very appetizing. In fact it looked more like dirty dishwater than anything else he could think of.

"Go for it," she told him.

He grimaced and took a small sip.

"Not too bad. Tastes kinda weird, but it's okay," he said.

They took turns sipping the hot soup from the bottle, since they had no spoons to eat it with, and when they were done they made sure to put out the fire before heading out again.

"That was a good idea, Raych," Brian told her as they walked along.

"Thanks," she smiled.

"There's just one problem with it, though," he added.

"What's that?" she asked.

"Too much time. We spent hours collecting all that food, and building the fire, and cooking, and then cleaning up. We've got to make better time than that or we'll never get anywhere," he said, hating to say so. The smile faded from her lips and she sighed.

"Yeah, I guess you're right. We'll just have to think of something else, or do without for a little while," she finally agreed.

"I'm sorry," he told her.

"Sorry for what?" she asked.

"For not thinking about this. We should have bought some supplies back when we went through that last little town. Then we wouldn't have this problem," he told her.

"I didn't think about it, either. Don't worry about it. We won't starve, even if we have to go hungry for a few days," she said grimly.

"I guess so," he agreed, unsatisfied, and then he thought of something.

"I do have one other idea," he suggested.

"So spill it. I'm listening," she said.

"What if I gave you the amulet? Then you could do everything I did, for seven days. Then we'd have plenty of food. You could turn a piece of driftwood into a steak, if you wanted to," he offered.

"Hmm. . . " she said.

"Hmm? What's that supposed to mean?" he asked.

"It means I'm not sure that's such a great idea, nice as it sounds," she told him.

"Why not?" he asked.

"Well. . . you remember what Miss Sadie and all the stories told us, don't you? That amulet was meant for *you,* not for just anybody. I doubt we could get it to work for me at all, and even if we did, it still feels an awful lot like breaking the rules," she said.

"So you're saying it might be dangerous even to try?" Brian asked.

"Something like that. I think at the very least we'd be taking a major risk of having the pointer close up again, like it was with you at first. And if something like that happened. . . " she said, and then trailed off meaningfully.

Brian didn't need to ask what she meant. They both knew exactly what would happen if they lost their only guide. The whole journey would have been for nothing, and then for Rachel and Brandon the last spark of hope would be extinguished.

This was a possibility Brian hadn't considered up till then, but he couldn't deny that it cast things in a whole new light. He very well might not have the *right* to pass on the amulet to someone else, and in that case the consequences for doing so might be severe. He knew all too well what could happen if you were careless about things like that.

"Yeah, I guess you're right. I hadn't thought of that," he finally admitted.

"I don't know for *sure* what would happen, of course, but I definitely think it's too much of a risk. Don't you?" she continued.

"Yeah, I'm just afraid the more time goes by and the hungrier we get, the less we'll remember that and the more we'll want to take the risk, even though we know what it might cost us," he told her.

She stopped dead in her tracks when he said that and turned to face him.

"No, Brian. We will *not* do that, no matter how hungry we get or whatever else might happen. We *can't*. Now swear to me you won't give me that amulet, even if I ask for it. Even if I beg for it. No matter what I say or do, you keep that chain around your neck till this thing is done. Okay?" she asked, grabbing his hands in hers and looking at him intently.

"All right, I promise," he said.

"Good," she said. They kept looking at each other for a moment after that, then she dropped his hands and they started walking again.

"How long do you think we can hold out with no food?" he asked. He knew what it was like to go on short rations for a week or so; there'd been quite a few times when Mama was broke and a school lunch was the only food he had for the day. But he'd never gone completely hungry, and he doubted Rachel ever had, either.

"I guess we won't know for sure till we give it a shot. We'll either make it or we'll die trying," she said.

"It might get really bad," he said.

"I'm sure it probably will. We just have to remember what the price will be if we crack, that's all," she said grimly.

It did get bad as the day wore on, bad enough that Brian was tempted again to bring up the idea of giving Rachel the amulet. Only the fear of what she might think of him if he did kept him from saying it.

These thoughts kept him too preoccupied to pay much attention to the world around him, other than to check the pointer from time to time to make sure they were still going in the right direction. But near dusk, Rachel suddenly stopped and whistled.

"What is it?" he asked, startled.

"Look there," she said, pointing through the trees to their right. Brian looked in that direction and immediately saw what she was pointing at. It was an old house or a cabin of some kind, unlikely as that seemed. The place looked deserted.

"Let's go check it out," she suggested.

"Might as well. I doubt we'll find anywhere better to spend the night," he agreed.

They made short work of the distance, and soon emerged into a ragged clearing. The cabin had a rusty tin roof and some of the boards had rotted around the foundation, but when they went inside they found that the floor was still solid enough. It was just one room, with a table and chairs and an old creaky set of wooden bunk beds by the wall near the door. There was a rock fireplace against the opposite wall, and a few shelves with various items sitting on them. Everything was coated in a thick layer of grime and dust, as if nobody had been there in a hundred years.

"What do you think this place was? Deer hunter's cabin?" she asked.

"Yeah, if I had to guess. Looks like nobody's been here for a long time, though," he said.

"Well, I guess it'll do for one night. Better than sleeping in the woods," she said, looking at the place.

"Yeah, no doubt," he said.

"Well, hey, why don't we look around a little bit? We might find some things we could use," she suggested.

"Sure, why not?" he agreed.

So they poked through the stuff on the shelves and looked under the bed and even outside in the yard. Brian found an ancient hammer with a rusty head, and then, much to his delight, an old guitar with a broken strap shoved into the closet.

But it wasn't till they went back outside that they found the pear tree.

"Look!" Rachel cried, spotting it first. Brian turned his head and saw it immediately. The branches were heavy with ripe fruit, some of it already fallen and rotting on the ground, but there was still plenty left on the tree. Rachel was already headed for it.

Brian hurried after her, and as soon as they reached it they helped themselves to several fruits apiece. Then Brian put a hand on Rachel's arm.

"Stop. Don't eat too much or it'll make you sick," he warned her.

"True," she sighed.

"Come on, though. Let's pick some and take them inside. We can eat some more later," he suggested.

They each collected a double armful of fruit, putting it down on the table inside the cabin. The fragrance of the pears soon filled the little room and made it seem almost cheerful.

"We should carry some with us when we leave tomorrow. I know they'll get old after a while but they're a lot better than nothing," Rachel said.

"Yeah, I'll empty the backpack and we'll fill that up, and maybe we could use one of the t-shirts as a sack, if we tied the arms and the neck closed," he suggested.

"Yeah, that'll work," she agreed.

Brian lit a fire in the old hearth, more for something to do than because there was any real need. It was a warm night. Then they both pulled up chairs and watched the dancing flames lick the wood. After a while, Brian picked up the old guitar to strum it thoughtfully. It was still in pretty good tune, surprisingly enough.

"Do you play?" Rachel asked, watching him curiously.

"Just a little bit," he admitted shyly.

"Play me something," she asked.

"I don't know, Raych. I'm not all that good," he said, and she laughed.

"Oh, come on. You're better than me, I'm sure. I promise I won't laugh," she said.

Brian thought about it, and decided he could make an exception just this once. If she laughed it wouldn't kill him.

"All right," he agreed. He took a minute to consider what she might like, and found himself at a loss. He didn't know enough about what she enjoyed. Then he decided to go with *Unclouded Day.* If he didn't let himself think about it too much, maybe he could pretend he was playing it for Brandon. That would make things a lot easier.

He started out uncertainly, his voice soft and his fingers slow, but after a while he got the feel of it and almost forgot she was listening. He shut his eyes to focus on the music, and when the song was done he opened them to see her crying.

"Is something wrong?" he asked, alarmed.

"No, I'm just sappy, that's all. Songs like that always make me cry," she said, smiling through her tears.

"I hoped you'd like it," he said, still uncertain.

"I loved it, Brian. I'm surprised you don't join the band. You're good," she told him.

"You really think so?" he asked, absurdly pleased.

"Yeah, I really do. Play some more," she asked.

So he did, all the songs he could remember, and for a while they were both lost in the music. It reminded Brian of the bonfire party before the football game, only better. Sharing something he loved with a friend was a rare pleasure for him. Happiness was the last thing he'd ever expected to find on a journey like this, but there it was, popping up in the oddest place and time he could possibly have imagined.

Not long afterward they climbed into the bunk beds for the night. It was still fairly early, but they were tired and had another long day ahead in the morning.

"You can have the top bunk," he offered, feeling generous, and she laughed.

"Mighty kind of you. Thanks," she said, and climbed up.

* * * * * * *

He woke some time later, with the smell of smoke in his nose. He coughed, and opened his eyes to the sight of flames. The cabin was on fire!

The smoke was already so thick that it burned his throat and made his eyes water, and probably the only reason it wasn't worse was because of the open windows and door. Through the smoke, he saw that almost the whole wall and part of the floor near the chimney were already engulfed in flames, and the fire was spreading fast.

It was already so hot inside the cabin that Brian was in danger of passing out, and he stumbled frantically for the open door close by.

He staggered outside, coughing and gasping for air, and quickly realized that Rachel must still be inside.

"Raych!" he cried, but there was no answer. He doggedly took a deep breath and plunged back into the house, looking through bleary eyes to see if she was still on the bunk.

He could see nothing, and in desperation he reached into the top bunk to see if he could feel her instead. His groping hand met her shoulder, and he shook her violently.

"Come on, Raych, the cabin's on fire!" he yelled, but there was no answer.

He grabbed hold of her arm and pulled her off the bunk, not caring about gentleness anymore. Her dead weight was more than he expected and he fell to the floor with her body on top of him, skinning his left elbow against the floor planks and nearly twisting his ankle.

He struggled out from under her and got to his feet. He couldn't carry her like that, but he was pretty sure he could drag her. It wasn't that far to the door.

He grabbed her hands and hauled her outside, choking and gasping, but he dared not stop so close to the house. He dragged her as far as the pear tree before his legs gave out, and then he collapsed onto the ground beside her, unable to get up or even to do anything except gasp for air like a beached whale.

Presently his head cleared slightly, and he was able to sit up and look at back at the burning cabin. His eyes stung and his cheeks were running with tears from the smoke. He could still feel the heat from the flames, even this far away.

He checked Rachel, and saw that she was still breathing at least. He turned his face away and hacked up a wad of black mucus into the grass, and he felt sick and exhausted.

After a while, Rachel opened her eyes and coughed up her own wad of smoky snot. Her hair was singed by the heat, and they both smelled like they'd just been wrestling in a giant ashtray.

After burning fiercely for a while, the fire had consumed most of the cabin and started to die back down. Brian and Rachel sat there and watched it burn, all too aware that they could easily have died. She reached out and grasped his hand, and he clasped it back, numbed by the almost-disaster.

"Thanks," she murmured.

"You would have done the same thing," he told her.

"Yeah, but thanks anyway," she said.

"Well. . . you're welcome," he said, for lack of anything better to say.

"Do you think it was the fireplace?" she asked.

"That's all I can think of. It must have had a crack in it, or maybe a coal popped out on the floor," he told her.

"It's a good thing you woke up when you did, or both of us would have been toast by now," she said.

"No doubt. But it's not over yet, though. What if somebody saw this? I bet you could see that fire for miles in the dark," he said.

"Does it matter? Even if somebody did see it, we'll be long gone by the time they could get here to check it out," she pointed out.

"I'm not so sure about that. We might not be as far from other people as we think. We better get gone pretty quick, if we don't want visitors," he said.

"I don't know if I can make it very far, at least not yet," she told him, apologetically.

"I'm not sure I can either, till we rest for a little while," he confessed.

"Then I tell you what. Let's pick some more pears to take with us, like we talked about earlier. Then maybe by the time we're done with that, we'll be rested enough to move on for a little bit," she suggested.

"We'll see," he said.

They both staggered to their feet and started reaching for pears, quickly filling the backpack as full as they could stuff it. Then Brian took one of his extra t-shirts and tied off the arms and neck, and they used that for a sack to hold more.

"All right, then. We better get a move on. Are you up to it, now?" he asked. He wasn't at all sure he was up to it himself, but it had the proper gallant sound.

"No, but if you can do it then I can do it," she said, setting her jaw firmly.

"Let's go, then," he said, and after consulting the amulet again, they moved off through the woods.

They were forced to go slowly, both because of the darkness and because of their recent ordeal by fire. But nevertheless, it didn't take long to put the cabin far behind them.

"You don't think it'll catch the woods on fire, do you?" she asked after a while.

"No, I don't think so. It's been pretty rainy lately, so it ought to just die down and not spread anywhere," he said.

"Do you think we're far enough away from the place so we can sit down and rest awhile longer?" she asked.

"Yeah, I think so. Let's start looking for a place," he said.

Eventually they came to a creek flowing beside their path, with a wide sandbar near the water. It wasn't much, but it would have to do.

"This is good enough. Let's stop here for a little while," she told him.

They hollowed out body-shaped depressions in the powdery sand to make it more comfortable, and then lay down.

Brian slept like a log for the rest of the night, perhaps not surprising after what he'd just been through. By the time he woke, the morning was already far spent, and the sun was halfway up to noon. Rachel still lay sleeping in the sand, and for the moment he let her be.

He felt horribly grungy from the sweat and the smoke, and he decided it was high time for a bath while he had the chance. He went a little downstream out of sight of the sandbar, stripped off his clothes, and dived into the water. He quickly scrubbed himself from head to toe, and then washed his filthy clothes before wringing out as much water as he could.

He put them back on still dripping, knowing the sun would dry them out soon enough. Then he went back to the sandbar and woke Rachel.

"Hey, Raych. Wake up," he said, shaking her. She took a deep breath and sat up, rubbing her eyes and reaching for her glasses.

"Slept late this morning," she said, with a weak smile.

"Yeah, me too. But I guess we needed it, after last night. You want a bath? There's a pool down the creek a little way. I already had one," he told her.

"I'd love one. You have no idea how nasty I feel right now," she said.

"Yeah, I've got some idea," he replied dryly, and she laughed.

"Yeah, I guess you probably do, at that. Wait just a sec and I'll be right back," she said, and quickly disappeared around the bend in the creek.

It didn't take her long to finish, and she returned in her dripping clothes looking much fresher than when she left.

"That was fantastic," she told him.

"Yeah, I think it was the best bath I ever had in my whole life," he agreed.

They both ate another pear for a late breakfast, and then got back on their way. Nothing interesting happened for the rest of the day, and they saw no one. If the burning cabin had attracted any attention, then they were far enough away from it to be safe from whoever showed up.

Brian was beginning to think they'd never find the Fountain, or that they'd have to walk through the woods for a hundred miles before they ever saw any sign of it. So far there'd been nary a clue.

But eventually they came to a rocky place in the side of a steep slope, and here they found a hole in the ground not much bigger than an oven door. It was almost hidden behind a clump of wild blackberry vines, so that Brian would probably never have seen it at all unless he'd been following the amulet.

His heart sank, but no matter which way he walked or turned, the pointer always swung around to point straight to the hole. Their journey through the woods was over.

Chapter Nine

"You've got to be kidding," Brian muttered under his breath. He was no caver, and he hated small enclosed spaces. Especially ones where you couldn't see where you were going or what might be down there with you.

"Have you ever been in a cave before?" she asked him, her eyes fixed on the hole.

"Yeah, a long time ago when I was little. Papaw took me somewhere that had a guided tour of one; I'm not sure where it was. All I remember is that it was dark and creepy and it scared me. I've hated them ever since," he said.

"Well, we've got a flashlight, as long as the batteries hold out. We haven't used it much so far," she said hopefully.

"That's a really cheerful thought, Raych," he said, laughing grimly, and she couldn't help smiling.

"I didn't mean it like that. But seriously, all we can do is try, you know. It's either that or turn back," she pointed out.

"I know," he sighed.

"Surely we won't be down there long enough to run the batteries dry," she said, trying to cheer him up, and maybe herself too.

"Yeah, I guess it'll be okay," he agreed grudgingly.

There was nothing else to be said, so they plucked up their courage and crawled headfirst into the hole, hoping it wasn't as bad as it looked.

The hole quickly led them into a small chamber about the size of a car, with a bit of leaf litter scattered on the floor. It was packed down in places, like something big and heavy had been sleeping on it. Brian had a vivid image of a bear hibernating there, right where his feet stood. Did bears sleep in their dens during the summer? He wasn't sure, but he glanced nervously at the opening and felt a strong desire to crawl right back outside.

"Scared?" Rachel asked, watching him.

"Yeah, a little. Don't want to run into a bear down here," he admitted.

"Me neither. Maybe we should hurry and get deeper inside, just in case," she agreed.

So Brian choked down his fear and consulted the amulet again, to see which way they needed to go. There were two passages that led deeper into the ground from the bear's den. One of them was big enough for a man to walk through, and the other one was so small and narrow that he seriously doubted if they could squeeze through it at all.

Naturally, that was the one the amulet wanted them to take. Brian shook his head and wondered why nothing could ever be easy once in a while.

Still, he got down flat on his belly and wormed his way into the hole as best he could, holding the flashlight between his teeth so he could see where he was going. It was a tight fit, and it didn't seem to get any better further ahead. As soon as he got far enough inside, Rachel followed him.

Brian's fear of bears was now replaced by the fear of getting stuck in this narrow crack in the ground until they died of hunger and thirst. It was almost certain that no one would find them in time to save them, if that happened. Would some casual explorer stumble across their skeletons years and years from now, and wonder what on earth they'd been doing down there?

It did him no good at all to think of such things, so he tried to focus on the Fountain instead, or Brandon, or anything at all except how narrow and tight the passage was. He squirmed and wriggled and inched his way along for what seemed like a week, until eventually the wormhole started to widen out again.

In a way, at least. He emerged into a place where the walls completely disappeared on both sides, but the floor and ceiling stayed uncomfortably close together. It felt like there was an enormous block of stone floating above his head with nothing to hold it up, and he kept imagining that it was about to fall at any second to crush him like a bug under a boot heel.

"Are you okay back there?" he called to Rachel, stopping to wait for her to come out of the passage he'd just left.

"Yeah, I'm fine," she said, emerging beside him.

They stopped to rest for a few minutes and give Brian time to check the amulet again. There hadn't been any need for directions while they crawled through the wormhole, but now they could go ahead almost any which way they pleased.

"Which way?" she asked, after he looked.

"That way," he said, nodding straight ahead and somewhat to the right.

"I'm sure glad we've got that pointer with us. We'd be lost for sure without it," she commented nervously, and he agreed wholeheartedly.

"Ready to head out?" he asked her.

"Yeah, let's go. This place is creepy," she told him. He couldn't have agreed more.

They passed through dozens of randomly shaped chambers and tunnels which meandered any which way, with no rhyme or reason that Brian could tell. The whole mountain seemed to be honeycombed with passages, most of them rough and wet and cold. Whenever they came to a fork in the way, Brian stopped to check the amulet. It never showed the slightest hesitation about which way they should go, but he was reminded every time of how completely dependent on it they really were. As Rachel had said earlier, they would have been totally lost without it.

Some of the passages were so tight he actually had to knock pieces of stone loose with his hammer before they could squeeze through, and others were so huge that they couldn't see the walls or the ceiling even with the flashlight. In a way Brian hated these places even worse than the tight ones, for there were absolutely no landmarks at all. It felt more like being lost in outer space than underground.

In one of these large chambers they came across a rushing stream that blocked the path, and the amulet showed in no uncertain terms that they were supposed to cross it. The current looked swift even in the weak glow of the flashlight. And deep, and cold, and therefore dangerous, too.

"Have we got to cross that?" Rachel whispered, wide eyed. Brian liked it no better than she did, but there was no hiding the truth.

"Yeah, it looks like it," he told her, reluctantly. He hesitated, and played the flashlight beam across the water to try and make out the farther shore.

It was there, but it was hard to make out any details except for a strip of sandy beach. The inky, pitch blackness had a way of playing tricks with your eyes if you weren't careful, and it seemed to soak up the light like a beach towel.

"I think it's about thirty yards to the other side," he told her, peering as hard as he could into the darkness as if that could help him see better.

"That's pretty far to swim, with a current like that," she said.

"Hmm. . . Let's see what it feels like, just in case," he said, sitting down on the floor to take off his shoes and socks. He dipped one foot in the water before quickly jerking it back.

"Cold as ice," he muttered.

"Is it really?" she asked.

"Well, no, maybe not quite that bad. But probably cold enough to take your breath away if you jumped in, and maybe freeze us to death if we stayed in there too long. Current's really strong, too," he told her, seriously.

"Let's look and see if there's any other way across it, then," she suggested.

They explored the stream bank for a while, trying to find a better place to cross. There didn't seem to be any, for at one end of the chamber the stream gushed out of the solid rock over a low waterfall just as swiftly as ever, and at the other end it formed a kind of pool backed up against the wall of the cavern. But that end was even worse, because Brian knew the water had to be escaping somewhere, probably through an opening below the surface. It would have to be one big monster of a hole to swallow a river as full and as fast as that one was, too. The surface of the pool was covered in swirling eddies and upwellings that seemed to confirm his guess.

Brian suppressed a shudder; what if they got sucked under by the whirlpool and carried off into some cavern where the water extended all the way to the ceiling? No, they dared not risk that at all. But the waterfall wasn't much better, and that left them with a problem. They had to get across, but how?

He looked again at the place where the stream gushed out from the wall, and after thinking about it for a few minutes he had an idea. The stream flooded out over a lip of stone, and the limestone below it was undercut slightly by the backsplash of the water. This formed a small space between the falling water itself and the rock behind it, and there at least the water was fairly calm.

It'd still be unbelievably cold and there was dangerously little room to maneuver, but he thought if they kept hold of projecting rocks and were very, very careful, and extremely lucky, they might just possibly make it across.

On the other hand, he didn't even want to think about what might happen if either one of them slipped. The falling water would snatch them under almost instantly, and they might be carried a long way downstream very quickly. Maybe even all the way into the whirlpool at the bottom of the cavern. Brian knew what that would mean, and he shivered at the thought. But there was no other way.

"I think maybe we could pick our way along that shelf behind the waterfall," he finally said, reluctantly.

"I knew you'd say that," she sighed.

"You did?" he asked, surprised.

"Yeah. Anybody can see it's the only way where there's any chance at all to make it across," she told him.

"So why didn't *you* say something, then?" he asked, confused.

"Well, you looked like you were thinking pretty hard over there, you know. I figured you'd probably come to the same conclusion yourself in a minute if I left you alone. Which you did," she added hastily, and in spite of his fear he laughed.

"So you thought I might like to figure it out by myself, is that it?" he asked.

"Sometimes people do," she shrugged.

"I don't think this is the time to worry about being proud, Raych. If you've got an idea from now on, just spill it," he told her, and she smiled.

"Okay, then. I'll try to remember that," she agreed, and then there was a pause while they both tried to think of something else to say, to put off the moment when they actually had to get started. Neither of them wanted to set foot in the water, but finally Brian sighed.

"I guess we might as well get going," he said, pointing out the obvious.

"Yeah, I guess," she agreed unenthusiastically.

He put the amulet in his pocket and zipped it up to keep from losing it, and peered across the river again to find a place where the other shore seemed closest. Then he tucked his socks into his shoes and threw them as hard as he could across the river. He didn't dare keep them on while he crossed, just in case he did fall in and had to swim. He couldn't afford to have anything dragging his feet down.

They landed somewhere on the gravel (he thought), and then he threw Rachel's shoes across, too. Then he picked up the backpack and hesitated.

"I don't think I can throw this all the way across, Raych. It's too heavy," he told her.

"Could you take some of the pears out and throw them across one at a time, and then throw the pack across when it's lighter?" she suggested.

"I can try," he agreed doubtfully.

He started lobbing pears across the river like baseballs, suddenly glad for all those years he'd spent rock throwing. He couldn't tell where they landed, but he didn't hear any splashes. He left about half of them in the pack, just enough to give it a little weight, and then he zipped it up and threw it with all his strength.

The pack sailed far out across the water, and then landed in the river with a huge splash, barely short of the far shore. The swift current carried it off in an instant, and Brian knew there wasn't a prayer of getting it back. He cursed out loud and kicked the ground in frustration. That was half their food and all their clothes and other stuff, gone in the blink of an eye. They had nothing left except the flashlight, the amulet, the money, and however many pears had made it across to the far bank.

"It's all right, Mad Dog. We'll make do without it," Rachel told him, doing her best to sound cheerful.

"I guess we'll have to," he admitted with clenched teeth.

"It'll be all right, I promise," she repeated.

"What makes you so sure? It looks pretty bad to me," he said, staring at the spot where the pack had landed.

"I don't think we made it all this way just to have it end like this, because we couldn't cross a stupid river," she said, and he couldn't help smiling a little.

"Maybe so. Sorry for losing my temper," he said.

"No problem. Happens to the best of us sometimes," she told him.

There was nothing else to wait for, so Brian looked at the river again and took a deep breath to steady himself before he waded out. The first few steps were stinging cold against his bare feet, and he was already shivering when the water was no more than knee deep. By the time he reached the edge of the waterfall he was in up to his chest, but most of him was too numb to feel much by then. The river was leaching the heat out of him, fast, and he knew there was no time to waste. With no more hesitation, he crawled in behind the curve of the waterfall.

It was worse than he'd thought. There was no more than two or three feet of space between the rock and the water. He could touch bottom with his feet, but he could also feel the edge of a drop-off. The roar of the falling water so near was loud enough to deafen both of them and make speech impossible, and even the slackwater they were wading through was full of cross-currents and surges of bubbles coming up from below.

Brian ignored all this and crept along as steadily and surely as he could toward the far shore, although it was rather like trying to ignore a rattlesnake in his bed. He dared not do more than glance back now and then to see how Rachel was doing, but she seemed to be getting along about as well as he was.

It was slow, scary business, but they did make progress, and after a while they made it perhaps three quarters of the way across, as best Brian could judge without being able to see past the curtain of water in front of him. Then they met a problem.

A boulder blocked the way forward, and there was absolutely no way around it except to plunge into the waterfall itself. Brian halted, appalled.

He'd barely been able to hold back his fear as it was, and the thought of swimming the raging torrent terrified him. The cross-currents swirling around his legs were just a feeble reminder of what the main flood would be like. His body was already so cold that he doubted he could swim very far, even with no current at all. True, there shouldn't be *that* much farther to go before they reached the other bank, but what if the river pulled them right back out to mid-stream? They'd drown, that's what. He didn't have a shred of doubt about *that*.

But there was no other way, unless they decided to turn back. And if they did that, then Rachel would most certainly die. So might Brandon, and even Brian for that matter, because the amulet offered them no help at all in finding a way back out of the cave system. All it did was point to the Fountain.

Brian had never been more frightened in his entire life than he was at that moment, not even on that awful night when Mama put the bullet hole in his bedroom wall. Any choice he might make seemed terrible.

He took deep breaths to calm his pounding heart. They'd have to swim and hope for the best; that was the only option. Anything was better than wandering the endless caverns until they starved to death alone in the darkness.

As gingerly as possible, he turned to face Rachel, who couldn't see past him to tell why he'd stopped. There was no way he could make her hear him over the roar of the falls, but he got as close as he could and put his mouth to her ear.

"There's a boulder up ahead, we can't get by this way!" he said, yelling so his words were loud enough for her to understand.

She grasped the situation instantly.

"Can you swim?" she asked, putting her mouth up to his ear. In this way they were able to talk, somewhat.

"Yeah, can you?" he asked.

"Yeah. How much farther is it?" she asked.

"I can't tell. I don't think very far," he said.

"Then we have to swim. It's no use going back," she said.

"Yeah, I was afraid you'd say that," he said, and for a second he thought she actually smiled at him.

"You better put the flashlight in your pocket and zip it up so we won't lose it," she reminded him, and he nodded. He switched off the light, plunging them into utter darkness, and quickly put the flashlight in his pocket with the amulet.

"Listen, the water will push us under when we jump into the falls, maybe a long way. Hold my hand, and before long we ought to pop back up top again. Then swim, *hard,* the same direction I do. Okay?" he asked.

"Okay," she agreed. She reached out to clasp his hand, and he was glad to feel some strength in her grip. He gripped right back. They took a deep breath together, and then jumped.

The river snatched them at once, and the weight of the falling water pushed them far under the surface. They plunged so deep that Brian felt his knee scrape against the bare rock bottom. He was dragged helplessly along for a short while, and then found himself caught in the upwelling below the falls. After that, he was launched quickly back to the surface. His head suddenly popped free into open air, and he took a deep gasping breath, fighting panic. He still had a grip on Rachel's hand, but that was the only point of contact he had with anything. He couldn't see a thing in the pitch black darkness, although he was conscious of being carried along at a rapid pace.

He knew he had to swim at right angles to the current to reach shore, but which way? He was too disoriented to remember. One of the banks was probably nearby, and the other one impossibly far. A wrong choice would probably be fatal, and he had only seconds to make up his mind. In desperation, he swam left.

It seemed like forever, but really it couldn't have been more than a minute before his hand struck bottom. Scant seconds after that he was crawling out onto a gravelly beach, but it was anybody's guess which side it might be. He wouldn't know for sure till he was able to get out the flashlight and look.

But for a while he lacked the strength to do even that much. He lay there and shivered violently, and then threw up what felt like a gallon of river water that he must have swallowed at some point, although he couldn't remember doing it. His head spun, and if he hadn't already been lying down he might have fallen. He felt someone patting his back and vaguely realized it must have been Rachel, but he was too far gone to care. The river had almost killed them both.

He could feel her body shaking violently from the cold, just as his was, and he quickly decided this was no time for modesty.

"We've got to get warm," he told her, between chattering teeth, and when she didn't answer he put his arms around her and pressed his body as close up against hers as he could. She didn't object, and they lay there together sharing body heat as best they could.

After a while, they both recovered enough strength to sit up and take stock. Brian unzipped his pocket to get the flashlight, and when he switched it on the first thing he discovered was that it didn't work.

"Just give it a little time to dry out. It'll be all right," Rachel reminded him, still shivering.

He did, and presently when he tried it again he was rewarded with a weak glow. The first thing he noticed was that they were dangerously far downstream, almost at the very lip of the whirlpool. Another ten seconds and they would both have been lost.

That scared him all over again, but he reminded himself sternly that they were safe now, and he needed to get a grip. The next thing he saw was his left shoe, and not long after that, his right one. They'd made it to the far bank after all.

They took a little while to wring some of the water out of their clothes and to rub some warmth back into their arms and legs, and when they felt halfway human again, Brian consulted the amulet to see which way they needed to go. Both of them were anxious to leave the underground river far behind as soon as possible. Brian had never been so close to death before, and he hoped he never would be again.

They found only seven of the pears that he'd thrown across the water, and they stuffed these into their pockets glumly. It wasn't enough food to last more than a day or two at the most.

But there was worse to come. It wasn't long after they left the river behind that Rachel put a hand on his shoulder and stopped him.

"What is it, Raych?" he asked, turning to look at her.

"My medicine bottle is gone, Brian. I guess I must have lost it when we crossed the river; I just now noticed it was missing," she told him, sounding scared.

"Are you sure?" he asked.

"Yeah, I'm sure. It was in my shirt pocket and I thought I had it buttoned shut, but it must have come open," she told him.

"Can you go without it for a while?" he asked.

"Maybe a few hours. Not very long, though. I'll start having seizures," she said.

"What should I do, if you have one?" he asked grimly.

"Just leave me alone. There's nothing you can do except wait for it to be over. I'll probably chew my tongue to pieces and I'll have to rest for a few hours before I can walk again, but I'll be okay," she told him.

"We'll just have to do the best we can, then," he said, hiding his own fear.

Again they went on for what seemed like days, although in reality it couldn't have been more than a few hours at the most. Sometimes they talked quietly, but more often than not they were both silent.

Then they came to the bat colony.

"What's that sound?" Rachel whispered, grabbing his arm again. Brian hadn't noticed anything, but when he stopped and listened carefully he could hear faint skittering noises above his head. It reminded him of rats.

He didn't like this at all, and quickly shone the light up above them. The ceiling was alive with bats, packed together in clumps like sardines in a can. Brian took the light off them immediately, but it had been there long enough to disturb a few of them already. These dropped from their perches and flew around the cavern noisily, until they finally disappeared somewhere.

"Cover up the light so maybe they'll settle down," Rachel whispered.

"Yeah, but then we can't see which way to go," he pointed out, also whispering.

They finally decided to cover the flashlight with one hand, and pick their way through the bat cave by the faint red light that welled up between their fingers.

This wasn't easy, because the floor of the cavern was piled deep with bat droppings, slick and greasy and fouler than Brian would ever have imagined it was possible for anything to be. It reminded him of wading through thick, sticky mud. At every step they sank in, sometimes thigh-deep, and more than once they slipped and fell. It was a slow and disgusting business to make their way across.

The filth was bad enough, but even worse was the thought of the bats swooping down to attack them. Didn't they carry rabies? Brian was almost sure he remembered reading or hearing that, somewhere. He could just imagine a long series of rabies shots if one of them bit him.

But that didn't happen, and just when he thought he couldn't possibly survive a single more step through bat crap, they reached the end of the colony and passed into a new tunnel.

Several hours later, still filthy and stinking, they sat down to rest for a while in one of the drier and sandier caves they'd come across. They had no way of telling what time it might have been in the world outside, but judging from how sleepy they both were it must have been late.

"All this sand gives me an idea about how to clean up a little, if you want to give it a try," Rachel said presently.

"What is it?" he asked, curious.

"We can take a sand bath. Take some of this sand and rub it all over the dirty spots. It'll help a little," she suggested.

"Yeah, I think I've heard of that somewhere before, now that you mention it," he agreed. Nothing but soap and water would get them completely clean, of course, but anything was better than smelling like a sewer all night. So they tried it, and found that it was slightly better than nothing. But not by much.

After the sand bath they both ate a pear, and Brian tried to ignore the fact that he was still gnawingly hungry even afterward. But they dared not eat any more. Five pears was all they had left to last them however much longer they had to stay underground, and who knew how long that might be? The caves seemed to go on forever, and Brian had kicked himself more times than he could count for overlooking the food problem. He'd assumed the Fountain was close, stupid as that was. He didn't know how much longer they could go on, if it didn't turn up soon.

He glanced longingly at the pears, unsatisfying as they were, and then he lay down on the sandy floor with a still-growling stomach. But nevertheless, he was so exhausted that even hunger couldn't keep him awake for long, and he was asleep almost before he could shut his eyes.

Chapter Ten

He must have slept for a long time, because he woke up feeling better than before. His body was so cold he thought he might never feel warm again, but he knew exercise would soon cure that. He was also hungry enough that he thought he might try eating a rock soon, if nothing better showed up.

He clicked on the flashlight and immediately noticed that Rachel was in a different part of the cave than he remembered. She lay crumpled in an unnatural heap on the sand, not at all like any normal person would choose to sleep. But asleep she surely was, and that puzzled him. He crawled over to shake her awake.

"Wake up, Raych," he said, and she only groaned.

Brian was uneasy. Rachel had been true to her word and never once complained about anything they'd had to do, no matter how dangerous or disgusting or difficult it might be. It wasn't like her to start doing it now.

"Is something wrong?" he asked, anxiously.

"I think maybe I had a seizure, Brian," she finally told him, her voice thick and heavy.

"You do?" he asked, stupidly.

"Yeah, I bit my tongue really bad, and this is always how it feels after it's over. Being really bone tired like this, like my whole body's made of lead," she said dully.

"Is there anything I can do?" he asked.

"No, there's really not. I knew it was coming, with no medicine. But you're right, I need to get up. You may have to help me, though; let me lean on you when I need to," she said.

He helped her struggle to her feet, and she seemed frail and weak in a way he'd never yet seen her. She had to grip his shoulder for support, just to stand.

"Can you make it?" he asked, worried.

"I've got to. I'll be all right, I promise. Just don't let me fall," she told him.

In this way they staggered and stumbled along as best they could, and after a while she seemed to recover enough so she didn't have to lean on him so much.

He was glad, but what if it happened again? He was afraid to mention it, for fear it might somehow make it happen. That was stupid, of course, but he couldn't shake the feeling. The possibility hung like a black cloud over his head, weighing him down. But as bad as that was, he soon had something even worse to worry about.

Before long, he started to notice how weak the flashlight batteries were getting, and he knew it was only a matter of hours before they died completely.

That was such a horrible thought that he stopped in mid-stride and switched off the light completely.

"What's wrong?" Rachel asked.

"The light's starting to get dim. We need to keep it off as much as we can," he explained.

"Yeah, I guess. But we better hold hands if we've got to walk in the dark, so we don't get lost," she pointed out. Brian shrugged and grabbed her hand, doing his best to feel his way along the walls by touch. But he was haunted by the fear of missing a turn, or stepping blindly off the edge of some yawning pit that might open up at their feet at any time, or who-knew-what else. Therefore he compromised, using the light in brief spurts to let them see what was ahead, and then groping their way through the darkness until he thought they needed another glimpse. Now and then he checked the pointer, but there seemed to be no turns in this region.

After a while, he felt Rachel's body suddenly go rigid as stone beside him, and before he could think to ask what was wrong she fell heavily to the floor like dead weight, her arms and legs thrashing violently while spit and snot flew everywhere. For a second he panicked, until he realized it had to be one of her seizures. Then he stood beside her helplessly, remembering what she'd said about waiting it out.

It wasn't very long before the convulsion was over, and when he was sure she was finished, he wiped the foam and blood off her face with the cleanest part of his t-shirt that he could find. There was nothing else he could do for her.

A minute or two later her eyes opened for a moment, and then closed again as she seemed to settle into a deep sleep. Brian sat beside her and ate another pear while he waited, thinking darkly of what might happen to them if things kept getting worse. After an hour or two she woke, and when he switched on the light he noticed that she had tears in her eyes.

"What's wrong?" he asked, bending down beside her.

"I can't go on anymore, Brian. I just can't do it," she said in a thick voice, and then started to sob uncontrollably. Brian awkwardly put his arms around her shoulders and shushed her like he might have done with Brandon, not knowing how else to comfort her.

"It'll be all right," he soothed, patting her back.

"No it won't. You have to leave me here and go get somebody, or else bring me some water from that Fountain and then we'll see if it can really do anything. But I can't go any farther," she said.

"You know I can't leave you here," he told her.

"Then you'll die too," she told him, with brutal directness.

"No I won't. Nobody's going to die, Raych. I know you can't walk right now, but can you hold on to my back and let me carry you for a while?" he asked. The very thought was exhausting, and he was already bone tired. But he'd never admit it until he collapsed on the floor. Until then, he'd try to make sure they both made it out of there.

She considered the idea.

"Yeah, I guess I could probably do that. For a while," she agreed.

"Then climb up," he told her, squatting down so she could get on his back. She did so, painfully slowly, and he had to hunch forward a little bit so she wouldn't slide off. She put her arms around his neck, and thus arranged piggy-back, they went on.

Several times, Brian was absolutely certain that he couldn't possibly take a single more step, but somehow he always did. He had to stop and rest several times, but he wasn't ready to give up yet.

He could feel Rachel's body twitching and jerking now and then and he was afraid she might have another seizure at any moment, but it was still the dying flashlight that terrified him more than anything else. No matter how carefully he tried to conserve the batteries, the light grew steadily weaker, and at last it winked out completely, leaving them in utter darkness.

Brian was strangely unmoved by this, by the time it happened. Perhaps he'd finally blown every fuse in his fear circuits, or maybe he was simply too worn out and too close to despair to care anymore. It would have been easy at that moment to simply sit down on the floor beside Rachel, curl up in a ball, and wait for the end to come. But he found that somehow he couldn't give up until the bitter end, if bitter was how it had to be. So he kept on doggedly putting one foot in front of the other, not willing to quit until he lacked the strength to keep going. The tunnel never divided anymore, although it twisted and turned repeatedly.

Rachel had two more seizures, one of them really bad, and each time he had to put her down on the floor of the cave and wait for her to revive enough to climb up on his back again. But each time she got weaker, and he could tell that after a few more episodes like that she wouldn't have the strength even to hold on to him anymore. Even if she did, he didn't know how much longer he could carry her. He was nearly at the end of his rope.

After a long time, a pale greenish glow began to filter into the cavern. It was so faint that he almost thought he was imagining it at first, and he wouldn't have been able to see it at all if his eyes hadn't been accustomed to pitch blackness for so long. But the light grew gradually stronger, until soon there was no mistaking it.

"I think there's something up ahead," he whispered to Rachel.

"Are we coming back outside?" she asked.

"I'm not sure. Maybe," he said, doubtfully. It didn't look like daylight, but what else could it be?

Still, it gave him hope, and along with that hope came a fresh surge of energy that he hadn't known he possessed. He straightened up and hurried forward, and though he staggered he didn't fall.

At last he rounded a final twist in the passage and stepped out into another immense cavern, almost full of water except for the sandy white beach where he stood. The water itself was the source of the light he'd seen, for it was somehow lit up from below and seemed to glow a bright, clear, emerald green. Small ripples cast dancing light across the ceiling and across Brian's face.

"What is this place?" Rachel whispered.

"I don't know," he confessed, staring at the emerald green water with wide eyes. Then he suddenly felt her shaking with laughter on his back.

"What's so funny?" he asked, confused.

"You, that's what. And me too, I guess, standing here staring at that pool of water like it's something spooky. It's just daylight, that's all, reflecting up from the limestone on the bottom. There must be a cave that leads outside, somewhere down below the surface," she explained.

"Yeah, I didn't think of that," he agreed, feeling foolish.

"It's beautiful, though," she said.

"Yeah, I guess it is," he agreed heavily, thinking to himself that neither one of them was in any condition for another swim. He shuddered at the very idea.

He could hear the sound of water flowing somewhere not too awfully far away, and he walked a little farther out onto the sandy fringe of the pool so he could see better. As soon as he did, he immediately noticed a flowing fountain to the left built of jet-black rock, quite thoroughly out of place amongst the white limestone.

From the fountain there gushed forth a stream of cold water, clear as glass, which overflowed the top and soon lost itself in the emerald depths of the lake. That was the source of the splashing sound.

"Is that the Fountain?" Rachel asked, in a hushed voice. Brian glanced at the amulet, and found that the pointer aimed straight for the black stone.

"I think it might be," he told her, hardly daring to believe it.

"I think I could stand for a little while now, if you put me down," she told him, and he allowed her to get off his back. She was still unsteady, but the rest seemed to have done her good, and she was able to stand on her own two feet by leaning on Brian's shoulder.

Neither of them said a word, but by mutual agreement they crept forward toward the Fountain together. And when they came near enough, they saw carven letters cut deep into the black rock, hard to make out until they got very close.

Then Brian was lost in wonder, for upon the stone lip of the basin were written these words:

The strong of heart shall drink of Me,
The life-giving Life, and the Beauty that makes beautiful.

Upon the edge of the Fountain there sat a golden cup, and Brian with trembling hand reached out to grasp it quickly, and dipped the cup in the gushing Fountain to fill it.

"Here, drink," he said, and offered the cup to Rachel first.

"No, say a blessing first. It wouldn't be right to just drink," she said. He nodded, and after a moment of thought he spoke aloud.

"To God Most High, may our taste of this Fountain give you glory forever," he said, holding the cup aloft with both hands. Then he lowered it and glanced at her, to see if he'd spoken too grandly and if she might laugh at him. It seemed the kind of solemn moment for which no less of a blessing would do, but he would have blushed bright red if she'd laughed. But she only nodded with perfect seriousness, so perhaps she felt the solemnity too.

She took the cup from him with hands that trembled, whether from illness and exhaustion or from awe, he knew not which. She closed her eyes and murmured something under her breath, then she lifted the cup to her lips and drank.

Nothing happened that he could see immediately, but she handed him the cup.

"Now you, Brian. Drink," she told him.

He dipped the cup again into the Fountain, but then he hesitated for a moment with the cup full to brimming in his hand, remembering Miss Sadie's warning. Did he love the world enough, and God enough, to live his life for nothing else, however long that might be? He wondered if anyone had ever stood before the Fountain like this, and then decided not to drink after all. The responsibility that came with it was a huge one.

Then he made his choice, and lifted the golden cup to his lips. The water was icy cold, as if it came indeed from the very heart of the earth, and he shivered as he drank deep, but he felt nothing else unusual. Just as with the amulet, there was nothing to tell him if it had worked or not. Nevertheless, he knelt down in that sacred place and gave thanks, and Rachel beside him.

When they were done with that, Brian reverently replaced the cup on the lip of the Fountain, and looked at Rachel.

"Do you feel any different?" he whispered, looking earnestly at her. Both of them were still filthy and exhausted, and then again the green light made everything look magical and half unreal, so that he couldn't tell for certain if she looked different or not.

"I feel stronger now, almost like I could walk again if I needed to, but still very tired. What about you?" she asked. He considered the idea.

"I guess I don't feel much different, but then I wasn't sick to start with," he finally admitted.

"So how can we tell for sure if it worked or not?" she asked.

"You can't tell if your eyes are better, or your tongue?" he asked. She thought about this for a minute, and then slowly took her glasses off.

"I can see without my glasses," she said wonderingly, and then broke into a huge grin.

"I think it worked, Raych," he told her.

"Yeah, I think so too, but surely there's some way we could tell about you," she said. Brian thought about this, and then he smiled.

"I think I know a way. Miss Sadie told me we'd be beautiful and perfect after we drank the water, didn't she? I have a scar from where I got cut with an axe pretty bad on my left foot one time, splitting wood. Maybe it's gone now," he suggested. He quickly stripped off his filthy left shoe and exposed the place. It was smooth and clean as a baby's foot, with no trace of the scar at all.

He quickly checked other spots. . . the chicken pox scar on his elbow, the deep scratch on his knee from a thorn bush last fall; they were all gone.

"Do you have any scars?" he asked, looking up. She nodded.

"Yeah, I have one on my side, where I had my appendix taken out," she agreed, lifting the edge of her shirt to show him the place.

It was gone, too.

They looked at each other with delight, and Rachel was the first one to break the spell.

"What do we do now?" she finally asked, and for some reason the question tickled him, though he couldn't have said why.

"Go home, I guess," he laughed. She smiled too.

"True. But how do we get out of here? I'm not sure we can find our way back the same way we came," she pointed out.

"No, not without the pointer to show us the way," he agreed.

"Well, *does* it show the way out?" she asked.

It was a good question, and Brian immediately looked at the amulet to see. In the back of his mind, he'd always had a vague hope that the pointer might perhaps swing around and lead them back out from the place of the Fountain again, once they'd found it and drunk from the water. But when he looked, he found that the back of the amulet was shut again, and nothing he could do would reopen it.

"I think we're on our own now, Raych. I can't get it open at all anymore," he told her.

"I guess it's done its job, now that we're here. We'd never make it back through all those caves with no light, anyway, even if it did show us the way. Not to mention we'd have to cross the river again," she reminded him.

"Yeah, I forgot about that. We'll just have to think of something else," he admitted.

Brian eyed the emerald green lake thoughtfully. There was definitely sunlight coming in from somewhere, so there had to be a way out beneath the lake, if they were brave enough to look for it.

He still had vivid memories of their near-drowning in the river yesterday, and he wasn't happy with the idea of going back in the water again so soon. He thought wryly to himself that he'd become awfully good at getting himself into situations where there was no way out except by doing something he hated.

"I think we could maybe get out through the lake," he finally told her.

"Yeah, I was afraid you'd say that," she agreed, with a humorless smile.

"I know; I don't like it either. But there's got to be a way out, down there. The light has to come in from somewhere, and it can't be all that far or it wouldn't be so bright," he said, talking just as much for his own benefit as for hers.

"What if it's too deep for us to swim, though?" she pointed out, and all he could do was shrug.

"Maybe it is, but do we have any other choice?" he asked.

"No, I guess we don't," she agreed.

"Okay, then, I tell you what. Let's rest for a little while to get our strength back, maybe sleep a couple hours if we can. Then we'll try it," he suggested, and she nodded.

"All right, but at least let's scrub some of this filth off, first. We've got water now," she said, waving a hand at the lake.

"That's a great idea," he said.

So they went to the edge of the emerald lake, stripped off their shoes and socks, and left them in a pile on the beach. There was no way they could take them along when they left the cavern. If someone else ever found his way to the Fountain, then maybe he'd come across two pairs of filthy Nikes and wonder who'd left them behind.

Then they walked barefoot out into the lake. Brian had been braced for freezing cold water like what he'd felt in the underground river, and he was all the more ready to expect this after drinking the icy water from the Fountain, but it wasn't so. The lake was no worse than cool, not even enough to make them shiver.

"At least it's warm," he commented.

"Yeah, at least. No current, either," she agreed, and he knew she was thinking about the underground river, just like he'd been doing.

There was a wide shelf of limestone near the beach, and then a sudden drop-off about ten feet out from shore. Brian couldn't tell how deep the water might be after that, for it was so crystal clear that it was hard to judge distances very well. Still, when he looked down he could see a jumble of white boulders, and vaguely make out the opening of a tunnel mouth through which reflected sunlight poured. There was no telling how far the tunnel itself might stretch.

But that could wait, and in the meantime, Brian and Rachel scrubbed themselves as clean as they could without soap. Then they sat down on the beach together and leaned their backs against the stone wall near the Fountain, quietly eating the last two pears while they rested. They both needed to get some strength back, before they tried a swim like that.

"I think you really do look different, Brian," she commented after a while.

"Like how?" he asked. He'd been thinking the same thing about her, but it was hard to put his finger on what the difference might be.

"Well. . . I know it'll sound weird to say it like this, but you're beautiful. Perfect, like one of those statues of a Greek god a long time ago. I couldn't tell what it was at first because the difference isn't much, and the dirt and the bat crap didn't help, but I'm sure, now," she told him.

"And it took you this long to notice that?" he asked her jokingly, trying to make light of it.

"I always thought you looked like that, Brian. It's just a little bit more, now," she told him. She seemed perfectly serious, although he noticed her knotting her fingers together like she was nervous to be saying it.

Her words embarrassed him, and he couldn't think of a good way to answer her. He suspected she was probably every bit as uncomfortable as he was, but unfortunately they couldn't just drop the subject. If the change was real, then they needed to be sure.

He studied her face carefully, and decided she might be right. The difference was a subtle thing, hard to notice at first, but it was definitely there. He could remember, vaguely, that he'd once thought she was something less than beautiful. But now she was just. . . perfect, like she'd said. She reminded him of Sadie Jones' roses, or one of his animals at Black Rock; flawless, with not a spot or a stain of any kind.

"You're beautiful, too," he finally told her, and she smiled like a girl who hasn't heard such a thing very often.

"Do you think other people will notice, when we get back home?" she asked, and he shrugged.

"If we can tell the difference then I imagine other people will probably see it, too. But I don't think it matters if they do. It's not enough to make us look freaky or anything," he said.

"Yeah, I guess you're right. It'll just take some getting used to," she agreed. They were silent for a while after that, thinking their own thoughts, until she spoke again.

"Brian?" she asked.

"Yeah?" he answered.

"Thank you for showing me this place. Even if we drown in the lake tomorrow, it was worth it, just to come here with you and see all this," she told him.

"I think it was worth it, too," he agreed, and reached out to clasp her hand. She squeezed back, and they said nothing more for a long time. Eventually they both slept.

When Brian woke, Rachel's head was lying on his chest, and his face was buried in her hair. He could almost have sworn it was softer and thicker than he remembered, and he couldn't help noticing the burnt spots from the fire and the sewer-smell from the bat cave were gone. He wondered what else the Fountain had done to them.

They must have been asleep for at least several hours; his body was rested enough to feel almost human again. He blinked his eyes and decided it was probably time to get moving.

"Wake up, Raych," he whispered, shaking her. She took a deep breath and sat up.

"How long did we sleep?" she asked, yawning.

"I'm not sure, but I think I'm strong enough to swim, now. What about you?" he asked. She considered.

"Yeah, I'm up for it if you are," she agreed, nodding.

They took a few minutes to stretch their arms and legs and get fully awake, and then they waded back into the green lake together, stopping at the edge of the drop-off. They both took several deep breaths, and then held the last one before they dived for the bottom.

Brian's ears popped as he went down, and he could feel the pressure building up all around him as he swam deeper. It reminded him unpleasantly of the underground river, and he shoved the thought aside. If he started thinking about that too much, he'd panic for sure.

He opened his eyes so he could find the tunnel mouth, and quickly entered it. He was already beginning to feel the need to breathe, but he didn't let himself think about that, either. He swam along the cavern wall, using handholds to pull himself along a little faster whenever he could. Then the cavern turned a corner, and he saw real, honest-to-goodness daylight streaming down from somewhere up ahead.

By the time they exited the cavern, Brian's lungs were bursting for lack of air, and he looked up to see the surface far above his head. There were several other cavern mouths all around them which might have led almost anywhere. Rachel was close beside him, and together they rushed for the surface.

Just when he thought he couldn't stand it even one more second, Brian's head broke out into open air, and a second later Rachel's popped up next to him a few feet away.

He took deep, gasping breaths of late afternoon air, treading water and unable to think of anything else except the blessed oxygen for a while. Only after he'd satisfied his body's craving for breath did he glance around to see where in the world they might be.

They seemed to be in a lake, very small but deep and clear, with steep cliffs all the way around, almost like a sinkhole. Of houses or boats or other traces of men, Brian saw nothing at all. They seemed to be in the middle of nowhere.

"Where are we?" Rachel called to him.

"I don't know. I guess we'll find out soon enough," he said.

The shore was close by, and as soon as Brian pulled himself out onto the rocks, he checked to make sure the amulet was still in his pocket. Then he looked at the cliff face above them. It was only about a hundred feet high, if that, but it might as well have been a thousand if they couldn't find a way to climb it.

He noticed there were breaks and cracks in the limestone all over the place. They shouldn't have a problem finding handholds, but the whole thing looked dangerously crumbly.

"I'm not sure we can climb that wall without a rope," he said worriedly.

"Do we have a choice?" she asked.

"Well. . . no, not really. Maybe if we tried to climb it over there where the cliff rises right out of the water, then it might be a little bit safer. That way, we'd just fall back into the lake if we slipped," he said, thoughtfully.

"That would hurt bad enough, if we were very high up," she said.

"Yeah, but at least it wouldn't break any bones and it wouldn't kill us. Not like landing on these rocks," he pointed out.

"Let's try it, then," she sighed.

They got back in the water and swam a short distance to reach the bottom of the almost sheer cliff. Then Brian reached up to grab hold of the lowest crack in the rock.

"Here goes nothing," he said, and heaved himself up, scrambling to get a foothold. Almost immediately, the weak limestone broke off under his weight and he fell backwards into the water with a huge splash. He came up sputtering and coughing, and Rachel laughed.

"It's not funny," he told her, when he could talk.

"I'm sorry, Brian. You just looked silly, that's all, falling backwards and grabbing air like that," she said.

"No doubt. Nothing to do but try again," he said, and moved toward the cliff again.

"Wait just a minute. I think the cliff leans backward a little bit, over there on the far side. I know it's not much, but it might help some," she told him, nodding her head toward the far shore.

Brian looked, and the cliff did in fact look a little less imposing over there. There was just enough slope to give them a decent chance of making it to the top without ropes. Of course, it also meant there was just enough slope to send them bouncing and rolling and smashing their skulls against rocks all the way back down to the water if they fell. Not long ago, Brian would never have dreamed of trying to climb such a thing. But then again, he'd been forced to do a lot of things lately that he never would have tried before.

He gazed at the steep slope uneasily, not liking the idea but unable to think of anything better.

"Let's try it," he shrugged, and took off swimming in that direction.

He reached it first, and grabbed hold of a rock just like he'd done before. This time he was able to pull himself up and cling to the stone without falling, and soon Rachel was up beside him.

"I think we can make it this time," she said.

It was a ticklish business, and they both had to climb slowly and carefully, testing the holds to make sure they wouldn't break. More than once they knocked loose stones that fell down into the water far below, and the higher they got, the scarier it looked.

But eventually Brian threw one hand over the top and grabbed a tree root to pull himself up the last few feet. He laid himself flat on his stomach and reached down to give Rachel a hand up, and for a few minutes they both sat there at the edge of the cliff, exhausted but happy.

"No wonder nobody ever finds this place. It looks just like any other sinkhole from up here; dime a dozen," Rachel commented, looking down. The emerald-green water far below them was set like a jewel at the bottom of the limestone cavity, not betraying the slightest trace that it concealed anything unusual.

"Well. . . maybe that's all it is, you know. Remember what Miss Sadie told us about how nobody ever finds the Fountain in the same place twice? It may not even be down there anymore," he said. That was a strange and novel idea, but no sooner had he spoken the words than it already seemed like an indisputable fact.

"You really think so?" Rachel asked, raising one eyebrow.

"We'll never know for sure unless we try to swim back down, but I really don't think it matters much either way. We found it when we needed to, and if somebody else needs to find it one of these days then I doubt they'll need any help from us," he said.

"Suits me," she agreed, still peering down into the green depths.

"Let's go, then," he finally said, and they both got up and walked together away from the cliff's edge. Neither of them looked back.

"Do you have any idea where we are?" Rachel finally asked, after they'd walked for a little while.

"Nope, not a clue. I'm just headed west so we can follow the sun and not get lost," he admitted, and she laughed.

"Sounds like we're already lost, but hey, it's a good enough plan for me," she agreed with a shrug.

They walked for several hours without seeing a single soul, and several hours after dark, they suddenly stumbled across an old timber road. It looked like it hadn't been used in a hundred years, but it had to go somewhere.

"That looks promising," Rachel said, eyeing the road. Brian knew how she felt; his feet were sore from trudging barefoot through the woods for so long, and he was ready for some easier walking.

So they took to the road and kept walking, and eventually they passed an old wooden bridge where they found a place to crawl up underneath and spend what was left of the night. It was a rough bed, but they were both so tired by then that they couldn't have cared less.

Chapter Eleven

Late the next morning they emerged onto a paved blacktop highway, and not long after that they caught a ride from a farmer in an old Ford pickup truck. Within fifteen minutes, they found themselves dropped off at a gas station in Jasper.

"Well, here we are, back in civilization," Rachel said, rubbing her hands together.

"Yeah, sort of. But we're still a long way from home, and we've got no way to get there," he pointed out.

"Well. . . let's get some real food for a change, and we can think about that while we eat, okay? I'm starving," she suggested.

"Absolutely. I don't ever want to see another pear in my whole life," he agreed, laughing.

They bought some cheap flip-flops at the gas station so they wouldn't have a problem getting inside a restaurant barefooted. Then they walked down the street a few blocks till they found a pizza joint and ate to their heart's content.

Brian was eager to get home, now, but he was having a hard time thinking of a way to make it happen. The car was still lost out there on some forsaken dirt road in the middle of nowhere outside Snowball, but he wouldn't even begin to know where to look for it. Nor did they have the time.

"Do you know anybody we could call?" Rachel asked around a mouthful of pizza.

"Not that I can think of. If I call my mom or my aunt then that'll probably just get me locked up for a while, and I can't let that happen till I make sure Brandon's all right, at least. Do you know anybody?" he asked.

"Not that I'd want to call just yet," she admitted.

"There's always Adam, I guess. He's got a truck," he suggested doubtfully.

"You mean Adam Crenshaw, the football player?" she asked, raising one eyebrow skeptically.

"Yeah, that's the one. You don't like him or something?" he asked.

"No, it's not that. I guess I just never realized you and him hung out together all that much," she explained.

"We didn't used to," he said wryly. Adam was the best friend that money could buy, but he was embarrassed to tell Rachel something like that.

"Would he come this far? And what would his mom and dad say about it?" she asked.

"Oh, he'd do it if I gave him enough money. And his family lets him do anything he wants, pretty much. No worries about that," he told her.

"How much have you got left?" she asked.

"About five hundred dollars, I think. I'm pretty sure he'd do it for that," he told her.

"I guess we could ask him. I can't think of any better plan," she admitted.

"He's at school right now, but I could still text him," he said, thinking out loud.

"You could if you had a phone," she pointed out.

"Yeah, true, but I bet we can find a cheap one somewhere in this town, don't you think? Let's ask the waitress when she comes back. She ought to know," he said.

They asked, and the waitress gave them directions to a dollar store just a few blocks away. As soon as they left the pizza parlor they went directly to the store to pick up a cheap phone, not to mention some clean clothes. Brian didn't bother buying a charger for the phone; he didn't expect to keep it long enough to need one anyway.

"There you go. I knew we could do it," Rachel told him after they left the store. Both of them had changed clothes in the bathroom, and thrown the old ones in the trash. Both of them still needed a real bath, but at least they didn't look like homeless people anymore. Brian stood in the parking lot and fiddled with the phone until he got it activated, then he looked up at Rachel.

"Guess I better text Adam and see what he'll do. What do you think I should tell him? He'll want to know how we got here and what's going on, I'm sure," he said.

"Just say you'll tell him about it when he gets here. I'm sure we can think of a good story between now and then," she said, and then Brian focused his attention on typing the text message.

"Okay, he said he'll come," he said after a few minutes of back-and-forth.

"Great!" she said.

"The only catch is, he can't leave till after school, so he won't be able to get here before probably seven o'clock or so. We're supposed to meet him at the courthouse, cause he can find that on the map without too much trouble. And he *did* ask what was up, just like I knew he would. So he's expecting the whole story as soon as he gets here," he said.

"We'll think of something before then," she repeated.

After that, Brian gathered up his courage and called Carolyn, reluctantly. He didn't think she could figure out where he was if he called her on a cell phone, and he was anxious about Brandon. A lot could have happened in three days.

"Hey, how's Brandon?" he asked when she picked up the phone. He half expected her to start yelling at him the second she heard his voice, but she must have decided to take a different approach this time.

"He's still not doing very well, Brian. He's got pneumonia. If that matters to you at all, and if you want to see him, come to the hospital tonight, if you can. He's in room 328," she said. She sounded tired beyond words, as if she didn't even have the energy to care whether Brian showed up or not.

"I'll try," he told her, not liking the news at all.

"Do you need me to come get you somewhere? Nobody's mad anymore, Brian, I promise. Just come home. Please," she asked him.

"It's okay, I've got a ride. I'll be home tonight as soon as I can," he promised.

As soon as he got off the phone, he looked at Rachel.

"Would you mind too much, if we stopped to check on Brandon first, before we go home? Aunt Carolyn says he's not doing too well. It'll be on the way, more or less," he told her.

"Sure. I'm in no hurry at all, if you think Adam won't mind waiting," she said.

"Adam would wait for ten hours barefoot in the snow, if he thought he could make a buck doing it," Brian said dryly.

When Adam finally got there at 6:45 that evening, Brian was so eager to leave that he had the door open almost before the wheels could stop moving.

"That much of a hurry, huh?" Adam asked, laughing a little. Patti Sue was with him, of course, even though he hadn't bothered to mention it earlier. It was a tight squeeze to fit all four of them in the seat.

"Yeah, I guess so. Let's blow this place," Brian agreed, and so that's exactly what they did.

"So what happened to you the past few days, buddy boy? You got no idea what kinds of things people been saying," Adam said as soon as they were out on the highway.

In fact, Brian had a pretty good idea what kinds of things people had probably been saying, but he didn't much want to think about all that. He'd find out soon enough without guessing.

But in the meantime, he told Adam the story he and Rachel had cooked up about deciding to run away from home together and getting lost in the woods for several days after her car broke down. It was true enough as far as it went, and if Adam wanted to think there was some secret romantic thing going on behind the scenes, then that was his own business.

He must have believed it, because he didn't question anything. But after a while Patti Sue said something that made Brian's skin crawl with uneasiness.

"You look different, Mad Dog," she said, looking him up and down.

"Different? Like how?" he asked, pretending he didn't know.

"I don't know, exactly. You're just. . . I can't quite put my finger on it. Did you cut your hair, or something?" she finally asked, lamely. Brian laughed.

"No, I'm just the same as I always was," he told her.

"No, she's right. Something's different about both of you," Adam said, glancing at him and then at Rachel for a few seconds before turning his attention back to the highway.

Brian shrugged and said nothing to this. What could he tell them, after all? That he'd drunk from the Fountain of Youth and had power and life they'd never dreamed of? He could imagine exactly what they'd say to *that*. All things considered, it was best if he simply let the subject drop.

But Patti Sue kept glancing at him from time to time, and it was hard to keep pretending he didn't notice. She was trying to be discreet about it, but she was getting more and more obvious. After a while even Adam started to notice it. Brian saw the scowl developing on the other boy's face, and he could see the way Adam's hands were gripping the steering wheel. He was angry, and sooner or later he'd say something, if Patti Sue didn't stop it.

Adam was doing the same thing himself, though, for he kept stealing glances at Rachel when he thought no one was looking, and the only thing that kept him from being as brazen as Patti Sue was the fact that he had to pay attention to the road.

Brian had no idea how to handle the situation. If he said anything, then that would only cause a fight later on between Adam and Patti Sue; in fact at this point they'd probably already have one anyway, even if Brian kept his mouth shut.

But he was blessed if he could think of anything to do about it, and he found himself forced to endure the increasingly uncomfortable ride for almost another two hours. He was glad when Adam dropped them off at the courtyard of the hospital.

"Hey, thanks for coming to get me, buddy," he told Adam, and gave him three hundred dollars.

"No problem, Mad Dog," Adam said, still glaring at Patti Sue.

"Uh, why don't you and Patti Sue go ahead home, Adam. I'm not sure how long we'll be here, and I'll just get a ride the rest of the way with my aunt or something," he suggested. He didn't think he could stand another hour with those two.

"Sure thing, bud. See you at school tomorrow," Adam said curtly, and left. Patti Sue couldn't resist looking back at Brian through the rear glass one more time before they pulled out of the circle drive, though, and he groaned inwardly. Was she really that stupid?

"That'll cause trouble. Just wait and see. I bet they're fighting already," Rachel commented, and Brian laughed.

"You think?" he agreed.

He shook his head and put it out of his mind. No doubt he'd soon hear all about whatever mini-scandal resulted from it; who called whom what names, and when, and whether it resulted in a break-up or not, and so forth. The gossipy details of such things were the bread and butter of social life at school, the juicier the better. But Brian had more important things on his mind at the moment than whether or not Adam and Patti Sue had the nastiest fight in the history of junior high schools everywhere. They could deal with their own problems.

"Come on, Raych, let's go," he told her, turning away from the drive and heading for the front door.

They entered the building, and it didn't take long to navigate the busy halls and elevators to reach Brandon's room, but here they hit a snag. There was no one there.

"Where is he?" Rachel asked, looking at the empty bed.

"I don't know. We better ask," Brian said, not liking this at all.

They walked back to the nurses' station, and Brian put both elbows on the counter.

"Can I help you?" one of the nurses asked.

"Yes, ma'am, I hope so. I went to my brother's room but he's not there anymore. Can you tell me if maybe they moved him somewhere?" he asked.

"What's the patient's name?" she asked, reaching for a binder full of papers.

"Brandon Stone," he told her. As soon as she heard that, the nurse looked hard at him, and then seemed to be at a loss for words for a few seconds.

"You're his brother?" she asked.

"Yes, ma'am. Can you please tell me where he is?" he asked, beginning to be a little scared.

"I know I shouldn't be the one to tell you this, but I'm afraid your brother passed away a little over an hour ago. I'm so sorry," she said, laying a hand on his arm.

It was Brian's turn to be speechless now, and he could hardly breathe past the hard lump in his throat.

"Would it be possible for us to see him, anyway, just for a minute? They were very close," Rachel asked, and the nurse hesitated again.

"I think they already took him down to the basement. I'm not sure what they'll say, but you could go down there and ask them," she finally said.

"Okay, thanks," Rachel told her.

Brian heard all this without really taking it in, so lost in his own grief that nothing else seemed to matter. But when he felt her grab his elbow and start pulling him down the hall, it roused him from his stupor just a bit.

"Where are we going?" he asked, dully.

"Down to the basement, to ask them if they'll let us see him for a minute, of course," she explained. Brian dug in his heels and made her stop.

"No, I don't want to go see him like that, Raych. I want to remember him like he was, not like. . . that," he said, unable to force his lips to form the word *dead.* It seemed too final, too real and ugly a word to utter.

"I understand how you feel, but come anyway, okay? Please? I need you for this; I can't do it alone," she told him.

"Need me for what?" he asked, confused.

"You're his brother, and you didn't know. They might possibly let you in to see him, but not me. I've got to have you with me," she said urgently, pulling him along again.

"But *why?* Why do you need to see him so bad?" he demanded, still refusing to move. She looked him in the eyes and sighed.

"Remember Lazarus, Brian," she told him, somewhat cryptically. It took him a minute to grasp what on earth she was talking about, and when he did, his jaw dropped.

"Do you really think. . . " he started, and then trailed off.

"I don't know. We can only try. Now come *on,*" she told him earnestly, yanking on his arm again. This time he followed her, all the way down to the morgue.

There seemed to be no one nearby when they got there, and they found the heavy steel door slightly ajar. Rachel knocked, and they heard a muffled voice from inside.

"Come in," it said. She pushed the door open and went in, followed quickly by Brian. There was man in green scrubs sitting at a desk filling out paperwork, and he looked up when he saw them come in.

"Oh, I'm sorry. Only hospital staff is allowed down here. You'll have to leave," he said, getting up from the desk. No doubt to usher them out.

"Please, sir. They brought a child down a little bit ago, his brother, and he didn't make it to the hospital in time to say his goodbyes. Could we see him, for just a minute? Please?" she asked, putting a hand on the man's arm and looking pleadingly into his eyes.

He must not have been an unkind man, for his face softened, and he hesitated.

"I could get in trouble, if anybody knew I let you down here," he explained, apologetically.

"I promise we'll never tell anybody. Please, sir," Brian said, and the man hesitated again.

"All right, but just for a few minutes," he agreed, reaching past them to shut and lock the door so no one would walk in and find them there.

"Thank you so much. You have no idea how much it means to us," Rachel told him, and Brian nodded.

"You're welcome, and I'm sorry," he told Brian, patting him on the shoulder. Then he went to one of the drawers, and they followed him.

"There he is, right in here. If you'll promise me you won't touch anything, and you won't answer the door if anybody knocks unless it's me, then I'll take my break and give you just a few minutes with him. If you decide to leave before I get back, just shut the drawer and close the door on your way out," he told them awkwardly.

"We promise," Brian told him, and then the man quietly excused himself.

As soon as he was gone, Brian braced himself and reached up to turn the handle and pull the drawer out, unsure if he could handle the sight. He hadn't been lying, when he told Rachel he'd much rather remember Brandon the way he used to be.

But he found the courage somewhere, and pulled open the drawer.

There indeed he was, pale as milk and cold as the water that flowed from the heart of the world. Tears filled Brian's eyes then, and though he tried to be strong, he couldn't help himself. He put his arms around Brandon, and pulled him close, and wept.

Rachel let him alone for a few minutes, although there were tears in her eyes too, but at last she interrupted him.

"Brian. . . we don't have much time," she urged him quietly. Brian saw the sense of this, of course, and pushed his pain deep inside. He laid Brandon partially back down, enough for Rachel to get close to him as well.

"I'm not sure how to do this," she confessed, swallowing hard.

"Just do the best you can," he whispered.

She put both her hands on Brandon's face, and then he heard her praying, though he couldn't make out the words. Then she put her head down, and kissed him on the lips, and blew her warm breath into his cold body. Then Brian did the same.

"The life-giving Life, and the Beauty that makes beautiful," he whispered to himself, repeating the words from the Fountain.

For an agonizing few seconds, nothing happened. Then Brandon coughed, and took a deep breath. Then his eyes fluttered, and he started to cry, and to shake from the cold.

Brian snatched him up and quickly wrapped him in his own shirt and held him tightly against his chest. Then he looked at Rachel, his heart too full for words. She came close, to add her body heat to his, for Brandon's sake, and then he tried to tell her what he was feeling.

"There are no words I can ever say to thank you for this," he whispered.

"Thank God, not me, Brian. I didn't do anything but pray," she told him.

"I know He's the one who did the miracle, but it was you that thought to ask for it and believed it could happen. I never would have come down here, without you," he told her.

"And I wouldn't be alive today without you, and I never would have drunk from the Fountain, and I never could have got in here by myself. You had a big part in all this, too," she reminded him.

She was about to say something else when the door opened and the man in the green scrubs came back in, holding a can of Coke and a half-eaten Butterfinger.

"What-" he started, and then froze when he saw Brandon turn his head to look at him. The Coke can clattered to the floor, spilling soda pop everywhere.

"Oh, my God," the man said, wide eyed, and he grabbed the edge of a table to keep from fainting.

Rachel disentangled herself and hurried over to help him, and Brian pulled up a chair so he could sit down.

"Maybe we should call the doctor back down here, don't you think?" he told the man.

This they did, as soon as the morgue keeper had sufficiently recovered himself. The news of Brandon's incredible "recovery" spread like wildfire through the hospital, so that he and Brian and Rachel soon found themselves minor celebrities.

It was a role Brian didn't relish at all, and he found himself forced to describe the entire event over and over again, from arriving at the hospital too late, to the part about he and Rachel breathing into Brandon's mouth. Most of the doctors seemed to think he'd lapsed into a near-death coma, from which the two of them had woken him just in the nick of time. There were, they told everyone sagely, several examples of such things in the medical literature.

Brian smiled and nodded, letting them think whatever they wanted to think, if it made them feel better. He knew it was a miracle, whatever they might believe, and told them so. Most of them smiled and nodded right back at him when he said this, but that was all right too.

They put Brandon back in another patient room, and Brian knew well enough that Mama and Aunt Carolyn would show up soon enough. He wasn't looking forward to that. But it would be at least an hour before they could possibly get there, and in the meantime the three of them found themselves alone. Brandon was still weak and felt awful, so it wasn't surprising that he fell asleep almost as soon as he had the chance.

Brian watched him sleeping for a little while, too happy to care much about anything else.

"Do you think he'll be all right, now?" Rachel asked after they were alone, speaking quietly to keep from waking him.

"Yeah, I think so. I'll stay here with him just in case, but his breath sounds fine, now. I think the pneumonia is all gone, too," he told her.

"Yeah, it sounds like it," she agreed, and then they were both silent for a few minutes.

"So what do we do now, Brian?" Rachel asked.

"About what?" he asked, not sure what she meant.

"I mean about things like this. We can't just go around raising people from the dead all the time, can we? I have a feeling life won't ever be the same again, since we've got this power now," she explained.

"Well. . . there's no hurry about anything, is there? I'll probably just go home, and go to school tomorrow, and see what happens from there. What about you?" he asked.

"Same thing, I guess. I don't want to do anything stupid. I'm not even sure what I'll tell my family yet," she confessed.

"Tell them the truth," he shrugged.

"You're crazy, boy. They'll never believe it," she told him.

"If they don't, then I think your next doctor visit might convince them," he pointed out.

"Yeah, there's always that. As far as I know, I'm the only person in the world who ever recovered from Batten's Disease," she said soberly.

"There you go," he agreed.

"I guess we'll find out soon enough. I'll probably be grounded for a while, but after things settle down, I think maybe I'll go see Miss Sadie and ask her how *she* managed it all," she said, thoughtfully.

"Yeah, I might go with you. I'm sure she could probably give us both some good advice," he agreed. There was a pause, and it was by no means an uncomfortable one.

"Didn't she tell you that the Fountain was just a way of making things beautiful and perfect, like God always meant for them to be?" she asked after a while.

"Yeah, something like that," he agreed.

"Okay, so maybe the reason we're supposed to do all these things is to touch people's hearts and pull them closer to Him when they see what might have been. I think that's what the Fountain is really for, to help people remember that," she told him.

"Do you really think so?" he asked. He hadn't thought of it quite that way before, but it made sense once she explained it for him.

"Yeah, that's what I think. But I'm just guessing right now, of course. I didn't know for sure that we could do anything for Brandon tonight; I just remembered Lazarus, you know. But we did, and maybe we could do that again. There might even be other things we could do, too. Maybe. . . we might even bring peace to a storm that would kill people, like Jesus did on the Sea of Galilee," she said.

"Maybe we should move to Oklahoma and become storm chasers," he agreed, poking fun because the thought of so much responsibility made him nervous.

"I'm being serious, Brian," she scolded him.

"I know you are. I'm sorry. It's just kind of a scary thing, you know," he said, apologetically.

"Yeah, I know. It is for me too," she agreed.

"It's good to know I'm not alone," he told her.

"No, never that," she promised, and kissed his cheek. He smiled, and reddened a bit.

"So what will you do with the amulet, now?" she finally asked when he said nothing.

"I'm not sure. It's really not much use to me anymore, except maybe as a keepsake. I think I might just put it away somewhere for now, maybe give it to Brandon for a souvenir one of these days, if I ever decide to tell him the story," Brian said, glancing at his sleeping brother.

"I think that sounds like a great idea," she told him, and Brian laughed.

"We'll see," he said softly.

At that point the conversation was cut short by the door swinging open, and Mama and Aunt Carolyn came spilling into the room with two nurses behind them.

No one paid Brian or Rachel any attention, so completely focused on Brandon as they all were.

"I think it's time for me to go; I'll call you later, okay?" Rachel whispered in his ear, and he nodded. No one seemed to notice her leaving, and Brian figured that was just as well.

But eventually things settled down, and then Mama turned her attention to Brian.

"You did this," she said, with a severe look on her face which he found difficult to figure out. He wasn't sure exactly what she was talking about, and he was afraid to ask. But she must have seen his confusion.

"You brought him back," she clarified, in a gentler voice. Then she did the last thing he would ever have expected, and threw her arms around him and held him tight.

"I thought I'd lost both of you," she whispered, and he was too stunned to say a word. She didn't seem to expect any answer right away, though, just wanted to hold him and make sure he was really there.

"You look different, Brian," she finally said, stepping back a little bit to examine him curiously.

"Yeah, I've heard that a few times today," he agreed, with a sheepish smile.

"Where have you been, these last three days?" she asked.

"Would you believe me if I told you?" he asked. For a second she showed a flash of her old annoyance, but then she checked herself.

"I think I would, Brian. I'll try," she told him. So he told her, and she listened, and then she looked wistful.

"I believe you," she told him when he was finished.

"You do?" he asked, skeptically.

"I'm inclined to believe almost anything tonight," she said, and he shrugged, not wanting to meet her eyes. She was being too nice, and he didn't trust it.

"Brian, there's something I want to say. I know I haven't been a very good mother the past few years. I know that's why you won't look at me right now. But all I can do is tell you that I'm sorry," she told him. He was almost as shocked by this apology as he'd been by the hug.

"I guess so," he shrugged, still looking down at the floor.

"It's all right if you don't believe me yet. I guess I can't blame you for that. But I promise you, I want to try to do better from now on," she told him.

"Really?" he asked, glancing up at her. She seemed to be sincere, incredible as that was to him.

"Yeah. I know I've said that before, but I really mean it this time. I don't know if I can do it, but I'll try," she promised. He took a minute to digest this.

"What changed things?" he finally ventured to ask.

"Well, sometimes when it seems like you might lose everything, it makes you remember just how valuable those things are," she said.

"I see," he said.

"I'm not the only one who thinks so, either," she said, mysteriously.

"What do you mean?" he asked, unable to guess what she was talking about.

"Somebody told your dad about Brandon, and he came by to see him yesterday," she told him. Brian's jaw dropped at that news. He'd thought he couldn't possibly be any more shocked than he already was, but that did it.

"Really?" he asked again, unable to think of any other reply.

"Yeah, he really did. I almost fell out in the floor at first. But we talked for a long time, and he said he was sorry for some things, and so did I. We both promised that if Brandon lived, we'd try to start talking more and maybe even doing some things together as a family, you know. I don't know how it'll all work out, but I thought you'd want to know," she finished.

"I don't know what to say," Brian said.

"No, I didn't think you would, right away. You and him have a lot of things to work out together, just like me and him do," she agreed.

"Do you mean. . . " he started, but she guessed what he was about to say and put a finger on his lips to stop him.

"No, I don't mean we're getting back together, if that's what you were about to ask. We're just talking and trying to do better for you and Brandon, that's all. Don't think it's more than what it is," she warned him.

Brian nodded. That was more than he'd ever dreamed possible just two weeks ago, and perhaps, in time. . .

He smiled, faintly.

"I know what you're thinking, Brian, and put it right out of your mind," she told him, a bit of her crossness returning.

"Okay, Mama," he told her lightly. Maybe sometimes wishes really *did* come true.

It crossed his mind that none of this would have happened if Brandon had never gotten sick. At the time, he'd thought that was the most awful thing that could ever happen, and yet it had turned out to be the key to everything. Who could have guessed it?

True, not everything had worked out quite the way he hoped it would; not yet, anyway, but he was content now to wait and see how things unfolded for a while.

He had all the time in the world.

Chapter Twelve

Time passed, and summer faded slowly into fall. The miracle of Brandon and Rachel's healing faded gradually into the realm of old news, as people found fresher things to talk about during the long evenings. Brian was glad to see it; he'd never liked being a celebrity in the first place.

By the time October rolled around, things had settled back into a calm and familiar pattern, for the most part. Mama quit drinking, and she was nicer in a lot of ways. True, she still had a tongue that was sharper than cats' claws now and then, but at least she didn't use her fists anymore.

The first few times his father came to visit were so awkward that Brian almost wished he could slink under a rock and hide, but after a while even that got a bit easier. There were still certain subjects that nobody was willing to mention, let alone talk about, but Brian was almost sure he could sense a slow thawing and loosening, and maybe eventually things would be better. Brandon seemed to take the whole thing in stride and never blinked an eye, but then of course he didn't remember very much.

Brian and Rachel both had problems with their newfound beauty. Adam and Patti Sue were only the first in a long line of jealousies and fights, and the two of them finally got to the point that they told everybody they were going out with each other, just to stop the headache. Neither of them really thought of the other like that, but at least the pretense gave them some peace.

Brian remembered what Miss Sadie had said about having to pay a price for all their powers and wondered sometimes if the constant flirting and jostling might be part of it. He strongly suspected so.

All the while, he was also gradually discovering just how amazing those powers really were. They were nothing at all like using the amulet; he found out quickly enough that there would be no more turning pebbles into gold, no more moving things around, no more growing full-size trees in thirty seconds flat. All that had disappeared forever.

But he didn't mind the loss of those things, or at least not too much. For he found that when he laid his hands on any living thing, he could do wonders. Scars disappeared, and sickness was cured, and even colors and textures became more subtly and variously harmonious than before. The roses grew redder, and the fireflies brighter, and even the grass under his feet turned greener and softer, flawless and perfect down to the tiniest blade.

More than anything else, it reminded him of what happened to him and Rachel when they drank from the Fountain. He brought beauty to everything he touched. It was almost like he had the power to pull a grimy, obscuring film off the world which no one had ever noticed was there because they'd never seen things any other way. Without it, everything looked fresh and bright and new.

He noticed other things, too. Animals that came near him turned tame, even wild ones. If he called them, even squirrels and birds and stray dogs would come sniffing at his fingers and eat from his hands without a trace of fear. He wasn't quite sure how that would work if he tried to tame a rattlesnake or a mountain lion, and he wasn't quite brave enough to try it yet, but so far he'd found no reason to think it wouldn't work.

But that was another marvel that came with a cost. Brian had always loved to hunt ever since the first time Papaw took him out in the woods with a gun when he was five years old, but this year he found himself uneasy with the idea for the first time. It seemed too much like betraying a sacred trust, when any deer in the woods would walk right up to him and nuzzle his face. So he sighed and shook his head and laid his rifle aside, and wondered how many other unexpected things he'd have to give up.

Besides all that, he found that he could blunt the edge of a storm so that no harm was done, he could take dirty water and foul air and make them clean again, and he suspected he might even be able to do other things he hadn't thought of trying yet.

He discovered all these powers little by little, in the course of going about his everyday life. He'd had enough of glitz and grandeur for a lifetime, and usually he wasn't consciously trying to do anything at all. It just happened, although the changes were always gradual and they always took at least a few hours or days before they showed up. After a while, he took to wearing gloves so he wouldn't touch things accidentally.

Now and then he discussed all these things with Rachel and compared notes. They were officially supposed to be going out, after all, so no one thought it was strange that they spent so much time together.

"It's weird, Raych. It's nothing like having the amulet at all," he told her one day not long before Halloween. It was the first chance they'd had for a really good talk ever since they'd got home from Snowball.

They were sitting on the edge of Black Rock together after school, and Brandon was playing in the sand down below, too far away for him to hear what they were saying.

It was a beautiful Indian summer afternoon, with a light breeze playing in the sweet gum leaves. It was still Brian's favorite place, in spite of everything. All of his white oaks were gone except one or two that he'd never touched with the amulet, but the gnarled old rock-tree was still there like always, and he'd found that fresh green grass had started to come back where everything had seemed completely dead not so very long ago.

"Well, I wouldn't know since I never had the amulet anyway," she pointed out, and he laughed.

"No, I guess you wouldn't. But it's different, trust me. You know Gina Powell?" he asked her.

"The girl with the really bad zits?" she asked.

"Yeah, that's the one," he nodded.

"Um. . . kind of. Not very well, though," she said.

"Well, I have science class with her after lunch, and a few days ago I had to take my gloves off during class, and I accidentally touched her hand with mine. So now her face is all clear as can be. I don't think anybody noticed it yet except me, but I bet they will," he told her.

"I bet *she* noticed, even if nobody else did," Rachel pointed out.

"Yeah, that's what worries me," he fretted.

"You mean she might figure out it was you that caused it, right? Honestly I don't see how she ever would. It's not like it happened instantly," she said.

"I know. It just worries me a little. Mama told me to keep all this stuff a secret as much as I can. She said if the wrong people found out, they'd just try to use me for their own purposes and then I'd never have a chance to do anything good in the world like I want to," he said.

"Your *mom* said that?" she asked.

"Yeah, believe it or not, she did. She's a lot different now than she used to be," he added thoughtfully.

"It doesn't sound like her at all," she said.

"No, and I wouldn't have believed it myself if I hadn't seen it with my own two eyes. She still has her bad moods sometimes, but it's nothing like it was when she used to drink all the time," he told her.

"She really quit this time?" she asked.

"Yeah, so far. She told me she doesn't even want it anymore, and she's never said *that* before. Sometimes I think maybe when I touched her it took away the craving, you know, like it took away Gina's zits. I'm not sure," he admitted.

"Maybe," she agreed, nodding.

"I think my dad being around has helped some, too," he added. He hadn't told this to anyone else, but Rachel was his best friend.

"Do you think so?" she asked.

"Yeah, he's been coming over on Sunday afternoons since Brandon got home, just like he promised he would, and he and Mama talk on the phone a lot. I don't know what they say to each other, but it seems like it helps her," he said.

"Does he not talk to you?" she asked.

"Yeah, but that's been. . . weird, I guess. I always said I wished he'd come back, but after he really did then it was hard to figure out what to talk about anymore. Three years is a long time to be gone," he said.

"Did he give you a reason for why he was gone so long?" she asked.

"Well. . . sort of. He said he's been down in Texas. He wouldn't tell me exactly where, but apparently I've got a couple of sisters I never even knew about. Jenny and Lisa. So he said he wanted to spend some time down there with *them* for a little while, since he couldn't seem to get along with Mama for long," Brian said. This also was a hard truth for him to admit, even though he knew Rachel wouldn't judge him for it.

"So how do you feel about that?" she asked. He could tell she was trying to choose her words carefully so as not to rub salt in his wounds, but he only shrugged.

"I honestly haven't had much time to think it over yet," he said. That wasn't quite true, of course, but the last thing he wanted to talk about at the moment was a laundry list of his father's misdeeds.

"I'm sorry," Rachel said.

"Aw, it's okay. Just a big nasty mess that'll have to get sorted out one of these days. In the meantime I think I'd just as soon let sleeping dogs lie," Brian said.

"You mean you don't even want to meet your sisters?" Rachel asked.

"Maybe someday. Not right now, though," he said.

"Really?" she asked.

"Yeah. . . that would be really hard, and it's not like I don't have enough on my plate already," he said softly, and she reached out to clasp his hand.

"Yeah, true," she agreed, and then there was a long pause.

"So what about *your* family?" he finally asked.

"I think they're too happy to ask many questions, honestly. It's almost like they think if they push too hard, it'll turn out not to be real after all," she said.

"They didn't say anything at all?" he asked, finding it hard to believe.

"Well, yeah, sure they did, at first. But that was before they realized I was cured. I think they're still in shock over that," she said, smiling.

"What about the car?" he asked.

"It's still up there in Snowball somewhere, far as I know. Your guess is as good as mine," she said.

"Nobody went to get it?" he asked, surprised.

"Nobody knows where to look. There are a lot of old dirt roads up there, and it's a long way off. It's like looking for a needle in a haystack, if you don't know which way to go. Sissy says it was just an old beater anyway and she doesn't care anything about it, as long as I'm all right," she explained. Then she looked down at the beach where Brandon was playing.

"How's the little guy doing?" she asked, nodding her head at him.

"He's fine, I think. No worse for the wear, it seems like," he told her, looking down at his brother with a faint smile on his lips.

"I'm glad to hear it," she murmured.

They both watched Brandon for a while, who seemed oblivious to the whole conversation. He was singing softly to himself while he piled up sand, an oddly beautiful tune Brian had never heard before. It reminded him of something he couldn't quite put his finger on, like the far green mountains on a rainy day. Rachel must have thought the same, for they both listened in silence till the boy eventually lost interest in his music and fell silent.

"It's pretty up here," Rachel commented after a few minutes, looking around.

"Do you think so? I've been working on it some more since we got back. It was awful at first, pretty much nothing but dirt and rock. I had to plant some grass seed just to cover it up. It'll take a while to be as nice as it was before, but I think maybe in a year or two it will be," he told her.

They sat in companionable silence for a while after that, feeling the warmth of the sun and watching Brandon slowly build his sand castle. Brian was happy, and it didn't matter to him if they talked or not. He was content just to sit there in his favorite spot, with the people he loved the best, and let things be.

"You're still wearing that amulet, I see," she pointed out after a while, nodding her head at his chest.

"Yeah, for now, until I can think of what to do with it," he said.

"I thought you wanted to save it for Brandon," she said, and he hesitated before answering.

"Well. . . I'm really not sure if that's such a great idea anymore, Raych," he finally said.

"Why not?" she asked.

"Because of something Mama told me awhile back. You know I always used to wonder how she knew anything about the amulet, right?"

"Yeah, I remember," Rachel agreed.

"Well, it turns out her brother found this thing, a long time ago when they were kids, and I guess he didn't use it very well. Some really bad things happened. I don't know exactly what all, but bad enough that he didn't live through it, and neither did my grandmother. Mama won't really talk about it very much," he said.

"That's awful! I'm so sorry," she told him.

"Yeah, I never even knew Mama had a brother. His name was Jack. That's his name over there, carved on the rock tree. I always used to wonder who that was. But anyway, Mama said Papaw took the amulet after Jack died and she always thought he got rid of it. But I guess he didn't. He just stuck it up there in one of his trunks in the attic and never said anything about it to anybody," he said.

"I wonder why he didn't get rid of it?" she said.

"Who knows? Maybe he was afraid somebody else might find it and so he thought it was better to keep it tucked away someplace where he knew he could keep it safe," Brian said.

"Maybe," she agreed.

"I don't know for sure, but I think it's a good guess. Papaw was like that, you know. He was always really protective. He would've done whatever he thought he needed to do to keep some other kid safe from finding it. Especially after what happened to Jack," Brian explained.

"But wasn't the amulet supposed to be just for you?" Rachel asked, furrowing her brow.

"Well. . . yeah, I know that's what we *thought* at first. But then after everything I heard about Jack it makes me wonder if maybe other people can use this thing, after all. Or at least *some* other people," he added.

"So maybe Jack was chosen to find it, too," she suggested.

"Yeah, I thought about that, but even if he was, then that only goes to show how even the chosen ones don't always pass the test. I don't have a clue what to think, honestly, but I know it sure does make things a lot more complicated than I thought at first," he continued.

"So what *will* you do with it, then?" she asked, and then there was a long pause while he considered the question.

"I don't know, Raych. I'm pretty sure if somebody's truly meant to have it then they'll find it no matter what I do, but it's everybody else that really worries me at this point. Maybe it wouldn't even work for them anyway, but who knows?" he finally said.

"Well. . . don't let it get you all tied up in knots. Just give it back to God and then let Him be the one to look after it. I'm sure He knows best," she said.

"But how am I supposed to do that?" he asked.

"You could always try asking Him, you know," she pointed out.

"You make it sound so simple," he muttered.

"Only when it is," she teased, and her smile drew a reluctant response from him.

"Maybe I will," he agreed.

That was the end of their conversation, and after spending several days in earnest prayer, Brian was sure he finally had his answer. The only thing he could see in his mind's eye was the little meadow at Black Rock, and it seemed to him that God wanted him to bury the amulet up there.

It seemed fitting, once he had time to think about it. Black Rock was probably the safest hiding place on earth, since nobody ever went there except Brian and Brandon; not even Mama. He'd always been curious as to why that should be, and then a week ago she'd let slip the fact that it was where Jack had died.

It was too long ago and too abstract of a thing to affect how Brian felt about the place, especially since he'd never known Jack. But he could finally understand why his mother might never want to see the place again, and it provided yet another poignant reason as to why the amulet should find its final resting place there.

He couldn't help wondering what it was that Jack had tried to do with the amulet that had turned out so terribly wrong, but that was one thing he could never get Mama to talk about. Whatever secrets she had, she meant to keep them a mystery.

So Brian waited for a time when no one else was home, and then fetched the very same cigar box from the attic where he'd found the amulet in the first place. Then he wrapped it in rice paper and sealed the box with duct tape, and finally he put the whole thing inside a Ziploc bag with all the air squeezed out of it.

As soon as that was done, he grabbed his package and a shovel from the garage and headed out.

The leaves were in all their autumn glory that day, more brilliant and colorful that year than Brian could ever remember. At least, all the ones he'd touched since he got back from the Fountain were like that. He noticed a few that he'd missed, and they seemed lackluster and dull in comparison. In spite of his hurry, he took a few minutes to fix that as he walked by, if the trees were close enough. Nothing changed immediately, of course; not like before, but he knew that within two or three days the new ones would be just as dazzling and beautiful as the others. The thought made him happy.

He reached the Rock before long and looked at the meadow with a critical eye. He wanted a place where there was some kind of landmark to let him find the amulet again if he ever needed to, but then again he also wanted something that wasn't too obvious.

There didn't seem to be any good options at first glance, but then his eye fell on a white oak tree at the edge of the woods, one of the very few that were still left from the old days. He'd touched it since he got home, of course, and it was as perfect and beautiful as any of the other trees now. There was nothing to mark it as unusual, except that it was the only oak nearby.

He decided it would do.

Brian quickly got to work with the shovel, digging a foot-deep hole between two big roots and then placing the plastic bag containing the amulet at the bottom. He took one last look before filling the hole back in, and then carefully tamped down the loose dirt and scuffed any leftover clods into the ground as best he could. Finally he scattered dead leaves over the top so no one would notice that he'd been digging, and that was that. One good rain would wash away all traces of his work.

"Peace be with you, uncle Jack," he murmured under his breath. It seemed like the right thing to do, and then he tipped his cap toward the rock tree in a silent mark of respect.

Satisfied, he headed back home with the shovel to put it back in the garage before anybody noticed it missing. He stopped to wash it clean with the water hose so it wouldn't be obvious that anyone had used it, and then he was careful to put it back in exactly the same spot he'd taken it from.

He knew he was probably being a little bit extreme, but he figured it was better to be safe than sorry.

When all that was done, he went inside and happily went to work on his newest project of repainting the stairs. No one had ever come around to ask about the disappearing gold, so Brian had finally decided it was all right if he used the money. There was no way for him to give it back even if he tried, after all. So he'd bought some things and started fixing the house the old-fashioned way, with his own two hands. It was hard work and it took a lot longer than using the amulet, but it was satisfying.

He'd already replaced all the worn-out wallpaper and put in some new carpet here and there. It would take a while, and he might not end up with marble floors when he was done, but that was all right. He was still enjoying himself in the meantime.

He hummed under his breath while he worked, a tuneless melody that he'd heard the day before on one of Brandon's cartoons and couldn't seem to get out of his head.

He was still painting when Mama and Brandon came home two hours later, and he looked up and smiled.

"That's really nice work, Brian," she told him, admiring the stairs.

"Thanks, Mama. What's for supper?" he asked. It was, of course, the most important question of the day.

"Ham hocks, mashed potatoes, and I think peas," she said.

"Sounds good to me," he said, putting down his paint brush. He quickly took a shower to wash the paint off and changed into some fresh clothes, and then he took Brandon outside to sit on the porch and wait for supper. Mama didn't like anybody else in the kitchen while she was cooking.

He could see the Crystal Range off to the north, green and mysterious as ever in the last light of the setting sun, and he smiled to himself.

"What are you smiling at, Brian?" Brandon asked, looking at him curiously.

"Nothing, Beebo. Just thinking how lucky I am, that's all," he said, and kissed him on the cheek. Brandon quickly rubbed it off like it was toxic waste.

"You left spit on me," he said, half disgusted and half laughing.

"Yeah, well; get used to it, kid," he told him, then he did it again and tickled his ribs for good measure. He loved to hear him laugh, partly because he still hadn't forgotten what it was like to lose him. Brian knew he'd never be able to forget that terrible moment when they opened the drawer to see him lying there dead. It was the most awful thing he'd ever experienced. But then again, he'd *also* never forget the moment when Brandon first opened his eyes. From blackest despair to joy sharp as needles in five seconds flat.

He often thought that Brandon hadn't been quite the same after that day. The change was so slight that sometimes he thought he must be imagining things, but other times, like now, he was almost sure of it again.

He could almost swear that Brandon's eyes were somehow *deeper* than he remembered, and sometimes he had a faraway look in them that made Brian wonder what on earth he was thinking about. He had that look in his eyes now, gazing out at the far mountains.

"What are you thinking about, Beebo?" he finally asked, curious.

"The green place," Brandon said absently, still gazing out with his deep blue eyes.

"The green place?" Brian asked. It was the first he'd ever heard of it.

"Yeah. There's water, and everything's green, with a gold cup to drink from," he said, as if Brian ought to know this already.

Brian furrowed his brow. It sounded like the cave where the Fountain was, but there was no way Brandon could know anything about that unless maybe Mama had said something to him about it. It seemed doubtful, but Brian himself had certainly never mentioned it.

"Where's that?" he asked lightly, not to make too much of it. Brandon turned and looked at him curiously.

"Don't you remember?" he asked, and at first Brian didn't know what to say. Then he decided there was no point in pretending, and so he smiled and pulled Brandon close.

"Yeah, Beebo. . . I remember," he said.

"Someday I'll go drink that water, too," he declared calmly, and again Brian wasn't quite sure how to answer.

"You think so?" he asked.

"Yeah, he promised," Brandon said.

"Who promised?" Brian asked, confused.

"The one who woke me up in the hospital that night. He said he wanted me to drink that water someday, but he needed me to do some other things first. That's what he said, and he promised," the boy said, with conviction.

Brian would have liked very much to ask him more, but he didn't get the chance. Just then, Mama came to the door and called them both inside to eat.

In the days that followed, Brian tried several times to bring up the subject again, but he never learned much more. Brandon's memories were vague and confused, and the only thing he seemed sure of was that he'd know what to do when the time came. Brian was mystified, but he had no choice but to be content. There was no more information to be had.

It didn't keep him from wondering (and worrying), but he kept his thoughts to himself and finally decided it was nothing he had any business meddling with. It would either happen or it wouldn't, and in the meantime there was nothing to be done about it anyway.

He took to roaming the town as quietly as he could and touching things here and there. Trees in the park, azalea bushes around the courthouse, songbirds and squirrels that came to him, things like that. He was pretty sure Rachel was doing the same thing whenever she got the chance, although she rarely mentioned it. As always, the effects were subtle and never immediate, but little by little he knew they were changing the valley. How *much* they might change it was still in doubt, but he knew it was happening.

He was much more cautious about handling people, for fear of getting found out. But still, whether it was curing Gina Powell's zits or getting rid of Mama's thirst for vodka, they were surely having an effect in that realm, too, and he knew the longer they stayed in one place the more emphatic that effect would be.

Brian never spoke of these things to anyone except Rachel and Brandon, and rarely even to them. But he was happier than he could ever remember being in his entire life, even when he'd had the amulet and thought that things couldn't possibly get any better. He was living out all the dearest wishes of his heart, just like Miss Sadie had told him he could do, and there were times now when he could look back and be thankful even for the hard days when he'd thought there was no hope and no chance. It was part of what had made him who he was, and he didn't think his new life could ever have tasted so sweet, if there had never been any bitterness to compare it to.

He visited Miss Sadie at the nursing home now and then with Rachel, and once he tried to explain to her how happy he was, but she only smiled and shushed him.

"That's exactly how it ought to be, child. The world has taught you to think it's not safe to be too glad, and that tears are more real than laughter. But that's not so. Joy is what the whole world was made for, even if people don't remember that very often nowadays. But you of all people should never forget it," she told him.

And Brian never forgot.

Epilogue

Brian always remembered Miss Sadie's words, and did his best to use his powers wisely. In time the whole valley became beautiful as Black Rock had been, for the ravages of time held no power there. Few people seemed to notice, except perhaps a stranger now and then, passing through on business of his own.

There were still, to be sure, the ordinary ups and downs of life to be faced and dealt with, for no one on earth can escape from pain completely. Yet if the stars shone a little brighter, and the grass was a little greener, and the music of the birds was a bit more sweet than in most places, that was only to be expected.

And if, perhaps, there were fewer pains and less sickness among the people than before, then no one seemed to notice anything unusual about that, either.

Yet there was a price to pay for all this, as Sadie Jones had warned him so many years ago. For there came a time when Brian and Rachel had to leave the valley behind, lest anyone begin to notice that they never aged.

Therefore they married and traveled the world, and now and again they would stay in some place that seemed good to them for a few years, and they did their best to fill it with joy for a time. But they could never stay for long, and after they departed the blessing gradually faded from whatever place they had brought it to. For nothing lasts forever in a dark and fallen world, and the best they could do was to plant memories of Heaven, to turn men's souls in that direction; not to make a heaven on earth.

But neither of them were sorry for this, and they labored long and gladly to do as much good as might be, even if they knew that it was only for a little while.

Brandon grew up, and many years later made his own journey to drink of the Fountain, for his own reasons and with his own burdens to carry. But that's another story, which may be told another time.

And so it may really and truly be said that they all lived happily ever after, and no words in a book could add more to their blessing.

And that was the best magic of all.

The End

If you'd like to read more about Brandon, his sister Lisa, and the rest of the Stone family, their story continues in:

Many Waters
Book Two of the Stones of Song series.

Enjoy the following sample chapters of:

Many Waters
Unclouded Day Series, Book Two
By William Woodall

Many waters cannot quench love,
Neither can the floods drown it.
-Song of Solomon 8:7

Prologue - Cody

Love has a way of sneaking up on you sometimes, especially when you least expect it.

So does evil.

I certainly never expected to find both of those things in the space of a single summer, but sometimes life is really strange that way.

I was mucking out the horses' stalls when it all started. Every now and then I had to stop and wipe the sweat off my face with my shirt-tail, and I think I would have traded my firstborn child for a cold Dr. Pepper right then. If you've never shoveled horse manure for two or three hours under a blistering Texas sun, then you've missed out on one of life's truly memorable experiences, buddy.

I wasn't expecting visitors that morning, so when I saw a black truck come bouncing across the cattle guard I was understandably curious. Strangers can be good or bad, but they always have to be watched carefully till you know which kind they are. I put down my shovel and started walking toward the front drive to meet whoever-it-was, secretly glad for the chance to take a break for a few minutes.

When I got close enough I noticed that the truck had Louisiana tags, and even though that's not *such* an oddity, it was unusual enough to elevate my curiosity another notch.

I was just in time to see a young man getting out of the driver's seat. He looked to be about two or three years younger than me, maybe eighteen or so, but I'd never seen him before in my life. He was wearing ratty jeans and a chocolate colored t-shirt that matched his hair and eyes, and he had the athletic build of a dude who runs or swims a lot.

"Can I help you?" I asked, when he was near enough to use a normal voice.

"Yes, sir, I think you can. My name's Matthieu Doucet, and I'm looking for the owner of the Goliad Ranch," he said. He had an ever-so-slight Cajun accent that marked him as coming from somewhere a lot farther south than Shreveport, and I wondered again what he could possibly want.

"Well, that'd be me. Cody McGrath," I said, offering my hand. Matthieu nodded and shook it, with a surprisingly strong grip.

"Pleased to meet you, Mr. McGrath. I'm afraid my business might take a little bit of explaining. May I come in for a few minutes?" he asked politely. I couldn't think of any reason not to hear him out, so I took him inside to the kitchen table and sat down. It's the place I always gravitate whenever there's a serious conversation afoot.

"I know you're probably busy, Mr. McGrath, so I'll get right to the point. We think your family might be in danger," he said.

That put me instantly on guard, of course, just like it would anybody, but I didn't let it show on my face.

"What do you mean?" I asked carefully, and Matthieu looked at me for a second, like he was sizing me up. I hate it when people do that; it almost always means they're trying to figure out how to get me to do whatever it is they want. I braced myself to be even more wary than usual, but what he said next totally blew me away.

"Mr. McGrath, do you believe in magic?" he finally asked.

Well, now *that* was a question I wasn't expecting. I *did* believe in it, of course; the Scriptures are chock full of stories about real-life witches and sorcerers. But they're also full of warnings about how we're not supposed to have anything to do with those kinds of things, so Matthieu's question alarmed me to say the least. I don't mess with stuff like that, and I don't allow it in my house, either.

"I think it's real, if that's what you mean," I said carefully.

"Well, then, maybe you can also believe it when I tell you that my job is to track down evil things like that, and put a stop to them whenever I can. That's why I'm here. Your name happened to come up recently during a fight with some especially cruel and powerful sorcerers, and that could mean you're a target. I don't know that for *sure,* but I'd be careful with strangers for a while, if I were you. Evil may not always look like you think it will, so please keep your eyes open," he said, cool as a cucumber. He seemed absolutely earnest and serious, like it was the most ordinary thing in the world.

"I see," I said, unsure what else to say.

"I'm also here to offer you some help if you *are* attacked at some point, but that's entirely up to you. I hope you never need to call on me, but if you do, please feel free," he said, offering me a business card which I took without thinking. It was cream colored, with shiny dark blue upraised italics that said *Matthieu Doucet, Avenger,* with a phone number listed at the bottom. I didn't know quite what to say to that, either.

Matthieu saved me the trouble of having to think of an adequate answer, because he got up from the table with an air of finality.

"Anyway, that's what I came to tell you. I hope you'll take it to heart, Mr. McGrath. Good luck, and God be with you," he said, offering his hand. I shook it, and that was that.

I stared at the dust trail from the disappearing truck, thinking to myself that I'd just experienced one of the strangest conversations of my entire life. I slipped the business card inside my billfold just in case, but honestly I hoped never to see or hear from Matthieu Doucet the Cajun Avenger ever again.

I went back outside to finish mucking out the stalls while I still had time, uneasy and full of foreboding. Mostly because Matthieu's warning wasn't nearly as much of a surprise as he probably thought it was.

You see, for as long as I can remember, I've had dreams.

I don't mean the kind that everybody has. I'm talking about *true* dreams. Visions. Glimpses of things yet to come. Most of the time they're incomprehensible; strange, vivid, unbelievably realistic tales that leave me baffled as to what they mean. Only rarely do I get a clear look at the future. But you better believe I pay close attention either way, just in case. Mama has always told me they're a gift from God, like the prophets in olden days used to have. All I can say is, if that's really true, then sometimes gifts are hard to bear.

Oh, not always, of course. I remember one time when I was eight years old and Mama lost her wedding ring while she was cleaning. That night I dreamed I saw it up under the dryer, and sure enough, when we looked the next day, that's where it was. It was a little bit uncanny, maybe, but nothing exceptional. That's how things were for a long time. I rarely dreamed at all, and even when I did they were usually fairly ordinary things like that.

But lately my dreams had turned dark and grim, full of monsters and blood. I didn't know quite what to make of them, but it didn't take a genius to figure out that whatever they meant, it was nothing good.

That's why Matthieu's warning was no shock to me. He was a little more specific about it, maybe, but I'd already known for weeks that I had some kind of ominous danger hanging over my head.

And then purely aside from the spooky stuff, it hadn't rained a drop since March, and the drought was killing us. We were losing money hand over fist, in fact, and even though you can run a business at a loss for a little while and still have a chance to make it up later, you can't do that forever. If something didn't change soon, I didn't know what I might have to do. Thinking about all that was enough to keep me awake at night sometimes, even if I didn't dream at all.

So what with one thing and another, I guess you could say I was pretty stressed out and preoccupied right then, jumping at shadows and inclined to think there were monsters hiding behind every tree. When you don't feel safe even in your own bed at night and you're also teetering on the brink of financial disaster, you tend not to care too much about other things.

Including girls.

In fact, I can safely say that I needed romance right then just about as much as a rooster needs a pair of socks. Maybe even less.

Which I guess goes to show what a really strange sense of humor God must have sometimes.

Mama came outside about ten-thirty to bring me a glass of tea and to make sure I hadn't collapsed from manure inhalation, I guess. It wasn't quite a Dr. Pepper, to be sure, but I was way past caring about that.

I drank the whole thing at one pull, then used the cold glass to wipe my forehead.

"Thanks, Mama, that was really good," I said, handing the glass back to her.

"Well, I thought you might need something cool to drink, it's so hot out here. Are you just about done?" she asked.

"Yeah, I'm finished now. Fixing to go load up some cows to take to the sale barn, as soon as Marcus gets back with the trailer," I said.

"Oh, all right. I don't guess you'll be back in time for lunch, then, will you?" she asked.

"No. Marcus said something about going over to his sister's place, and I'll probably stop in Ore City and grab a burger at the Dairy Dip on the way home. Don't worry about cooking anything," I said.

"All right. I hope you do good with the cows," she said, and I nodded. I hoped so too; God knows we needed the money.

I crossed my fingers and prayed for a good day, and never had the faintest clue how that prayer would be answered.

Chapter One - Lisa

I didn't recognize Cody at first.

The lunch crowd had finally trickled out from the Dairy Dip, and I was sitting at the register for a while to rest my aching feet and read a little bit of my brand new Scarlett Blaze romance novel. It was only my third day on the job, and it takes a while to get used to standing up so much.

It had been one of those days when it's hot enough to make the devil sigh, when nothing wants to move but the flies against the window panes and the dirt devils on the empty highway. It was hot even with the air conditioner on full blast, and I remember hoping there wouldn't be any more customers to have to deal with before I went home at three. I was ready for a shower.

All that changed when Cody walked in. All I noticed at first was a particularly handsome young cowboy, with the broad shoulders and lean muscles that come from a lifetime of ranch work. He was wearing boots and dusty Wranglers, with a white straw hat and a horsehair belt with a silver buckle that had a golden letter C in the center of it. He had close-cropped dark brown hair and bright blue eyes like a Siberian Husky, and that's when I knew him; no one has eyes like Cody. . . bluer than gas flames or corn flowers, blue as the lupines that blossom in spring. I hadn't seen him since I was twelve, but I'll never forget those eyes.

"*Cody?*" I asked, getting up so fast I almost dropped my book. He glanced at me carelessly for a second, and then his face lit up with recognition.

"*Lisa!*" he cried, and immediately swept me up in a ferocious bear-hug. He smelled like sweat and horse manure, but I was too glad to see him to care about that. I hugged him back, and then stood back and looked him up and down again.

"So where have you been, boy? You've changed a lot," I said. And he had, too; he was nothing like the thin, rangy kid I remembered.

"Oh, same old place, you know. But what about you, Miss Stone? I bet it's been eight, ten years since I saw you last time," he said.

"Well, we just got back in town about three months ago. Mama dragged us off to South Carolina for a while, and then Florida. But we're back now, as far as I know. Jenny's working down in Tyler and I'm going to nursing school and working here part time," I said.

"That's awesome. Well, listen, why don't you give me a call sometime? We can catch a movie or somethin', catch up on old times," he said.

So we traded numbers, and after he left with his cheeseburger and coke, I thought to myself that the world can be a really small place sometimes.

There was a time when I used to think I was in love with Cody, back in seventh grade when we both thought the whole meaning of the word was to hold hands in the hallway and keep pictures of each other on our phones. But still, he was the first boy who ever kissed me, at the fall dance that year, and when we had to move away at Christmas I thought I was heartbroken forever.

But time passes and you tend to forget about such things after a while. My childhood love was long ago and far behind, and life tends to be a lot more complicated at twenty-one than it ever was at twelve. But the memory of loving him was still sweet, and I was unattached at the time, and I confess the thought did cross my mind that there might still be some lingering embers between us. Maybe it was silly to think so, but then again I'd never know unless we spent some time together.

So I went with him to the movies in Longview on Friday night, mostly just for fun but also out of curiosity to see if anything might develop. I don't remember what we watched; a forgettable creature feature with enough of a love story to make it interesting for me and enough explosions to make it interesting for him. We brushed fingers in the popcorn tub now and then, and I could almost-but-not-quite swear he lingered a fraction of a second longer than strictly necessary whenever we touched. I don't think he was even aware of doing it, but I smiled to myself.

He took me out for frozen yogurt afterwards, something I hadn't done in years. I got a single scoop of mint chocolate chip (my favorite), and he had two scoops of strawberry vanilla swirl.

"So what did you think of the movie?" he asked.

"Eh, it was pretty good. The monster looked fake, though," I said.

"Yeah, I agree. No real monster would look anything like that," he agreed, and I laughed.

"You know what I meant, silly," I said.

"Sorry, couldn't resist," he said, taking another bite of his strawberry vanilla.

"I bet not," I said.

"So what brings y'all back to town after all this time? Any special reason?" he asked.

"Well, yeah. Mama had a stroke a few months ago, and things got hard after that. Grandma's old house in Ore City was just sitting there empty, so we decided to move back home to be closer to family and cut down on expenses and things like that," I said.

"Oh, I'm sorry to hear that," he said.

"It's all right. She's doing a lot better now, but she still needs somebody to help her out with things," I said.

"Well that's good, at least. So you think you'll be around for a while, then?" he asked.

"Yeah, for the foreseeable future. It's good to be back home, though. No place else is ever quite the same," I said.

Cody smiled a little, and I knew what he was thinking. He's always been the kind of boy who had dirt in his blood, as they say; he loved the land almost the way you'd think a hickory tree might love it, with roots planted deep in one spot and limbs reached out to taste the sunshine and the rain beneath a sheltering sky. He was strong that way; full of life and sure of where home would always be. It was one of the main things my younger self had always loved him for, and I was glad to see it hadn't changed.

We talked for a long time that night about all kinds of things, sitting on the tailgate of his truck and eating our yogurt till it got too drippy to be any good. After that we just talked. I told him about how I liked to do landscape painting with oils and watercolors, and he told me about his calf-roping days on the high school rodeo team. But the most interesting thing I found out was that he had a band called the Mustangs along with two other boys.

"What kind of stuff do y'all play?" I asked, curious.

"Red-dirt mostly, sometimes southern rock or gospel," he said.

"That's so cool. You really get paid for it and everything?" I asked, suitably impressed.

Red dirt music is basically homegrown Texas country, just in case you never heard of it before. The kind of stuff local bands like to play on small-town summer evenings, mostly for love of music and home. There's nothing better than a good red dirt band and some spicy beef barbecue at a Friday night tailgate party, and a case of cold Dr. Pepper to wash it all down with. What's not to love? Maybe I'm letting my southern country girl roots show, but hey, that's who I am.

"Yeah, sometimes we get paid a little bit, but we mostly play for tips. We have to take whatever we can get, pretty much. Coffee houses, county fairs, things like that. Sometimes even bars and honky-tonks if that's all we can find. And then we do the music service at church every Sunday, but we don't get paid for that. You ought to come listen sometime," he said.

"Where at?" I asked.

"At the cowboy church in Avinger. Starts at eleven, if you want to come. Just wear jeans or whatever; it's not formal at all," he said.

"I'll see what I can do," I agreed.

And so it was that I found myself driving out to Avinger on Sunday morning, dressed in nothing fancier than a pair of jeans and a t-shirt. Mama would have died a thousand deaths before setting foot inside a church in anything but a dress, and I have to confess I was more than a little uneasy with the idea myself. I had to keep telling myself I'd been specifically told to wear jeans.

I'd never actually been to a cowboy church before, even though I'd seen them often enough. The one in Avinger looks more like a barn than a church, although I have to admit it's the only barn I've ever seen that had stained glass windows. It helped when I got there and saw that everybody else was wearing jeans and such, too, and when I got inside I soon found out the reason. The church was built like a barn on the inside, too. Everything was rough wood and bare concrete with sawdust sprinkled on the floor. People were sitting on bales of hay rather than pews, and the only modern-looking spot in the whole place was the podium and the altar. It was quite a sight, to me at least.

I spotted Cody and a few others up on the stage area behind the podium, setting up sound equipment and fiddling with instruments. I waved at him when he glanced my way, and he smiled and bounded down off the stage.

"Hey, Lisa. I'm glad you could make it," he said, giving me a quick hug.

"Aw, I wouldn't have missed it for anything," I said.

"So what do you think of the place?" he asked, sweeping his arm around at everything.

"It's definitely different," I admitted, and he laughed.

"Yeah, that's what everybody says at first. I guess it seems ordinary to me by now," he said.

"When are y'all playing?" I asked.

"In just a minute. We'll go first, and then preaching, and then some of us at least will go out on the trail ride for an hour or so. Want to come? I know you don't have a horse but I guess we could ride double if you want," he offered.

"Sure. Wore my jeans, didn't I?" I said.

"Yup, that you did," he agreed.

He had to get back up on stage after that, and then they played for about thirty minutes. They were pretty good, as far as I could tell. They played several songs I'd never heard before, and a couple of hymns straight out of the hymnal.

Cody came down and sat next to me on the hay bale when the music was over, and from then on out the service progressed more or less like I was used to.

After church he led me out the back exit doors to the corral; another anomaly. I'd never been to a church that had a corral before. It was full of horses, and Cody seemed to know exactly which one he was after.

"Be right back," he told me, climbing up and over the metal pipe fence and landing on his feet. It didn't take him long to catch a pretty brown-and-white splotched horse, which he led up to the fence by his halter.

"This is Buck," he said, as if introducing me to an old friend.

"Buck?" I asked.

"Yeah. Short for Buckwild. I named him that because he was so crazy when I first went to break him. Threw me in the dirt more times than I can remember. He's my buddy now, though," he said, stroking the horse's mane affectionately.

"How long have you had him?" I asked, reaching out to pet the horse's soft nose and being careful not to let him nip my fingers.

"I got him when I was fourteen. We went to a place where they let you adopt abused and neglected horses. He was an orphan so I had to bottle feed him for a little while," he said.

He led Buck outside the corral and quickly and expertly slipped his bridle on.

"I think we'll ride bareback, if that's okay. Not really good for his kidneys to ride double with a saddle on there. Just hold on tight to me and not him, and sit as far forward as you can, okay?" he said, and I nodded.

He got on first and helped me up behind him, and I laced my fingers together around his stomach and stayed as close to him as I could, just like he told me. I could feel his taut muscles and smell the clean scent of his skin through his t-shirt, and I won't deny that I enjoyed it very much.

We rode along a dirt track that wound through the wooded hills behind the church along with a group of several other people, and it was hot even with the breeze that day.

"Y'all played really nice today. I really liked that song about *Nebo's Crossing,*" I said after a while.

"Thanks. Me and Cyrus wrote that one, actually. I think I've got some demo disks out in the truck, if you'd like one. That song's on there," he said.

"I'd love one," I said.

"Okay. Just remind me about it when we get back so I don't forget," he said.

It wasn't all that much longer before we did get back, and he swung me down with one arm before dismounting himself. He took Buck's bridle off and turned him out in the corral while I waited beside the truck.

"So what about that disk you promised me?" I asked when he got back.

"Hold on a second and I'll see if I can find one," he said, rummaging through the console.

"Here you go," he finally said, handing me a disk in a paper sleeve. The name of the group was written on the disk itself with a black marker, along with a website address and a phone number.

"I'll listen to it later sometime. I'm fixing to have to get home and check on Mama, but you can stop by about one thirty and have lunch with me at work anytime you want to. That's my break time," I offered, and he nodded.

"We'll see what we can do," he said, with one of his little smiles, and then he gave me another hug before I left.

On the way home I found myself thinking a lot about the way his muscles felt under the thin cotton of his t-shirt, and the deep but musical drawl of his voice, and a dozen other things like that. He was no boy anymore, and I couldn't deny there was definitely still some chemistry there. I couldn't help wondering if he felt it too.

I suppose I've always had a certain romantic streak. My father was like that; he loved poetry and music, and I remember him telling me he hoped I might find such a love as that someday, so fiery and strong that naught on earth could ever break it. Those were the very words he used, too. He fed me on Marlowe and

Coleridge from my earliest memories, and after that, how could I not be an idealistic dreamer?

Unfortunately he wasn't exactly the faithful type himself, and he finally disappeared completely when I was twelve; that was the main reason we moved away that year. I had a hard time with it for years, but Mama always told me to love the good in him and forgive the bad, and never to drink the poison of hating him. I've been grateful to her many times for that, for casting aside her own pain and showing me by example that we live for God and not for the world. She's my hero, and always will be.

Another thing she's always told me is that whenever I meet a man who seems interesting, the very first thing I should do is to pray about the situation. Cody was definitely appealing, so I murmured a silent prayer that God would touch his heart and inspire some interest in return, if that was something which would make both of us happy and if that was what He wanted for both of us.

No, I wasn't exactly thinking about running down to the church to get married before the sun set; I'm not that silly. But it's always something to consider, at least in an abstract, long-term kind of way. I certainly didn't want to end up as one of those frumpy, starchy old spinsters who talks to her tomato plants and lives in a run-down house with forty cats.

On the disk, Cyrus was singing *Nebo's Crossing,* a verse about how Moses stood up on top of Mount Nebo at the end of his life and saw the Promised Land across the Jordan River, and how God is always faithful to keep His promises even though it might take longer than we like, sometimes. Very true, and good to remember.

As soon as I got home, I went out to the back yard to weed and water the garden, but my mind was a million miles away from such a mundane chore. We'd had a vegetable garden for as long as I could remember, no matter where we lived; mostly tomatoes and squash and a few other things, and cabbage and broccoli in the winter. It was a quiet and satisfying kind of hobby, even though I was having to keep a close eye on things to make sure the plants didn't burn up in the heat.

But the whole time I was busy digging and weeding, I kept thinking about Cody; the sound of his voice, the roughness of his hands, and perhaps what his lips might feel like, pressed up to mine. A little bit of bare skin contact on a hot afternoon goes an awfully long way, when it comes to putting thoughts like that in your head.

But in the meantime, I was content to wait and see.

Chapter Two - Cody

Old flames die hard, it seems.

I could tell Lisa still liked me, just from the way she held me a little closer than she really had to, and the way she put her face against the back of my neck once or twice. You can always tell about things like that, if you pay attention.

That was bad.

Even worse, I enjoyed it myself. She was pretty and sweet and fun to spend time with, and I swear the way she pressed the tips of her fingernails up against my stomach muscles that day was enough to make me forget my own name. If circumstances had been different, I might have taken the bait, so to speak. No, scratch that; I *know* I would have.

But as it was, I knew better than to take even the first step down *that* path. She didn't have a clue what she was getting herself into, but *I* did, and so I owed it to her to keep my distance, much as I might regret it. I had too much going on in my life to think about getting close to anybody.

Ominous dreams and business headaches were bad enough, but there was yet a third issue that bothered me when it came to forming any kind of potential relationship.

It so happens that I like to study my family history. A pretty harmless hobby, for the most part. But one of the things you start to notice after a while is what killed everybody. Not to sound morbid or anything, but you can't help seeing patterns if there happen to be any. I guess I was about sixteen when I first noticed an odd pattern in the way my father's family died. Not a single one of them ever lived to see his thirtieth birthday. It wasn't obvious at first because it didn't seem to affect people who married in; only the natural-born members. But once you *did* notice, it was plain as a pikestaff.

My father drowned at twenty-five. My Aunt Linda was killed in a car wreck at eighteen. Grandfather died of cancer at twenty-nine. And the list went on, and on, and depressingly on. It was always something different every time, but always something commonplace like that. Nothing you could put your finger on and say it was anything unusual.

At first I thought I was imagining things, that it was just a string of nasty coincidences which didn't really mean anything. But when the list gets as long as your arm and there are still no exceptions, then you have to start wondering if there might be something else at work.

In fact, in my darker moods I was almost certain the McGraths had our own private version of the Mummy's Curse, and I was the next one whose head was on the block. Sometimes I felt like I might as well have an expiration date stamped on the bottom of my foot, like a carton of milk.

Of course I didn't *know* that. I couldn't prove it, the way you'd prove something in a book. But I'd seen the dates on the tombstones. I watched my father drown. I drove past the spot where Aunt Linda died, every time I went to Longview. It was hard not to at least semi-believe it, after all that, and Matthieu's warning about evil sorcerers only inflamed my fears even more. I never talked about it much, but it was always there in the back of my mind, a dark suspicion that I didn't really want to think about too often.

But suffice it to say, I believed it enough to take it seriously. And that along with everything else made me hesitant to get involved with Lisa, or anybody else for that matter.

I've always believed it was cruel and selfish to knowingly drag another human being into danger and heartache, if you have any choice in the matter. Least of all a person you claim to love. I'm not that selfish, or at least I hope I'm not. There's such a thing as honor, you know, even when it hurts.

But still. . . I'd be lying if I said I never thought about love and family and all those things. I was always brought up to believe that family is everything, that I have an obligation to the past and to the future, to honor my parents and love my children. In my heart of hearts, nothing would have pleased me better than to find my one and only true love and then settle down to raise corn, kids, and tomatoes at Goliad and live happily ever after.

Sound funny, coming from a young guy? Well, maybe so. But that's who I am and I'm not ashamed of it, and I know well enough that I'm not the only boy who ever thought likewise. You might be surprised how many of us think that way, if you took the time to ask.

But they say you always wish the most for the things you know you can never have, and for that reason among others I could almost wish I'd never bumped into Lisa again at all. I liked her too much, and that made things hard.

I probably should have found something more productive to do when I got home, but I grabbed my guitar and went to sit under the hickory trees in the back yard to play a few songs. They say music soothes the savage beast, or I guess in my case the troubled spirit. I love all music, but besides red-dirt, my favorite is southern gospel, or blue-eyed soul as Mama always likes to call it. Her father, my Grandpa Tommy, used to play in a band called *Southern Psalms* when he was young, and when me and Marcus and Cyrus Clay decided to start up a band after high school, he gave me his original 1939 twelve-string Martin acoustic guitar as a graduation present. It's from him that I get my love of music, and my middle name, and the color of my hair. On a small bronze plate at the foot was the name *Tommy Lee Grey, Avinger, Texas* and below it the inscription:

> *To the Lord God Almighty, the Creator of all Music,*
> *May the Hands that play these strings give You glory.*

I always liked that, although I've wondered many times why old folks always seem to want to capitalize every other word that way. Anyway, if you don't know anything about guitars, then I'll go ahead and tell you Martins are the best that money can buy, especially the old ones. At first I'd been so intimidated by such an awesome instrument that I'd been afraid to actually play it much, but Grandpa Tommy only laughed and told me to use it for what it was meant for instead of treating it like it was made of gold leaf. So that's what I did, and ever since then I've hauled that guitar around with me all over half of Texas and parts of three other states. It's one of my most prized possessions.

So I played *His Life is an Open Book*, and then *Send the Fire* and *Nebo's Crossing,* singing the words when I felt like it and sometimes not. I can't sing quite as well as Cyrus, but I've been told I have a nice voice. And just like always, it gave me some peace in the midst of my troubles.

We'd been up till two a.m. the night before, playing a hundred-dollar gig at the *Little Brown Jug* down on the Longview highway. That's a honky-tonk place where guys get busted over the head with pool cues and beer bottles pretty regularly, and the smoke is so thick it'll make your eyes water and it feels almost like walking through a big bowl of tapioca pudding. I don't much like to play at bars, but when money's tight then it sure does make it hard to turn down a paid gig. At least there hadn't been any fights, but I was still tired from the late night.

So after a while I gave up playing and lay down on the ground instead, looking up at the hickory leaves dancing in the sunlight and using my guitar as a headrest. I pulled my hat down over my face to shade my eyes from the sun, and soon enough I dozed off in spite of myself.

And dreamed.

I found myself standing on a rocky hill under a grove of enormous pine trees, disoriented and not sure where I was. Below me was a stony path under the light of a full moon, and presently I saw a girl in a white gown walking silently along. She was paler than usual, but I recognized her immediately as Lisa.

She passed by me, and I silently climbed down to follow her, till we came to the mouth of a cave in the side of the hill. It was dark inside once we passed beyond where the moon reached, but not quite. A faint gray glow seemed to come from everywhere, just enough to find our way. I followed her down a winding staircase cut out of the living rock, and at last the tunnel opened out into a huge cavern. And here was a wonder of wonders.

The path went on through a forest of trees, but not like the kind I knew. These were of crystal and glass, brittle and glittering even in the weak light. They were exquisitely beautiful, and as we passed by I broke off a twig from one of the crystal branches.

Then we came to a lake with troubled waters dark as soot, and far off on an island in the middle of the lake was a palace blazing with light. A bridge of silver filigree crossed over to the island, and when we arrived I saw a finely-dressed young man awaiting us.

Up till then I hadn't seen anything especially alarming, but when we got close enough I saw that the man was nothing but a skeleton dressed in fine clothes. Lisa seemed not to notice, and she laughed and joined hands with him. Then for several hours I watched them dance, till morning came and she climbed the stone stairway back to the outside world. I couldn't help but notice that she looked even paler then, weak and sickly, indeed almost at the very edge of death. It was only when we reached the sunlit world again that she seemed to revive a little, but somehow I knew the man in the blazing palace hadn't turned her loose for long.

I pulled the crystal twig from my pocket and watched it crumble to black dust in the morning sunlight, and then a voice from above me spoke.

"Save her from the evil one," it said.

Then I woke up, covered in sweat and gripping the grass with my fists. I hate the ones like that, when I know they mean something really important but I can't guess what it is. Who was the evil one, and what did all the rest of it signify? I couldn't tell, except that like all the others lately it was obviously something really bad. And worst of all, what was I supposed to do about it?

I did *not* need this. It wasn't like I didn't already have enough of my own problems to deal with.

"What's wrong with you, boy?" Marcus's voice cut through the haze of reverie, startling me.

"Huh?" I asked, still half-dozing. I pulled the hat from my face, shielding my eyes from the light. Marcus was looking down at me, and I yawned and sat up.

"You were twitching and talking to yourself, so I wondered what was wrong," he said.

"Oh. I was only dreaming, sort of. That's all. Sorry about that," I said.

"Dreaming about what? Hot mermaid babes in real estate jackets again?" he teased, and I laughed a little. Back when I was eighteen I had a dream about a mermaid who was also a real estate agent and came up out of the sea wearing an old-fashioned gold-colored Century 21 jacket. I never did figure out what that one was supposed to mean, although I have to admit she was a smokin' hot babe and it sure was entertaining. I told Marcus about it years ago, and he's never ceased to think it was hilarious.

"No, not this time. It was about a skeleton, mostly," I said.

"Dang, boy, you're weirder than I thought," Marcus said.

"Ha, ha, very funny," I said.

"So what do you think it means? Anything?" he asked, and I hesitated. Marcus knows all about my dreams, with good reason. But he also knows I don't like to talk about them much.

You see, on Christmas Eve my senior year, I dreamed I saw a boy about my age sitting in his bedclothes at the pole barn in the Ore City park, fifteen miles away. I never would have had any reason to go nosing around over there ordinarily, and especially not on Christmas morning. But to make a long story short, I went out there to check, and sure enough there he was, exactly like I saw him in my dream, shivering in the cold and wrapped in a blanket with nowhere to go.

You probably guessed by now it was Marcus. Turned out his dad got drunk and kicked him out of the house that morning, so he wandered over to the pole barn and tried to think what to do. Christmas Day is a bad time to be out on the streets; everything is closed, and nobody wants visitors. We didn't even know each other at the time; he went to school at Ore City and I went to Avinger, and we'd never had a reason to meet before then. He was already eighteen, barely, so I guess Mr. Cumby had a right to throw him out if he wanted to, but I thought then as I think now what a sorry thing it was to do.

So I offered him a place to stay for a while and a job helping out around the ranch. I guess I probably should have asked first, but when I brought him home that day Mama treated him like a long-lost son, just like she would have done with any other lost kid who needed a place to be loved. He's been here ever since, and in all that time I couldn't ask for a better friend.

Except when he gets some kind of bright idea in his head, and then he can be stubborn as a green-broke stallion. Like now.

"Cody, I've been thinking. I was listening to the radio the other day and there's a preacher down in Longview that was talking about dreams and visions. Why don't you go see him? Maybe he could help you figure somethin' out, you know?" he asked.

That was actually one of the more sensible suggestions Marcus had come up with lately, and I frowned, thinking about it. The simple and obvious dreams I never needed any help with, but what was I supposed to think about crystal forests and dancing skeletons? I'd tried most everything I could think of at one time or another to help figure out the obscure ones like that, from psychology textbooks on dream interpretation to simply praying for understanding, but so far nothing had ever worked. I knew in the old days there were people who could understand the meaning of dreams and visions, like Daniel did for the king of Babylon, and Joseph did for Pharaoh and others. I'd often wished I knew somebody like that; it would make the whole thing so much simpler. But since I didn't, I was ready to try just about anything.

"Who is he?" I asked.

Marcus gave me the name and address, and I decided it was worthwhile to go ahead down there and see the man.

It turned out to be a non-denominational church over on the east side of town, and of course those are always a gamble when it comes to what they teach and believe, but I figured I didn't have to listen if I didn't want to. It's not that I hadn't asked my own pastor about the dreams before; I had, several times. We'd even prayed together about it. But nothing had ever come of that, and I decided I had nothing to lose by asking somebody else.

So I went inside and sat down in one of the pews to think for a few minutes, not sure what I wanted to say or even who to say it to. The office was empty and there didn't seem to be anybody around, although I knew there had to be, since the building was open.

I hadn't been there five minutes when a janitor appeared from one of the doors beside the podium.

"Excuse me, sir, can you tell me where I can find the pastor?" I asked him, getting up from the pew. He gave me a long look, and then shook his head.

"Nobody here but me, son," he said.

"Oh, all right," I said, disappointed. I was just about to ask him what time I needed to come back, when he got close enough to hand me a folded-up sheet of notebook paper. I took it without thinking.

"What's this?" I asked, looking down at it.

"Go see him. He can tell you what you need to know," the man said.

I looked down at the paper, which had the name *Brandon Stone* written on it, along with an address in Ravanna, Arkansas. I didn't know who that was, but Ravanna is only about thirty miles from Goliad. I looked up to ask for clarification, but during the second when I glanced at the paper the janitor had already disappeared.

Well, I've had my share of odd experiences now and then, and I guess compared to some of them, a disappearing janitor doesn't amount to much. I looked at the paper again and figured I had nothing to lose by going to see Mr. Stone, whoever he was.

My first thought was to wonder if he might be some relation of Lisa's, unlikely as that seemed. I left the church mighty puzzled, but at least I had something concrete I could *do* for a change.

There were still a good three or four hours till it got dark, and I decided that was plenty of time to run over to Ravanna. It wouldn't take more than an hour or so to get out there and find the place.

Chapter Three - Cody

Ravanna sits right on the edge of the biggest cypress swamp in the world, in case you didn't know. It fills up all the wide valleys that drain down into Caddo Lake, but there's still quite a bit of high ground where the towns and things are.

Brandon Stone didn't live on high ground.

He lived in an old school bus at the end of a muddy track that barely deserved to be called a road, amongst a thicket of cypress trees at the edge of a blackwater bayou. A rusty stovepipe stuck out one of the windows near the back, and the yard was littered with trash and three or four rusty vehicles up on blocks. Three mongrel dogs lay curled up under the bus in the shade, watching me. Maybe they were too lazy to bark; it wouldn't have surprised me, if they took after their master.

I went up to knock on the door of the bus, only to find a double-barreled shotgun pushed right out into my face.

I really don't like having guns aimed at me; there's just something that really bothers me about that, you know? But I put my hands up where the dude could see them and backed up real slowly, making sure I didn't make any sudden moves.

The door opened, and there stood a young boy no more than fourteen at the most, barefoot and bare-chested, with nothing on but a pair of overalls that were way too big for him. He looked just like the boy on the Tennessee Pride sausage wrappers, red hair and all, and I might have laughed if he hadn't had a gun pointed right between my eyes. Somehow that killed all the humor in the situation.

"What do you want?" he asked, not even pretending to be friendly.

"I'm looking for Brandon Stone," I said.

"You found him. Now what do you want?" he asked again, and I decided this was no time to beat around the bush.

"I was told you could tell me what I need to know. I have dreams sometimes. True ones. But I don't always understand what they mean. I need your help," I said. I didn't know if he'd believe me or if he'd think I was crazy, but I couldn't think of anything else the janitor could have meant by telling me this kid could tell me what I needed to know.

The boy looked hard at me for a while longer, and then slowly lowered the shotgun to his side. He had intensely blue eyes almost the same color as mine, something I'd rarely seen before.

"I see. Don't know that I like that, much. Who told you where to find me?" he asked.

"A janitor at a church in Longview. I don't know his name," I said truthfully.

"Hmm. Well, you best come inside, then," he said.

I followed him inside, and when I got closer I caught a whiff of body odor so strong it could have gagged a maggot at thirty paces. Not just body odor, either, but *old* body odor. I wondered when the kid had last taken a bath.

The smell was even stronger inside the bus. Dried sweat, wood smoke, and mildew all combined in a way that made me wish I could stop breathing for at least an hour.

The bus seats had been ripped out and the place had been refitted into a one-room house, sort of. There was a stack of ancient mattresses in one corner which passed for a bed, a table and chairs, a potbellied wood stove, and some canned goods and such on a shelf. Not much else.

I sat down in one of the chairs, and Brandon took a seat on the bed.

"So spit it out. I can't tell you anything if you don't cough up the story," he finally said, with more than a hint of impatience in his voice.

So I told him the dream about Lisa, making sure not to leave out any details whether they seemed important or not. He listened without saying a thing, and when I was finished he did the last thing I would ever have expected. He got down on his knees beside the bed and prayed for at least five minutes, leaving me to sit there watching him.

When he was finished, he got up and sat back down on the bed again, watching me curiously.

"Well?" I finally asked.

"This is what God is saying to you. The cave means a time of doubt and uncertainty, and the crystal forest is a time of happiness that you and the girl will pass through. The silver bridge over dark waters means that you'll face a dangerous time which you'll need money to get through. But when you find it, that will lead you directly into the palace of the worst danger of all. The skeleton means death. Death to the girl, and to you too. But both of you will go willingly to meet it, because it'll be cloaked in beauty. Don't be fooled," the boy said.

"Is that all?" I asked, chilled.

"Not quite. In spite of the disguise, you'll still be able to see the evil underneath the surface, if you pay attention. The bones will still be visible underneath all those fine clothes, so to speak. The evil one will ask you to do something you know is wrong, just like the skeleton asked the girl to dance. Don't do that thing, no matter how minor and harmless it might seem. If you do, it'll cause you more grief than you could ever imagine. Once all is said and done, and final happiness seems to be in your hands, you'll find that it suddenly crumbles to dust before you can stop it. That's the meaning of the crystal twig falling to ashes in your hand," he said.

"It seems awfully gloomy," I muttered.

"I'm sorry to have to give you bad news," the kid said, softening a little bit.

"Yeah, well, I wish I knew what I'm supposed to do, that's all," I said.

"Follow her, just like you did in the dream. That's your job right now. Stick to her like glue. That's all I know," he said.

"Thanks, I guess," I said.

"You're welcome, maybe," Brandon said with a scowl.

"I'm sorry, I didn't mean it like that," I said.

"Yeah, whatever," he said.

"So how old are you, anyway?" I asked, changing the subject to something less disturbing. It had nothing to do with what we'd been talking about and it was really none of my business, but finding a kid living alone in the middle of a swamp *is* a little strange, you've got to admit.

"Thirteen and a half, and before you even ask, yeah, I live here alone, I take care of myself, my parents are gone, and that suits me just fine. Anything else you want to know?" he asked, hostile again.

"No, I guess not," I said.

"Good. And if you're thinkin' about telling anybody I'm here, you better think again. I *will* come after you," he promised. I stared at the dirty boy across from me, with his twelve-gauge shotgun still within easy reach if he needed it, and somehow I wasn't inclined to doubt he'd try his dead-level best to make good on that threat.

Well, I wouldn't rat him out. Not because I was scared he might hunt me down later, but just because he helped me and you don't betray people who do you a favor. He seemed to be surviving, at least, even though that was no way to live to my way of thinking.

I still had two hundred dollars left in my pocket from selling cows. We needed it, to be sure, but not as much as this strange kid did. Maybe I couldn't help him any other way, but money might buy him food and clothes for a while. Better than nothing. I took it out of my pocket and offered it to him.

"Please take this, so I can thank you," I told him. He eyed the cash, looking from it to me and then back again, like a coon watches a sweet plum in your hand while it decides whether it's safe to grab it or not. Slowly he reached out and took it, stuffing the money inside his dirty overalls without even counting it.

"Much obliged," he said.

"Least I could do," I said.

I left after that, trying not to let it show how sweet the air smelled after that fetid bus. I didn't want to offend Brandon; I might need his help again someday. Dream interpreters are hard to come by.

So I went home, thinking hard about what he'd told me and what all it might mean. I was supposed to stay close to Lisa; well, okay, I could handle that. The rest of it still seemed pretty murky, but if I kept my eyes open and paid attention, then there was a good chance I might spot the signs while there was still time to do something about them.

I hoped.

Many Waters
is available now at your favorite retailer

Author's Note

Unclouded Day began as a short story which I composed as a teenager, and it has undergone many refinements and changes over the years, but I think the core of the story has always been the same: the yearning for what is true and beautiful and right, the sense that evil is a thing that ought not to be, if all were as it should be. I think we all have this same deep certainty that ultimate reality is both fair and good, a certainty which almost no amount of earthly suffering or injustice can shake.

One need not enjoy symbolism to like the story, of course, but for those who do enjoy such things, the story is rich with subtlety. The title, *Unclouded Day,* is a reference to the hymn of the same name, which is a song about the glory of Heaven and yearning for that.

I gladly acknowledge my debt to William Morris for his beautiful story *The Well at the World's End,* which is referred to rather obliquely in my book as the tale which prompts Brian to go looking for the Fountain in the first place. The language is rather archaic and sometimes difficult to understand, but I would encourage anyone who likes such tales to read it.

The Crystal Range is in fact a real place in western Arkansas, and yes, I have often thought the white mist after a rain made them look just like I described them. Glenwood is a typical little mountain town to the southwest of Hot Springs, in the same region that Zach Trewick likes to go hiking and bear-hunting, and where he escaped from the werewolves in *Behind Blue Eyes.* Although it isn't named in this book, Brian and Brandon live in a little town called Langley.

The name Brian means "noble" and Madaug means "good", so those were chosen intentionally.

I wrote this story because I wanted to show that pain and sorrow are never the end of the story. Keep your eyes lifted up, and if you have the heart to believe, you'll always be able to see the glint of gold beyond the bitterness. Brian always believed this, and never doubted that there had to be something more than the harsh world he lived in. His faith was rewarded, and so will ours be if we do likewise. Those hints and promises of unspeakable joy that glisten in a golden sunset or a misty landscape are no lie and no cheat.

Authors of Christian fiction are sometimes hesitant to address subjects like child abuse or alcoholism, for various reasons. That impulse to shy away from harsh topics is understandable in some ways, but the unfortunate truth is that we live in a fallen world. Such things go on, and sin won't disappear just because we pretend it doesn't exist. Darkness can only be drowned in the light of God, and in no other way. I hope this book will make some contribution to that effort.

Brian and Brandon are both curse-breakers, of course, although they haven't quite realized what that means yet. Brandon goes on to become a very important character in the rest of this series and in the *Tyke McGrath* series which follows, although Brian isn't forgotten, either. God has very long-term purposes for both these brothers, in ways that nobody could guess at this point. I hope readers will enjoy their further adventures.

William Woodall
March 31, 2012

Discussion Questions

1. Characters often change during the course of a story. In what ways do you think Brian and the other characters changed during this one?

2. Brian's mother has serious problems with alcohol abuse and bad temper. What kinds of experiences do you think she might have had which led her to become the kind of person she is?

3. From the beginning, Brian's deepest wish was to remake the world so that there are no bad things anymore. Why do you think he had this wish?

4. The Fountain can only be found by those who are chosen and found worthy. Why do you think this is true, and why do you think Brian was chosen? What might happen if anyone could find it?

5. Sadie Jones told Brian that he should drink from the Fountain if he had the courage, implying that not everyone does. What are some reasons why a person might reach the Fountain, and then choose not to drink from it after all?

6. Some of the mysteries in the story are never explained and some problems aren't resolved. Puzzles in real life aren't always answered; some things we learn in time, and other things we never understand. What are your thoughts about this? Do you prefer stories that are neatly wrapped up, or ones that leave you wondering about some things?

7. When Brandon dies, Brian thinks that all is lost, until Rachel reminds him of the power they now have. Are there times when you needed someone to remind you of things you already knew?

8. There were several times during the story when Brian and Rachel nearly died. What do you think kept them going in spite of these difficult events?

9. People who drink from the Fountain are given the power to wipe away ugliness in the world, to turn men's eyes toward Heaven. Do you think beauty is a reminder of God? Why or why not?

10. The "theme" of a story is the underlying message or messages about life the author is trying to convey. It is the lesson or moral of the story, such as "Love conquers all". What do you think the theme of *Unclouded Day* is? (There can be more than one.)

11. Brian came to believe that using his power to fix the hurtful things in the world is the right thing to do, in spite of how much it will cost him (and others). Do you agree? Have you ever done something because it was the right thing to do, even though it was dangerous or other people thought it was foolish? What?

12. In the beginning, Brian carelessly overlooked the instructions carved on the amulet, which caused several awful things to happen, including Brandon's death. Has there ever been a time when you were careless and it caused serious problems for you or others?

13. The inscription on the Fountain reads *"The strong of heart shall drink of Me; the life-giving Life, and the Beauty that makes beautiful."* Explain what you think this means and why it would be on the Fountain.

14. Near the end, the story mentions that Brandon goes to drink from the Fountain for his own reasons and with his own burdens to carry. What do you think these burdens might be, and how would drinking from the Fountain help him?

15. Brian makes several mistakes throughout the story, and he isn't always wise. What are some of the mistakes you think he made, and what should he have done differently?

16. Sometimes, bad and hurtful things happen because they help us to become better people than we could have been without them. In what ways do you think the bad things in Brian's life helped him to become a better person?

The Stones of Song Series
By William Woodall

"There's a thing called magnanimity, or greatness of heart, and to me it's the most beautiful thing that ever there was. It means courage, but it's more than that. It means to cast aside all thought of yourself for the sake of another, like Moses in Gilead or the martyrs who died with a smile on their face. In its own small way it's a reflection of the Lord Jesus at Calvary, and therefore of God, the Light so beautiful that no one who sees it can ever turn away."

So says Cody McGrath, and in many ways that statement is the central theme of this series; the casting away of self for love of another, the scorning of selfishness in all its forms.

These are the stories of Cody and his girlfriend Lisa Stone, and of Lisa's half-brothers Brian and Brandon, and the ways in which all of them were called for great and glorious things, though sometimes only after great suffering and many mistakes. No two were ever called alike, but all did well.

Unclouded Day: Brian's life isn't easy. Abandoned by his father, abused by his alcoholic mother, and mocked by his classmates, his only treasures are his beloved little brother and his old guitar. This is the tale of his journey to find the Fountain of Youth, and perhaps to save the world.

Many Waters: Lisa is a small-town waitress with heavy burdens to bear. Cody is a young cowboy with big dreams and some very dangerous enemies. But when the two of them must face down an evil witch who tries to destroy their very lives, it seems that only a miracle can save them.

Bran the Blessed: Brandon hasn't always made the right choices in life, but he's never found himself in quite such deep trouble as this. But even though his life seems ruined forever, Bran still has a high calling to answer. . . if he can find the courage.

* * * * * *

"I would absolutely, without reservation, encourage you to read this wonderful novel, even if you aren't the fantasy genre type. It was a blessing."
-Sue, *Reflections and Reviews*

"There are so many nuggets of truth in this book. It's about Heaven. It's about bad things happening for a reason. It's about deciding for yourself what truly matters most in life. It's a really good book!"
-Tattie, *Christian Fiction Ebooks*

The Last Werewolf Hunter Series
By William Woodall

Zach Trewick always thought he'd become a writer someday, or maybe play baseball for the Texas Rangers. What he never imagined in his craziest dreams was that he'd find himself dodging bullets and crashing cars off mountainsides, let alone that he'd ever be expected to break the ancient werewolf curse which hangs over his family.

But Zach is the last of the werewolf hunters, the long-foretold Curse-Breaker who can wipe out the wolves forever, and he's not the type to give up just because of a few minor setbacks. . .

Cry for the Moon: What would you do, if your family wanted you to become a monster? What if they wouldn't take no for an answer? When 12 year old Zach faces questions like these, he seems to have only one choice; *run*. Thus begins a long search for refuge, and perhaps redemption also.

Behind Blue Eyes: When a stranger kidnaps him from his own back yard, Zach soon finds that the past isn't quite as dead as he might wish. For the time has come at last for him to break the werewolf curse forever; and his family has no intention of letting that happen.

More Golden Than Day: When his girlfriend and then his cousin fall into the hands of the wolves, Zach has no choice but to take on his enemies for a second round. Only this time the stakes are horribly high, and if he fails he may end up losing everything he's ever loved.

Truesilver: When a family of wicked ex-wolves is accidentally awakened, Zach soon finds himself locked in a desperate fight for survival that he never anticipated. And even though he's sworn an oath to fight evil to the utmost of his power, sometimes courage is awfully hard to come by.

Lion's Heart: Cameron never imagined he'd find himself embroiled in the ex-werewolf Andrew Garza's secret plan to destroy the world, let alone that he'd be expected to fight without Zach. But sometimes the most unlikely heroes turn out to be the only ones who can save the day.

* * * * * * *

"If you are looking for a story about a boy who learns valuable lessons about family, love, friendship and God this is the book for you. I recommend this book to a pre-teen or adult. I truly enjoyed this book." **-Rae, *My Book Addiction Reviews***

"I found myself captivated with the story and could not stop reading until I reached the final page. Everything about this story is thought-provoking. Readers of all ages will appreciate this wonderfully told story," **-Jancy, Kansas**

The Tyke McGrath Series
By *William Woodall*

In the year 2154, the world has become a dangerous place. Extremist groups would like nothing better than to wipe out humanity completely, and even the people sworn to defend civilization against such threats have become deeply corrupt and untrustworthy.

When a virulent plague destroys all warm-blooded life on Earth, a small band of survivors clings to life on the partially-terraformed Moon. But fresh dangers lie in wait for the unwary; nor have they left behind all the wickedness in the hearts of men.

Nightfall: When Micah McGrath suddenly finds himself thrust into a dangerous and ugly future after a lab accident, his only choice is to make the best life for himself that he can. But when the secret police get wind of his research into time travel, he soon finds himself in deep trouble indeed.

Tycho: Tycho McGrath is a high school honor student in Florida when he discovers a terrifying secret: a man-made bacterium is about to wipe out all warm-blooded life on Earth within days. The only hope for survival is to flee at once, a plan which carries its own set of unexpected dangers.

Avenger: After spotting an SOS coming from the abandoned Moon, the survivors must organize a rescue mission. But the expedition quickly becomes far more complicated, leading them to the icy world of Titan in search of a holy mountain that no human eye has ever seen.

Freedom: When a cruel and power-hungry military commander on Venus decides to reconquer Earth, the only thing he needs is the formula for Tyke's Orion vaccine. The survivors soon find themselves locked into a bitter battle over the future of mankind, and who will inherit the Earth after all.

Elysium: What began as a simple mission to recover lost comrades in the Martian desert quickly turns deadly when Tyke and the others find *themselves* stranded on the Red Planet, with only the slimmest of chances to make it home again, or to fulfill the destiny which God has in store for them.

* * * * * * *

"Reminiscent of Freedom's Landing, by Anne McCaffrey, Tycho combines the best of traditional space-exploration sci-fi with modern apocalyptic fiction. For any fans of hard science fiction, it doesn't get much better than this."
- Liz, 0H2 Reviews

"This story was awesome! A must-read book if you like sci-fi."
-Scott, Georgia

Curse-Breaker Family Tree

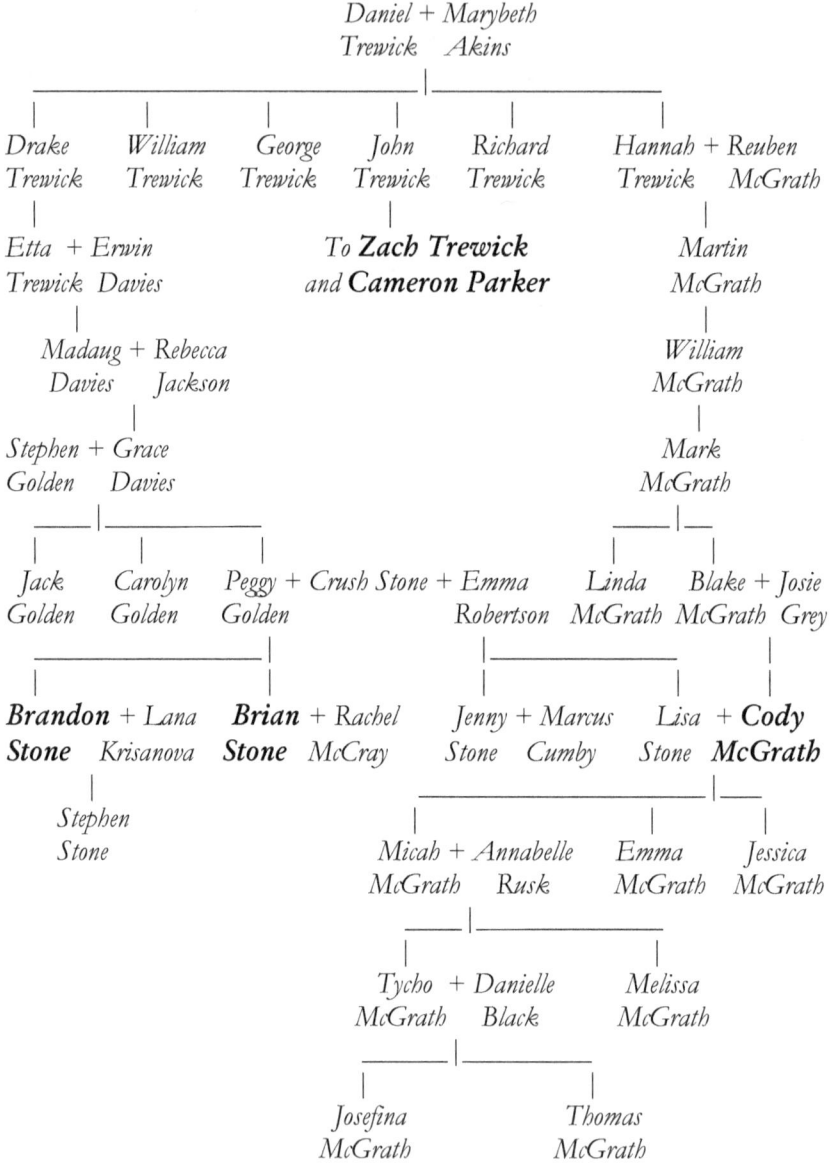

Daniel + Marybeth
Trewick   Akins

| Drake | William | George | John | Richard | Hannah + Reuben |
| Trewick | Trewick | Trewick | Trewick | Trewick | Trewick   McGrath |

Etta + Erwin   To **Zach Trewick**   Martin
Trewick Davies   *and* **Cameron Parker**   McGrath

Madaug + Rebecca   William
Davies   Jackson   McGrath

Stephen + Grace   Mark
Golden   Davies   McGrath

| Jack | Carolyn | Peggy + Crush Stone + Emma | Linda | Blake + Josie |
| Golden | Golden | Golden   Robertson | McGrath | McGrath Grey |

Brandon + Lana   **Brian** + Rachel   Jenny + Marcus   Lisa + **Cody**
Stone   Krisanova **Stone** McCray   Stone   Cumby   Stone **McGrath**

Stephen
Stone

Micah + Annabelle   Emma   Jessica
McGrath   Rusk   McGrath   McGrath

Tycho + Danielle   Melissa
McGrath   Black   McGrath

Josefina   Thomas
McGrath   McGrath

Curse-breakers are in bold.

Curse-Breaker Family Tree

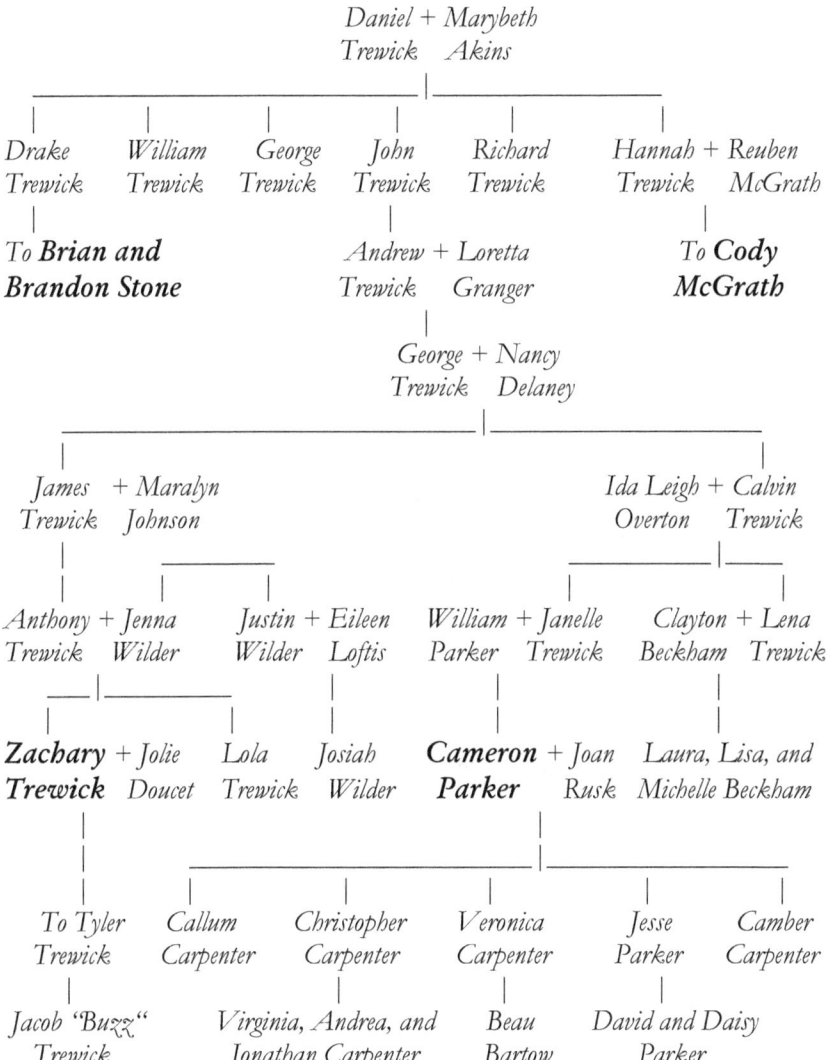

If you'd like to find out more about
The Stones of Song and other books,
please visit:

William Woodall's
Official Author Website

www.williamwoodall.org

Here you will find:

Free short stories
Discussion questions for teachers and book clubs
Free sample chapters of all my books
Photos of characters and locations for each story
Articles
Interviews
Quotable Quotes
Contact Information
And much, much more!